THE SECRET AT SEA GRAPE COTTAGE

A Drake Marlow Mystery

Sally J. Ling

To contact the author, you may email her at: info@sallyjling.com

The Secret at Sea Grape Cottage is a work of fiction. Names, characters, locations, and incidents are either the product of the author's imagination or are used fictitiously.

Cover designed by Andy Massari.

ISBN: 979-8-9916822-5-1

TABLE OF CONTENTS

THE SECRET AT SEA GRAPE COTTAGE

Chapter 1

Palm Beach, Florida
1933

I pushed the door open to Marlow Investigations and found Betty Lou tucked behind her desk, nose buried in a thick book. She didn't look up. Didn't even flinch.

I cleared my throat loud enough to rattle the blinds. "Good morning to you, too," I said.

She blinked, startled, then looked up like I'd just yanked her out of a dream. "Oh! I'm sorry, boss. I didn't hear you come in."

"Must be a real page-turner."

"It is," she said, holding up the book so I could see. *Sea Grape Cottage* brushed across the cover in sweeping script set against a pale blue background. Below, an artist depicted the cottage's silhouette framed by sea grapes and soaring gulls.

I raised an eyebrow. "*Sea Grape Cottage,* huh?"

"Everyone's talking about it," she said, half-defensive, half-excited. "It's technically fiction, but reads like something that actually happened. Supposedly, the events occurred right here in Palm Beach forty-three years ago at Sea Grape Cottage. People are whispering the story is about a real scandal."

"That so? Nothing like fitting in with all the rest of the scandals Palm Beach has had over the decades." I walked toward my office.

"Oh, I meant to ask," said Betty Lou. "How's Constance doing in her new Social Secretary job at Mrs. Anderson's?"

I stopped mid-stride and turned back. "So far, so good. Little rattles her after working for Isabella Somerset, but I'm sure she'll give me the full update tonight. I'm taking her to dinner at the Green Turtle."

"Tell her I said good luck. I envy her if she gets to work in luxury while I'm here with dust and case files." Betty Lou gave me a half smile.

"You love those files, and you know it."

She smirked. "Maybe, but working surrounded by polished floors and a view of the Atlantic would be nice."

I laughed. "Maybe someday. Right now, we've gotta pay our dues."

As I turned for my office, the phone rang, sharp and sudden. Betty Lou picked up the receiver. "Marlow Investigations… Yes, sir… He's here… Yes, of course." She covered the mouthpiece. "Drake, it's Alan Cummings. Says it's urgent."

She raised her brows, and her index finger jabbed at the author's name—George Cummings—on the front cover of *Sea Grape Cottage.*

The son's name hit me like a cold splash of water. I'd seen his name in the papers. He was a rising political star, handpicked for a possible federal appointment. He didn't just walk in off the street. Someone had to tell him I could be discreet.

"Put him through," I said, slipping into my office. The door shut with a click, and I lifted the receiver.

"Drake Marlow."

"Mr. Marlow. An urgent matter has come up, and I must see you." His voice carried the slow cadence of authority, deliberate and unhurried, the kind of tone that came from years of shaking hands, cutting deals, and never blinking first.

I rested back in my chair. "I'm between appointments, if you'd like to come now."

A pause, long enough to let me know he'd considered it, short enough to show he wasn't accustomed to waiting. "I'll be there," he said, and the line went dead with a decisive click.

A half-hour later, he stepped into the office. He was in his late thirties, tall, clean-cut, and wearing a neatly pressed suit. Every inch reflected the polished political climber, yet his eyes betrayed him. They were tight with worry, shadowed with something else.

After introductions, I invited him and Betty Lou into my office. She brought her notepad and sat in a chair opposite my desk.

"I appreciate you seeing me on short notice," he said. "This is... a bit delicate."

"Most of the work I do is," I said, gesturing to a chair. "What's the trouble, Mr. Cummings?"

He sat, ran a hand through his dark hair, and leaned in. "My father, George Cummings, is a novelist. Maybe you've heard of his new book?"

I glanced at Betty Lou. She didn't say anything. "Betty Lou has started reading it. Seems half the town has."

"Yes, well, that's the problem. It's fiction, of course, with the setting in Palm Beach. People are already whispering that the story is based on real events involving specific individuals and locations. And some of those places, even disguised, feel too close to home." He paused and studied me. "I'm not concerned about the literary merit. I'm concerned about what's true. There are things in that book, implications, let's say, that could be disastrous if the public starts making inferences. Especially with the press sniffing around and a potential nomination for a prominent position in the U.S. government coming down the pike for me."

"If I may ask, what kind of rumors have you heard?"

"I'd rather not say. I don't want to taint your investigation one way or the other," he said, then sat forward. "But I can tell you this. If what they say is true, it could destroy my chances of getting the appointment."

"You think your father based the story on real events?" I asked.

"I *know* he drew from life. He always does. But if certain rumors are true… well, I need to know if there's a skeleton in the family closet. And I need to know before the rest of the world does."

"And you want me to find out," I said.

"Quietly. Discreetly. No paper trail. My father's in Palm Beach now for a book talk tomorrow night. He's staying with Mrs. Anderson, who is hosting the event."

Mrs. Anderson? Constance's Mrs. Anderson? Betty Lou and I shared an intrigued glance.

"I want you to come. Listen to my father's talk and read the audience's reaction. You can speak with him afterward," Cummings continued. He pulled a check from his breast pocket and slid it toward me. "I'm sure that will cover your retainer and then some."

"Mr. Cummings, if your father wrote the book and you have questions about the story, why haven't you asked him about your concerns?"

He shifted in the chair. “It’s not that simple. My father and I don’t see eye to eye, and discussions like this are challenging. Thus, why he’s not staying with us. I’d rather not involve him and see what you turn up.” He smiled, but there was a slight tremble to his lips.

I gazed at the check and nodded slowly in quiet understanding. “I’ll need a copy of the book and any names, places, or leads you suspect are real.”

He pulled a book with a folded sheet tucked inside, along with an invitation from his valise, and passed them over. “The invitation will get you and a guest into The Breakers for the event, and the paper contains the names used in the novel. I’ve jotted down who I think they *might* be in real life. But you didn’t get that from me.”

I took the objects and slipped them into a drawer. “Understood.”

As he stood, his eyes met mine with an unspoken plea. “Mr. Marlow,” he said, pausing at the door. “If there’s something in my family’s past, whatever it is, I’d rather face it now than have it explode later. Just be thorough.”

When the door closed behind him, I turned to Betty Lou. “Looks like we’ve got ourselves a new case,” I said.

She looked up, eyes wide. “And to think we’ll be part of the real story. You going to tell Constance?”

“I’ve never kept a case from her, but this one?” I shook my head. “I can’t tell her I’m investigating the guest of her employer. That would be unethical.”

~~~

Constance was waiting on the porch of Mrs. Crippen’s Boarding House for Women when I pulled up, the glow of the porch light brushing her shoulders in amber. She wore a pale, aqua blue dress with white trim and had an easy smile that could quiet the worst days. I stepped out and opened the car door for her.
~~~

“You’re right on time,” she said, sliding in with a graceful sweep of her skirt.

“I try to be reliable. Especially when it comes to dinner,” I said, winking as I shut the door and circled back to the driver’s seat.

The Green Turtle was humming when we arrived. Candles flickered in the small lanterns on the tables, and the scent of lemon butter and fresh herbs hung in the air. We took our usual quiet booth near the back, away from the regulars, and ordered the night’s special: grilled pompano with rice pilaf and asparagus.

Constance handed me a wrapped package as our waitress brought the iced tea.

“What’s this?” I asked. “Today isn’t my birthday.”

“I know, silly. But I thought you might like a distraction from your daily investigations.” She smiled expectantly.

I pulled off the bow and opened the paper. A familiar invitation sat atop the book *Sea Grape Cottage.*

Another copy of the book and two extra tickets. Just what I needed.

“George Cummings, the author, is staying with Mrs. Anderson and will be giving a talk on his book tomorrow night at The Breakers,” she continued. “I was responsible for coordinating the event. It’s her last one of the season, and she’s wrapping it up with a bow.”

I raised an eyebrow and leaned in. “I guess that’s why I haven’t seen much of you lately. Too busy planning this exclusive affair. Why didn’t you tell me?”

“And spoil my little surprise for you? No, I wanted you to see what I’m capable of.” She tilted her head and gave me a proud, knowing smile.

“Betty Lou’s reading this book right now. She’s completely mesmerized, from the look of things.”

"She's not the only one," Constance said. "Everyone in Palm Beach seems to be absorbed in the book. Mr. Cummings gave Mrs. Anderson several complimentary, signed copies as a gesture of appreciation for hosting the event. That book is one of his signed copies."

"Have you read it?" I asked, raising an eyebrow.

She shook her head. "Not yet, I've been too busy. But Mrs. Anderson says it'll help if I know what all the fuss is about."

"I imagine Betty Lou would love to go," I said, reading the invitation and tucking the card back into the envelope.

Constance smiled. "Bring her. The invitation is for two."

"She'll be thrilled, I said. I glanced toward the kitchen, where Cookie stood in the threshold of the swinging door. I gave him a nod of approval. "This place still knows how to treat a man right."

"And a lady, too," Constance added, raising her glass toward him.

The rest of the dinner passed in easy conversation, the kind that flows when the food is good and the company better. Afterward, I drove Constance home under a moonlit sky. The warm hush of a Palm Beach night wrapped around us as I walked her to the door.

She turned with a soft smile. "Thanks for tonight."

I leaned in and kissed her gently. "You're welcome. I'll see you tomorrow night," I said, watching her disappear behind the screen door before heading back to the car.

~~~

The bungalow was still and silent when I got back, the type of quiet that hung in the air when the ocean breeze forgot to stir. Before I loosened my tie or kicked off my shoes, I phoned my parents and offered them the extra
~~~

invitation. Mom was thrilled and would pick up the invitation tomorrow.

The clock on the dresser ticked like a steady old friend, but I wasn't quite ready to call it a day. I changed into my bedclothes, the cotton cool against my skin, still warm from the evening air, and padded over to the nightstand. The invitation Constance gave me, thick cardstock with gold embossed lettering, sat where I'd dropped it and the book on the bedside table beneath the lamp. I turned the card over in my hand, then set it aside and picked up *Sea Grape Cottage*.

I hadn't planned on reading, not tonight, anyway. But if Betty Lou could barely put the book down, and the whole town was talking about the story like it was gospel, maybe there was some truth tucked between the pages. Besides, I'd never ignore a good mystery, especially one brought to me by a client.

I climbed into bed and propped a pillow behind my back. The first page cracked like old leather, and I thumbed through the dedication before settling into the opening lines.

Palm Beach, Florida -1891

The train exhaled steam as it came to rest at the end of the line—a place less constructed than surrendered to. Lake Worth Station was not much more than a platform stretched beneath an aging awning, its boards bleached gray by sun and storm. The Jacksonville, Tampa, and Key West Railway had done its duty, laying iron tracks as far south as men dared challenge the swamp and salt of South Florida. Beyond this depot, the land yielded nothing. It watched. It breathed.

The Hadleys disembarked in a silence born of awe. Mr. Hadley, trim and resolute; his wife, gloved and composed; and their only son, Kevin, seventeen, sullen, half-grown, and wholly displaced. A Negro porter, his shirt sticking to his back beneath a faded cap, pulled their trunks from the train with the solemn grace of a man used to arrivals and departures not his own.

No town stretched from the platform. Instead, the jungle pressed close—palmetto fronds bristled like green spears, slash pines swayed with secrets, and dragonflies hovered in shimmering clouds above sawgrass. The civilized world ended here in a tremble of wood and steel. From this moment on, the Hadleys would be at the mercy of the subtropics.

A wagon met them for the journey east, a canvas top stretched taut over sun-bleached ribs. It bore them down a sandy track that bled into the edge of the lake, where a flat-bottomed skiff waited. No engine, just oars, sweat, and current. Kevin leaned over the worn railing, peering into the heart of the green water, the color of tarnished coins. Eelgrass rippled with the slow outgoing tide.

Across the lake, a different world awaited. Mangroves twisted their roots into brackish shallows, white sand flared like bone between the trees, and here and there, a thatched roof showed through the tangle like something half-remembered from a dream.

Waiting at the landing was a wagon shaded beneath the sweep of coconut palms. Beside it stood the Travers, the Mr. with a sun-hardened smile and Mrs. with the poise of someone who had learned to command with a glance. They waved, their voices bright as silver bells across the water.

"Welcome to Palm Beach!" Mr. Travers called, his cheer rising above the tide.

Embraces and reaffirming introductions followed the Hadleys' disembarkment. A sturdy Negro man dressed in a rough shirt and suspenders quietly lifted the Hadleys' trunks and secured them in the wagon with a practiced hand. No words passed. None were needed.

They traveled south on a track that wasn't a road so much as a memory of one. Wheels found their way between sand ruts and broken coral, the wagon swaying with each turn. Kevin sat stiffly, his eyes wide, not with wonder but wariness. Yet, the place did not allow indifference. Pines rose like columns, live oaks bent under veils of moss, and hibiscus flowers bled red against the green. Somewhere just beyond the dunes, the ocean whispered, constant and unseen.

Kevin hated it. Or thought he did. The heat clung to his neck, and his shirt had long surrendered to sweat. The air, salt-wet and perfumed with something wild, crept into his lungs and would not leave. Gulls wheeled and screamed overhead, laughing at the absurdity of propriety in a place like this.

Sea Grape Cottage revealed itself as the wagon curved inland. Whitewashed and clean-lined, it stood among the palms and sea grape trees with the dignity of something unbothered by time. Green shutters blinked in the sun, a wide porch beckoned shade-seekers, and bougainvillea poured across the railing like wine spilled on linen. Two rocking chairs moved faintly, stirred by a breeze Kevin could barely feel.

He stepped down, his boots sinking slightly into the sand and shell. He didn't know what to make of it—the house, the heat, the absence of noise. No trolleys. No sidewalks. No friends. He hadn't wanted to come, fighting the trip every step of the way and making his objections plain.

And yet.

There was something here, just out of his reach. Not a welcome, not yet, but an invitation. A possibility. The scent of the ocean wrapped around him like a hand on his shoulder.

He'd expected tedium. He'd braced for exile.

He was wrong. Very wrong.

What happened at Sea Grape Cottage would rewrite everything he believed—about himself, about the past, about what lives in the depths of a secret.

Chapter 2

When I stopped by Willie's newsstand, the morning sun hadn't yet burned off the mist. He stood there already set up, his sleeves rolled to his elbows and his cap low.

I picked up the *Post* and *Herald*, nodding toward the stack of glossy-covered books nestled between the usual magazines. "You heard anything about that *Sea Grape Cottage* book?" I asked.

Willie's eyes lit up. "Heard? Mr. Marlow, it's all Palm Beach is talking about. Half the ladies who come by here say the story's true. The other half is trying to figure out where the real cottage is. Some swear it's that old house near Sloan's Curve. Others think it's down near the inlet."

I raised an eyebrow. "So, some people think the story's real?"

He chuckled. "Ain't that the fun of it? The author weaves enough truth between the fiction to make the story believable. Palm Beach folks eat that up. Mystery, romance, and scandal all wrapped up in a tidy little novel. What's not to like?"

"I just started it last night," I admitted, folding the papers under my arm. "It does pull you in."

Willie gave me a knowing look. "Told ya. Gets its hooks in you."

"That's what I hear," I said. "Constance is planning a big reception at The Breakers tonight. The author is here and giving a talk on the book."

"Well, now," Willie said, scratching his head and tipping his hat. "That oughta be somethin'. Bet the garden club's all aflutter."

"No doubt," I said, smirking. We gave each other our two-finger salute in departing, and I headed to the office.

Betty Lou sat hunched in her chair, eyes glued to the book, a loose curl hanging across her brow.

I set the papers down. "Let me guess," I said. "Someone gets murdered in chapter twelve, and you're too spellbound to speak."

She looked up sheepishly. "Sorry, Drake. I just hit a part I hadn't seen coming. This book's something else."

"So I've heard." I hung my hat and leaned against her desk. "How about being my date tonight at The Breakers? Constance is the one who's coordinating the event for George Cummings."

Betty Lou's eyes went wide. "No kidding? That explains why *everyone* is reading the book. Even *you*."

I gave a crooked smile. "Started it last night. It's not my usual fare, but the writing's sharp. And there's something about it that sticks."

Her lips curled up into a slight smirk. "Maybe you're turning into a romantic."

"Don't push it."

We both chuckled, and then I tapped the desk. "Take off early to get ready. I'll pick you up at six o'clock.

I entered my office, closed the door, sat, and opened the papers. The *Post* pleaded for my attention, but my thoughts drifted to *Sea Grape Cottage*. I needed to scan the entire book and try to place the names Alan gave me into the story. Otherwise, I'd have nowhere to start.

Pulling the list Alan gave me from my desk, I scanned the names. There weren't many, but they were names I recognized, all wealthy Palm Beach winter residents. Some were elderly, while others inherited their parents' homes and were likely around the same age as Alan.

I'd left the book Alan had given me here at the office, so I picked up the tome and turned to Chapter Two.

Kevin stepped through the threshold of Sea Grape Cottage and into a world that seemed to exhale warmth and memory. Gone was the crisp bite of Denver air, replaced by a heavy, salt-laced heat that clung to the skin and seemed to permeate the walls.

While the staff moved quietly up the stairs with trunks and satchels, the Traverses conducted introductions with the effortless poise of people long accustomed to welcoming guests.

"This is Bella Knowles, our cook," said Mrs. Travers, gesturing toward a stout woman whose apron bore the faint smudge of flour and whose expression was one of steady composure. "And her daughter, Hattie."

Hattie stood a step behind her mother, hands clasped neatly in front of her. She looked to be a year or so younger than Kevin, with dark skin and hair pinned back with precise simplicity. But it was her eyes that caught him—calm, observant, unflinching. There was quiet in her, yes, but not emptiness; rather, the kind that made a room feel fuller somehow, more deliberate.

When Mrs. Hadley asked where they were from, Hattie answered.

"Abaco," she said. "In the Bahamas."

The name lingered in the space between them, softened by her accent as though she had brought the island with her in her voice. Kevin gave the polite nod his mother had long ago instilled in him, but something stirred beneath the surface. Curiosity. Sharp and sudden, like the flick of a match.

After a short rest in their rooms, they sat in the dining room in wicker chairs that creaked gently beneath them. Bella poured iced tea into tall glasses, the ice clinking. Then, she retreated into the kitchen, and Hattie remained, moving with silent grace from one place to another. She served the evening meal with ease, setting down dishes without a sound, her movements unhurried and precise. When she refilled Kevin's tea, he watched the way the light caught the surface of the liquid, and again, the name rose in his mind... Abaco... though he wasn't sure why.

After the meal, the Travers rallied Kevin's parents for a tour of the property.

"Long ride," Kevin said, and excused himself with a shrug that required no further elaboration. Left alone, he wandered through the parlor, its windows shuttered against the sun. After a time, his feet led him back toward the dining room. And there she was again.

Hattie stood by the sideboard, gathering the last of the plates into a large porcelain basin. She didn't turn at the sound of his approach, only spoke, her voice light, even.

"You didn't go with them?"

He leaned against the doorframe and shrugged. "Too hot."

A small smile touched her lips as she reached for the silverware. "You'll get used to it."

Her voice had the same soft cadence and British lilt, like water over smooth stones or wind through palms. He wanted to ask her about the island, about what the sea looked like from Abaco, about the stories hidden in her voice. But the questions caught somewhere in his throat. Instead, he watched the sunlight as it slanted through the shutters, casting golden bands across the table, her hands, her wrists.

Upstairs, Kevin lay back, arms folded behind his head, and listened to the distant hum of insects, the breath of this strange new world. And in that stillness, she returned to him.

He thought of her hands, her voice, the way she'd said Abaco with neither apology nor pride. Just certainty. The word stayed with him, like something unfinished or unopened.

Something had begun. Kevin didn't know what it was, only that it had.

What I read was a nice description of Sea Grape Cottage and Hattie and Kevin's budding relationship, but I needed to reach the heart of the story, where whatever bothered Alan Cummings still nestled among the pages. I skipped ahead to somewhere in the middle of a chapter.

Kevin walked along the sandy path winding from Sea Grape Cottage through the dune grasses, heading toward the beach. The sun hung high, painting everything in gold, and the humid breeze carried the scent of salt and marsh. Just ahead, the sea murmured steadily, a vast expanse of shimmering dark blue meeting a pale horizon. Then he caught movement down by the shore, a figure dancing in the distance, in and out of the waves, as if she belonged to them.

Hattie.

She hadn't seen him yet. The hem of her skirt was tucked into her waistband, revealing strong, muscular legs that moved across the wet sand with grace. Her bare feet brushed the surface as she spun, stooped, scooped up a shell, then twirled again. Her laughter, light and unguarded, carried on the wind.

Kevin stood still, watching, mesmerized. This was the first time he'd seen her outside the house, outside of work. Free. Her hair caught the sunlight in dark, copper strands; her arms stretched toward the open sky as if she were part of the landscape—alive, wild, beautiful.

She turned suddenly and saw him.

She paused, hand shielding her eyes. Then, a smile.

He walked toward her, his shoes crunching softly over shells and sand. "Didn't mean to interrupt," he said.

"You didn't," she said. "I come out here when I can between my duties. Ocean's got a hundred stories if you know how to listen."

"Yeah?" he asked, curious. "Like what?"

"Pirates," she said with a grin. "Ships sunk in storms. Gold washing up after hurricanes. Fishing tales. Sometimes, even voices in the wind if you stay quiet enough."

He chuckled. "I wouldn't mind finding gold."

"Most folks wouldn't. But all that glitters isn't gold. Ever heard that saying?"

"Of course," he said.

They walked side by side along the edge of the surf, their footsteps swallowed in the lapping waves as fast as their next step.

"You ever swim in the ocean?" he asked.

"Every summer. When I was little, Momma used to tell me not to go out too far. But I didn't listen." She looked up at him, her eyes bright. "Do you swim in Denver?"

"We don't have any ocean," he said with a grin. "But we have lakes and lots of snow. And mountains so tall they scrape the stars."

Her face lit up with wonder. "What's snow like?"

"Cold. Real cold. But quiet, too. When it falls, it hushes everything. And hiking those mountains—" Kevin glanced at the horizon "—like climbing to heaven. Hard work, but it feels good when you reach the top. Makes you feel strong. And the views! Can't see anything like that here."

She studied him, then looked down.

"You look strong," she said softly. "Like you could lift a tree if you wanted to."

He laughed, embarrassed. "Hiking'll do that. Especially if you've got gear strapped to your back."

They kept walking, the silence between them stretching easily. She explained about the Bahamas, a string of islands off the Florida coast, and her home there. He didn't know how long they'd been there, only that the sun was lower now.

Then he noticed a figure farther up the beach. Someone strolled along the dunes and glanced their way now and again.

Hattie noticed, too. Her mood shifted in an instant.

"I have to go," she said quickly.

"I'll walk you back," he offered.

She shook her head. "No. You can't. A white boy and a Negro girl walking together?" She didn't finish the sentence; she didn't need to.

He watched her hurry away, skirt untucked, trying to catch her flying hair and gather it back with a ribbon. The waves rolled in, indifferent to the world's rules and borders.

Kevin stayed there a while, staring out at the sea, thinking of gold, snow, Hattie, and stories not yet written.

Now, we were making progress, and the relationship between Kevin and Hattie was possibly growing into something taboo. But I hadn't seen any other characters that alerted me to the names Allen had given me.

I closed the book, my hand lingering on the cover. No doubt there would be more hidden clues as the story unfolded, but Kevin's walk on the unspoiled beach reminded me that I hadn't taken an afternoon off and walked on the sand or swum in the ocean in a long time. With Betty Lou already out of the office, I decided to close up shop early and head for the beach. I did my best thinking while swimming. Perhaps the exercise would trigger a starting point in my investigation.

Chapter 3

The Breakers never did anything halfway. From the moment Betty Lou and I stepped out of the car, I handed my keys to the valet, and we joined the tide of evening coats and silk gowns flowing toward the entrance, it was clear tonight was meant to impress.

"Not bad for a Thursday night," I muttered to Betty Lou, offering my arm as we moved with the crowd through a pair of arched doors into a side reception room where marble gleamed underfoot, and chandeliers shimmered overhead.

She took it all in, eyes scanning the crowd with a mix of curiosity and calculation. "You think they're here for Cummings's talk," she said, "but I think most of them came to be seen."

The reception room was already vibrating with expectation. A string quartet in the corner played something light, the kind of melody that makes champagne feel more expensive. Servers moved effortlessly through the crowded room, offering drinks and canapés that could fit on a dime.

A courteous nod of recognition came from Alan Cummings from across the room, which smelled of gardenias and Palm Beach's regal past.

Betty Lou nudged me gently with her elbow. "There's Max and your parents," she whispered.

Sure enough, Maxine "Max" Shelton, a reporter for the *Palm Beach Post*, stood near my parents, one hand resting on a camera slung over her shoulder while the other balanced a glass of champagne. She'd traded her usual nondescript shirt and slacks for a midnight blue dress that fell just below the knee. Her dark hair, usually jammed under a cap, fell in soft waves that framed her boyish features. She looked, for once, like she belonged on the other side of the lens. We walked over.

"Well, don't you clean up nice," Betty Lou said, slipping up beside Max.

Max turned, blinking in surprise, then gave a crooked smile. "Don't start," she said, her voice low and husky, so deep that if I hadn't known better, I might've sworn a man had spoken. "I only wore this because Mrs. Anderson gave me the eye when I showed up in trousers last time."

Betty Lou chuckled. "You look beautiful. I mean it."

"She does, doesn't she," said Mom, smiling.

"Thanks," Max muttered, clearly uncomfortable but pleased in her own way. "I figured if I'm going to shoot society folks talking about scandal, I might as well pretend I'm not just the help."

I offered a nod of greeting. "Got enough film to catch a confession?"

She grinned at that, a glint in her eye. "Wouldn't that be something? I'm just hoping for good lighting and nobody spilling champagne on my lens."

Mom giggled politely.

“Think it’ll be worth all the fuss?” Betty Lou asked, glancing toward the curtained doors that led into the main hall.

Max shrugged. “Palm Beach loves a secret. And a man like George Cummings dangling half a dozen of them in a book? You bet they’ll be holding their breath.”

We weren’t halfway through our first round of cocktails and canapes when I spotted Constance.

She stood near a cluster of town matrons, a coupe glass in hand, looking like she’d just stepped out of a *Vogue* spread in a navy crepe gown, white gloves, and her hair pinned into a sweep that defied gravity and humidity alike.

“Excuse us,” I said, as Betty Lou and I drifted toward her.

“Drake,” she said when we approached, her smile bright. “And Betty Lou, you look lovely.”

“Likewise,” Betty Lou returned with a smile. “This is quite the turnout.”

Constance gave a modest shrug. “You know how Palm Beach is. Everyone loves a bit of literary scandal, especially when it’s dressed up in respectability.” Her eyes flicked briefly to her watch. “We’ll be starting shortly. Please excuse me. I’ve got to make the announcement.”

She moved to the front of the room with practiced grace and spoke into the floor microphone just loud enough to rise above the strings and chatter.

“Ladies and gentlemen, if I may have your attention. The lecture will begin in fifteen minutes. Please make your way to the main hall and find your seats. We’re honored tonight, and I promise it will be worth your time.”

There was a ripple of polite laughter and a rustle of silk and linen as the crowd began to drift toward the hall.

Betty Lou and I found our seats several rows back on the outside edge. Constance sat in the front row beside

Mrs. Anderson. The lights were low, the stage framed by tall palms in brass urns. Excitement buzzed in the air.

At precisely 7:00 p.m., Mrs. Anderson, a formidable woman in emerald satin and pearls thick as macadamia nuts, rose and stepped onto the stage and behind the podium. She waited until the crowd quieted before speaking, her voice rich and commanding.

"Good evening and welcome. It is my great pleasure to introduce tonight's speaker, whose depiction of Palm Beach is both vivid and unflinching. His prose captures not just the sunlight and splendor but the shadows, too, the things we whisper about but rarely name. Please join me in welcoming the bestselling author of *Sea Grape Cottage*, Mr. George Cummings."

Applause erupted, enthusiastic and prolonged. The kind that doesn't just signal respect but anticipation. I clapped along, though not as robustly as Betty Lou. Something in me, instinct, I presume, was already watching the edges. Cummings emerged from stage left, tall and tanned, with a slow, steady walk that said he knew precisely how long applause should last. He gave a modest bow, then raised one hand, calling for quiet.

"Thank you, Mrs. Anderson, for that generous introduction. And thank you to all of you for being here this evening. It's always a rare gift to speak in a place that understands its own myth."

The room quieted. Cummings smiled. The kind of smile meant to disarm and impress.

"And Palm Beach," he said, "is nothing if not myth and memory stitched together in sunshine and salty air."

Laughter and exchanged glances. We were off to a smooth start.

Cummings had been speaking for nearly ten minutes, and the audience was utterly still, the way a crowd only quiets when something in the air turns serious. He'd charmed them at first, self-deprecating, wry, with that dry New England polish that made his sarcasm land gently. But now, his tone had shifted.

"I know," he said, resting his palms on either side of the podium, "that some of you believe *Sea Grape Cottage* to be more than fiction." A faint smile etched his lips, though his eyes betrayed something else. "Too vivid, too detailed. As if only memory could have supplied it."

He paused, glanced out over the sea of faces, and then added, "The truth is, I did come to Palm Beach all those years ago. And I did stay in Sea Grape Cottage. And—"

Here, his voice wavered. Not just with emotion, though, at first, I thought it was. His throat caught on the words like something dry and sharp had lodged in it. He coughed softly into his fist and reached below the podium for a glass of water.

He took a long swallow. His brow furrowed, and for a moment, it looked as if he might put the glass down, but he pressed on with another gulp.

"I think it's time," he said, placing the glass back on the shelf behind the podium, "to finally put the rumors to rest. To tell you..." He paused. "... what really happened..." Another pause. "At Sea Grape Cot—"

His breath hitched. Just a fraction. Then he froze as if a string inside him had pulled his vocal cords shut.

From where I sat, I could see Cummings's knees give way, a slow buckle as though gravity clawed at them. His grip tightened on the edges of the podium. A murmur rippled through the audience. People shifting. Whispering. And then, without another word, he dropped.

Not forward, but sideways, collapsing behind the podium where the crowd could only see the sudden lurch, then the jarring sight of his polished shoes jutting from behind the rostrum, heels kicking once, then again, sharp and convulsive.

Gasps swelled through the room. Chairs scraped. Somewhere to my right, a woman stifled a cry. Mrs. Anderson, sitting in the first row, stood, then fainted, those on each side of her catching her as she crumpled.

Constance and I were already on our feet. She moved toward the door. I rushed toward the stage, the hum of confusion swelling as I reached its edge. “Is there a doctor?” I called out, scanning the crowd. “Doctor, please!”

By the time I reached George Cummings, I already knew. He was beyond saving.

Max, already there, snapped away, and as I knelt beside Cummings’s crumpled body in the narrow space behind the podium, his head twisted toward the floor, one arm tucked beneath him like he’d tried to break the fall and failed. His face was flushed, lips slightly parted. No blood. No struggle. Just silence.

The doctor dropped to his knees beside me and checked for a pulse.

Constance rushed onto the stage. “I’ve called the police,” she gasped, horrified by the scene.

Beside Max, Constance, the doctor, and me stood George’s son, Alan, his expression frozen in shock. His mouth hung open, lips slack, eyes wide. Another man, someone I didn’t recognize, rushed to his side. He wore a pressed suit, his posture rigid, fists clenched until the knuckles shone white. His gaze was fixed on the body, and he didn’t flinch, as though his limbs were drained of function and his mind locked in alarm.

I scanned the small gathering, then stepped to the mic. “Ladies and gentlemen, no one is allowed to leave this room, so please remain in your seats. The police have been alerted and will be here momentarily to take statements."

Someone in that breathless room, surrounded by the elegance of The Breakers, had just committed murder.

Minutes later, the sea of murmuring guests parted as uniformed officers pushed through the main doors. Chief Borman led the way, his broad shoulders squared beneath his tan summer-weight jacket, followed by Detective Holcomb and a squad of men, including two from the coroner's office wheeling a collapsible gurney. I met them near the doors, stepping away from a huddle of shaken spectators.

"What happened?" Borman asked in a low voice, his eyes already scanning the room.

I gave him the quick version. "He started strong, maybe ten minutes in. Reached for a drink under the podium. A glass of water, he thought. Took a big swig, went back to speaking, and then he buckled. Never got back up."

Borman grunted and glanced at Holcomb, who gave a sharp nod and began barking instructions to the uniforms. Then, the chief stepped behind the microphone and addressed the crowd with a calm, even voice.

"Ladies and gentlemen, I'm Chief Borman of the Palm Beach Police Department. We appreciate your cooperation during this investigation. No one is under suspicion at this time, but we will need to speak with each of you before you leave. Officers will be dividing you into groups and taking your statements."

A few guests gasped, others whispered behind gloved hands. A woman near the aisle dabbed her eyes with a monogrammed handkerchief. The rest of the crowd seemed suspended in a mix of curiosity and polite dread.

Max was still near the back, camera slung low now, her face a mask of reluctant professionalism. A uniformed officer motioned to her and asked for her film. She gave me a harsh stare before handing the case over and melting into the group ushered out for interviews.

The forensic team met me at the top of the stairs.

"It was the glass," I said, pointing. "Cummings reached under the podium for it. Thought it was water. Something was off about the taste, but he kept talking." I stepped back to give them space.

The police photographer focused on the podium, the glass of water, George's body, and the small spread of collapsed papers that had fluttered down as he fell. When he finished, the forensic boys nodded and donned rubber gloves. One poured the water into another container, sealed it, and placed it in a paper evidence bag, while the other took the glass, dusted the rim and sides for prints, and then put it into a second bag.

Meanwhile, the men from the coroner's office opened the collapsible steel gurney; its scissor legs clattering slightly as they locked into place. Its canvas stretcher sagged somewhat in the middle, and the leather straps hung loose at the sides, waiting. It wasn't fancy, but it did the job quietly. They placed George on the gurney, covered him with a sheet, and strapped him in, then wheeled him out of the room.

Borman joined me a few minutes later. "Poison?"

"Seems that way. Fast-acting. Not cyanide, no frothing. Maybe strychnine slipped into the water before he even came out on stage."

He frowned. "And you're tied up in this, how?"

"Cummings's son, Alan, hired me," I said. "He wants me to find out whether stories in his father's novel, *Sea Grape Cottage,* are based on real events. His father was about to tell the audience when the incident occurred. Somebody didn't want them told."

Borman's mouth tightened, but he nodded. "All right, Marlow. We'll work this one together."

"Same arrangement?" I asked.

"You keep me informed. I keep you breathing."

"Fair enough."

I watched as Constance escorted Mrs. Anderson, pale and trembling beneath her cloche hat, to a waiting officer who would give them a courtesy ride home. Betty Lou walked up.

"Here," I said, handing her my keys. "Go on home. The Chief will give me a ride to your place, and I can pick up Celia II there."

She opened her mouth to argue, then thought better of it. An officer guided her to the side door with the others, and the crowd began to thin.

Alan Cummings found me before he left. His tie had come loose, and he held a folded handkerchief in one hand like he didn't know what to do with it. "Mr. Marlow," he said, his voice hoarse, "I'd like you to continue."

I looked him in the eye. "You still want the truth?"

He swallowed hard. "More than ever."

"All right, Mr. Cummings," I said. "I'll find it."

"By the way, who was the man next to you on the stage?" I asked.

"Dad's literary agent, Mr. Slater." He gripped my hand and then walked out alone.

I stayed behind with the others until the hall emptied, the stage cleared, and the last camera bulb flashed. The hush that followed felt heavier than the crowd.

Whatever secrets lay buried in *Sea Grape Cottage*, someone just killed to keep them there.

Chapter 4

Late the next morning, I stepped onto Worth Avenue. I spotted Willie behind the counter of his newsstand, thumbing through the comics.

"You're late," he said without looking up.

"I was up half the night watching a man get wheeled out like a buckled display."

He grunted. "You and half the island." He reached under the stack and held out a folded copy of the *Palm Beach Post*. "They held up the press for this. Said they were waitin' on Max's column."

I took the paper and scanned it. There it was in bold block letters across the front page:

"BESTSELLING AUTHOR ABOUT TO REVEAL SECRETS DROPS DEAD"

A photo showed George Cummings holding his book in a publicity shot supplied by the publisher. Below the image, Max's byline stretched like a victory flag.

"She get all this in one night?" I asked.

"She stayed up typing while half of you were still giving statements. They say she was gonna beat *The Herald* to the story or die trying."

I gave a low whistle and turned the page. There was Max's voice, sharp, clean, and fast-moving, like a camera shutter. She didn't speculate, but she painted the scene in tight brushstrokes: the crowded hall, the hush that fell as Cummings reached for his glass, and the way the enthusiastic applause at the start turned into gasps by the end.

"She make you look good in there?" Willie asked, a glint in his eye.

"Barely mentioned me." I folded the paper. "This means she's saving something. And now, with her appetite whetted for the complete story, she'll be on this like a dog digging up a bone."

Willie chuckled. "You gonna beat her to the bone?"

"Have to. The author's son hired me to find out who killed Cummings, and you can help. I've been reading the book. The story got me wondering what the mainland and Palm Beach were like in those days. Especially the folks who lived and worked here before Flagler and the big money rolled in."

Willie leaned an elbow on the stand, giving me that patient look he reserved for old friends. "Well, this area back then was swamp and salt marsh, mostly. You had folks movin' down from Georgia, the Carolinas. They were freemen, formerly enslaved people lookin' to start over. Then you had the Bahamians, comin' over by boat, bringin' farmin' know-how and toughness you needed to survive here."

I nodded, thinking about Kevin stepping off that boat and gazing at the raw, wild land around him.

"Most of 'em farmed, at first," Willie went on. "Pineapples, tomatoes, anything that would grow in this sun. When the land boom hit in the 1920s, they shifted. Became carpenters, domestics, business owners, you name it. Built half the homes and hotels you see now."

I hooked a thumb in my pocket. "I need to talk to someone who remembers the island back then. Who these people were, their names, where they worked, their way of life."

Willie didn't hesitate. "Mama Dawson," he said, reverence in his voice. "She's got a hundred years of stories in her. Still sharp as a barber's razor. She watched this island grow from a patch of sand and scrub to what you see now."

I smiled. "Think you could introduce me?"

Willie grinned. "Wouldn't dream of sendin' you without a proper vouchin'. Mama don't waste her time with just anybody."

"Would you know by tomorrow?" I asked.

"Sure enough."

I thanked him and tucked the papers tighter under my arm. Kevin Hadley had stepped onto this island with wonder in his eyes. Maybe I wasn't so different when reading *Sea Grape Cottage*.

~~~

The Building Department at Town Hall would be my next stop after checking in with Betty Lou. Mrs. Weston, the head clerk, had a knack for filing the day's headlines alongside blueprints, permits, and property records in her mind. In a town where gossip moved faster than the tide, she seemed to be the rare soul who could separate fact from fiction, at least regarding walls and roofs. If anyone could trace the long, winding history of Sea Grape Cottage, if it had been a real house, it would be her.
~~~

I didn't know yet whether George Cummings had chosen the house for his novel because of its lush, secluded setting, the kind that soaked into a man's imagination, or if he had truly walked its halls and listened to the wind rattle the shutters at night as he intimated in his talk before he collapsed. Either way, I intended to find out. There were stories buried in those floorboards, and with any luck, the head clerk would help me pry them loose.

Mrs. Weston beamed as I entered the records room in the Town Hall, and she nearly leaped from her chair to greet me.

"Mr. Marlow!" she exclaimed, grasping his hand warmly. "I'm simply *thrilled* to see you again. I read the article in the *Post* about The Breakers case involving the stolen jewels. Imagine my delight when you credited me for helping you find those hidden passageways!"

I chuckled. "You deserved the mention, Mrs. Weston. Your memory of old blueprints saved me days of searching. I'm the grateful one."

She patted my arm affectionately. "You're too kind. Now, what brings you by? No doubt George Cummings's abrupt departure has stirred something in you."

I lowered my voice slightly. "I'm looking into *Sea Grape Cottage.* The book, and more importantly, the real house."

Her eyes twinkled with mischief. "You're not the only one. Everyone in town is whispering about that novel and the house, especially after what happened last night. I just bought a copy myself, though I haven't had a chance to start it."

I leaned against her desk. "What can you tell me about the cottages constructed on Palm Beach back then?"

Mrs. Weston tapped her fingers thoughtfully. "Well, in the 1890s, nobody filed blueprints or building plans around here. Palm Beach wasn't a real town yet. It was all raw land, wild vegetation, and a handful of settlers. West Palm Beach didn't become a city until 1894. Filing building plans didn't become a thing until the 1910s and wasn't formally required until the Land Boom in the 1920s."

I nodded, following closely.

"As for the cottages," she went on, "most structures built around that time were constructed of Dade County Pine, a sturdy wood impervious to insects. These folks were early land investors, part of that first wave who saw potential here long before Henry Flagler laid down his railroad. The Carlisles were part of that wave."

I nodded for her to continue.

"From what I remember from stories my mother told me, the Carlisles built Sea Grape Cottage as a winter retreat, a sturdy two-story frame house with a wide porch facing Lake Worth. It would have been simple but elegant, surrounded by croton, sea grapes, and palm thickets."

"Were there other houses nearby?" I asked.

"Very few. You could walk for twenty minutes in any direction without seeing another roof, although you might have seen a shack or two. It was still a frontier in those days."

I smiled. "Anything else about the Carlisles?"

"They would have been respectable, but like many early settlers, they'd have depended on Bahamian workers to help build and maintain the property. Most laborers came from the islands. They were hard workers with a British colonial influence." Her eyes glinted knowingly. "Especially if you're looking into the parts of the story people are starting to whisper about."

She turned, rummaging through a wooden file cabinet with little brass pulls, and pulled out a folder. From inside, she drew a faded, sepia-toned photograph. "There," she said, handing it over carefully. "That's Sea Gull Cottage, a real house on Palm Beach built around 1890."

I studied the photo. The house stood proudly against a wild backdrop of cabbage palms and sea grapes, its wide front porch sagging slightly at the edges from the Florida humidity. There was nothing but sand trails and tangled underbrush around it. No manicured lawns. No paved roads.

I whistled softly. "Looks like Sea Grape Cottage, the same structure Cummings described in his book."

"The McCormicks built Sea Gull Cottage. They hosted friends from up north and stayed for a few winters. Then, in 1893, along came Henry Flagler, scouting land for his new hotel, which would become The Royal Poinciana. He needed somewhere to stay while he built his empire. He bought Sea Gull Cottage from the McCormicks and moved in."

She smiled, then continued.

"And after Flagler moved into the Royal Poinciana Hotel once it opened, Sea Gull Cottage passed through a few hands. Some private owners. Some seasonal rentals. Today, it's one of the oldest surviving homes on the island, a reminder of the rougher, simpler days before Palm Beach became the glittering resort it is now."

I stared at the photo. See Gull Cottage vs Sea Grape Cottage. The names were so similar. If Cummings tried to disguise the dwelling in his book, he hadn't done a very good job.

I handed the photograph back carefully. "This helps a lot. Thank you, Mrs. Weston."

She gave me a wink. "Always happy to help a sharp young man with a good memory."

Just as she slid the photograph back into its folder, Mrs. Weston leaned in closer, lowering her voice to a confidential murmur. "You know," she said, glancing around like someone might hear her, "my mother knew the McCormicks and said there were always rumors circling them."

I raised an eyebrow. "What kind of rumors?"

She gave a slight shrug, as if reluctant to share the gossip but unable to resist the thrill. "Oh, nothing ever written down, of course. But I remember my mother saying they kept to themselves. 'Friendly enough, but guarded,' she'd say, 'as though they had something to hide.' Some whispered that they were eager to sell to Flagler and leave Palm Beach behind."

I tucked that little nugget away carefully. In my experience, where there was smoke, there was usually a bonfire someone tried hard to stamp out.

I left Miss Weston and drove up to Mrs. Anderson's house. A widow, she resided in one of those grand Palm Beach homes featuring tall hedges trimmed to perfection and a circular drive paved with coral stone. The kind of house where even the sea breeze seemed to straighten its tie before blowing through. I felt a flicker of hesitation as I approached the wooden door with its polished brass handle. Coming unannounced wasn't exactly polite society's way, but polite society hadn't hired me to solve a murder.

The door swung open before I could knock twice. A maid in a crisp uniform scrutinized me, her expression neutral.

"I'm Drake Marlow, Private Investigator, and Miss Grimley's fiancé," I said, giving her my best respectable smile. "I was hoping to speak with her and Mrs. Anderson if they're available."

The maid's face softened just a touch. "Yes, sir. Please come in."

I entered a marble foyer where sunlight filtered through leaded glass, casting little rainbows on the floor.

The maid disappeared down a hall, and I caught the faint scent of fresh lilies from a massive arrangement on a side table. Everything in the place whispered money, from the gilded mirrors to the Persian rugs plush enough to show footprints.

Constance appeared a minute later, looking as polished as the house but with a tightness around her eyes that told me the last few days hadn't been kind. She blinked in surprise when she saw me.

I gave her a small smile. "Alan Cummings has hired me to find out who killed his father. I need to ask you and Mrs. Anderson a few questions."

Her lips parted, but she caught herself and just nodded. "Of course. I'll get her."

I sat in the formal living room a few minutes later, all pale upholstery and delicate antiques. Mrs. Anderson walked in, her silver hair pinned up haphazardly. She gave me a sad but gracious smile. "So you're Drake Marlow. Constance speaks very highly of you, Mr. Marlow."

I stood. "Thank you, ma'am. And I appreciate you seeing me on short notice, considering what happened."

She gestured for me to sit. I got to the point once we settled in.

"First, I want to offer my condolences. I know Mr. Cummings was staying here, and I hate to trouble you at a time like this, but I need to ask some questions. I'm trying to understand his last days and whether he had visitors, if he seemed bothered by anything, or if he mentioned where he was going when he left the house."

Mrs. Anderson's face grew thoughtful. "Detective Holcomb asked much the same things. I told him, and I'll tell you, I didn't notice anything unusual. George seemed in good spirits, though perhaps a bit tired. He did have a few callers. His son, of course, and his agent, Mr. Slater, who came down from New York for the event, though they seemed to share words."

"What kind of words?"

"Let me think." Mrs. Anderson closed her eyes for a moment. "Oh, yes, now I remember. Mr. Slater said, 'You can't do this,' and George said, 'Watch me!'"

"Do you know what they were referencing?" I asked.

"I just assumed they were talking about George's upcoming talk."

I jotted that information in my notepad. "Do you recall any names? Of the other callers?"

Mrs. Anderson shook her head slowly. "Some I knew by face, not by name. And I'm afraid I didn't keep track. Constance might remember more."

I turned to Constance, who was already slightly frowning as if trying to pull details from the back of her mind. She offered what she could, but nothing concrete.

"Sometimes it takes a little while before someone remembers other details," I said, jotting down notes.

Constance leaned back a little, her eyes glancing toward the big picture window where the palms swayed. "There *was* one thing," she said slowly. "The day before his talk. I remember Mr. Cummings got a phone call while having coffee on the terrace. He seemed irritated afterward. Muttered something about 'old ghosts' and that he needed to get rid of his baggage. Then, he made another call. I didn't think much of it at the time."

Mrs. Anderson's brows lifted faintly. "Now that you mention it, Constance, I recall he left abruptly late that night. Said he had an errand in West Palm. That was unusual for him as he preferred not to cross the bridge unless necessary."

I nodded, filing that away. "Did George say where in West Palm? Or who he was meeting?"

They both shook their heads.

"When did he return?" I asked.

Mrs. Anderson pressed her hands together. "I'd say around 12:30 a.m. You know, Mr. Marlow, there was also that gentleman who came by earlier in the week. I didn't recognize him. He was of medium height, with reddish hair and a distinct limp. He stayed only a short while, but George seemed pensive afterward. Spent the evening in his room and didn't join us for supper."

"A limp?" I repeated, ears perking. "Did either of you catch a name?"

Constance bit her lip, thinking hard. "Something with an M, I think. Malone maybe. He had a Florida accent and wore a signet ring. I couldn't make out the design, but I think it was initials, not an image."

What they gave me wasn't much, but more than I had five minutes ago. I let a slow breath out. "Thank you both. Even small details help."

Mrs. Anderson gave me a tight smile. "I hope you find whoever did this, Mr. Marlow. What happened to George was awful, and this book event would have been his crowning glory."

"If I may, I'd like to see George's room," I said, standing.

"Of course," said Mrs. Anderson. "Thank you for coming, Mr. Marlow. I'm sure Constance can show you his room."

Mrs. Anderson left while Constance led me up the broad staircase, her steps soft against the thick runner. At the top, she glanced back. "Detective Holcomb and his team have already been through the room. They dusted for prints and took his things to the lab."

I gave her a thin smile. "Doesn't hurt to give it another go. Sometimes fresh eyes catch what others miss."

She stepped aside at the door. "I'll leave you to it. I know how you work."

Before she slipped away, I pulled her to me and gave her a long, passionate kiss that stirred more than my lips. But I had a job to do, and so did she.

"Thanks. I needed that." She slipped out of the room, leaving me alone with the silence and whatever secrets still lingered.

The room carried the faint scent of expensive cologne, mixed with the sharper smell of fingerprint powder left behind by Holcomb and his boys. Sunlight cut through the slats of the tall windows, striping the heavy drapes and the neat, impersonal furniture that came with these old Palm Beach houses—high-backed chairs, a carved writing desk, a bed with posts thick enough to hold up a dock.

I moved slowly, my eyes tracing every aspect of the room. Holcomb had done his job, no doubt. The suitcase was gone, the dresser drawers open and empty, every surface smudged with the ghostly residue of dusting powder. But I wasn't looking for what was obvious.

My search came up empty, and I crossed to the windows to look at the view and maybe clear my head while I thought. I grabbed the edge of the drapes to pull them back. That's when I noticed. One curtain dragged more heavily than the other, as if it hesitated to move.

Curious, I ran my hand along the hem and found the stitching loose in one spot. A little work and something solid and small, a little larger and heavier than a quarter, dropped into my palm.

It was a coin, but not like any I'd seen in circulation. Heavy and misshapen, hammered gold with rough, clipped edges. A bold cross flared out on one side, crowded by little lions and castles in the corners. The other side showed a shield divided into strange patterns, waves etched along the bottom, and a number stamped clean as day: 8.

I didn't know much about old coins, but I knew enough to recognize this wasn't pocket change. Spanish, maybe. The kind of thing sunken fleets and treasure hunters whispered about along the Florida coast. I slipped it into my pocket. Holcomb might've missed this little prize, but I wasn't going to. Yet, the puzzle remained. What was the coin's significance, and why had George hidden the precious object in the hem of a curtain?

~~~

The Green Turtle was quieting down by the time I wandered in for dinner. A few regulars were nursing what looked like their second slice of pie and third cup of coffee. The soft clang of plates in the kitchen and the low murmur of a saxophone on the radio gave the place its usual easy rhythm. I sat at the counter, nodded to the waitress, and ordered the usual.

After the last bite of coconut cream pie disappeared from my plate, I slipped behind the swinging doors into the kitchen. Most of the staff was winding down for the night, rinsing pans, sweeping the floor, and dousing burners. Cookie stood at the sink, overseeing his dishwasher, whose arms were slick with suds as he worked on a roasting pan that looked like it had survived a war.

Cookie glanced over his shoulder. "Surprised you're alone tonight, mate. Where's Constance?"

I leaned against the wall. "She's recuperating. I just left Mrs. Anderson and her. They're both still distraught. Constance will stay there until Mrs. Anderson feels better.

Cookie wiped his hands on a towel. "Crimey, Marlow, folks out front can't stop talking about the book. 'Did you read *Sea Grape Cottage*?' 'Do you think it's about someone real?' 'Must be if George Cummings died because
~~~

of it.'" He threw the towel over his shoulder. "Feels like the circus came to town."

I beckoned him over and lowered my voice. "What I'm about to say doesn't leave this kitchen."

His eyes narrowed slightly, but he nodded once. "Right, mate."

"I may need to head over to the Bahamas," I said. "A case I'm working on. Quiet stuff for now. Research, mostly. But I could use a second pair of eyes. Thought I'd see if you'd want to come along."

He didn't hesitate. "The Bahamas?" His grin stretched wide. "Man, say the word, and I'll pack. I've been lookin' for an excuse to get back across the water. It's been too long. You thinkin' soon?"

"Not sure yet," I said. "But I'll keep you posted. It may involve tracking down some old family names. Deep roots."

Cookie rubbed his hands together like I'd just told him we were chasing pirate treasure. "You know I'm in. Besides, we can always find trouble somewhere between here and there."

That made me smile. With Cookie, we usually did.

~~~

Back at the bungalow, the wind had picked up, rustling through the fronds and brushing against the screens. I settled into the armchair by the window, kicked off my shoes, and opened *Sea Grape Cottage* to the bookmarked page I'd left behind.

The next chapter followed Kevin as he delved deeper into his first summer on the island. Long walks under the moonlight, secret glances exchanged across the kitchen while Hattie peeled mangoes. Pretty stuff, sweet even, but nothing that cracked the case wide open. If this book held a secret, it still lay hidden.
~~~

I closed the book and rested it on my chest, staring at the ceiling fan as it turned in slow, lazy arcs. A car engine sputtered, coughed, and died somewhere in the distance. Probably someone leaving the beach after one too many warm beers.

My mind drifted to Mama Dawson. I couldn't wait until tomorrow when I'd hear back from Willie. If anyone could get past the hundred-year-old fortress of stubbornness, it was Willie. With any luck, I'd be sitting in front of Mama Dawson sometime tomorrow and hearing truths wrapped in Bahamian riddles.

I placed the book on the bedside table and pulled the lamp chain. Time to get some shut-eye. I had a feeling things were about to get interesting.

Chapter 5

April hadn't quite finished, yet the morning was already warm, and the breeze off the ocean felt like a blessing. I strolled my usual route from the office to Willie's newsstand, tipping my hat to the early risers and those staffing the stores and restaurants along Worth Avenue.

Willie was already manning his newsstand, sleeves rolled up, as he set out the latest editions. He looked up as I approached and gave me his wide grin, the kind that let me know I was welcome but not immune to ribbing.

"Well, well," he said, handing me the *Palm Beach Post* and *Herald*, folded and ready. "Look who's still making headlines without trying."

I raised an eyebrow and scanned the front page. "Don't tell me they printed my grocery list again."

He chuckled and shook his head. "Not this time. But folks are still talkin' about what happened at The Breakers. Seems that George Cumming's death has pushed your last caper with secret passages, ruby necklaces, and foreign agents into the rearview mirror. It's better than the serials."

I slipped a coin into the little cigar box beside the stack of papers. "Maybe I'll pitch it to the radio. You hear from Mama Dawson?"

Willie's expression shifted, just a tick. Not quite serious, but something more careful behind his eyes. "She knows of you," he said. "Not just from me, neither. Said she's been reading the papers. Says you don't just chase trouble, you untangle it. That counts with her."

"I'll take that as a compliment."

Willie reached into his shirt pocket and pulled out a folded slip of paper. "She wrote this for you. Said to give it to you when the air still smells like morning paper ink."

I unfolded the note. The handwriting was neat, though somewhat shaky: *Come when the sun is past its shoulders. Bring nothing but your questions and your manners.*

An address followed, scrawled in faded blue pencil.

I looked up at Willie. "Any idea what time that is, exactly?"

"'Bout an hour after noon, give or take. She don't work off clocks." He gave a knowing smile. "Just don't be late. And don't bring that revolver you keep under your coat."

I gave a dry smile. "Marvin only comes out when necessary."

Willie tipped his hat. "Then I reckon you two'll get along just fine."

~~~

I entered the office and found Betty Lou at her desk, flipping through a small notepad with a pencil tucked behind her ear. She looked up as I crossed the room to my office.
~~~

"I think I'll read a few more chapters of *Sea Grape Cottage*, and then I have an errand to run." I slipped into my office and closed the door.

After a few chapters, I gazed at my watch, which read just past one. I had enough time to get across town before the sun slid too far off its shoulders.

"Where are you off to now?" Betty Lou asked.

"Mama Dawson's. She left me a note."

Betty Lou's eyebrow arched. "That old woman from the Glades?"

"That's the one."

"Take Marvin," she said. "And don't drink anything you didn't see poured."

~~~

Mama Dawson's place sat hunched under a jacaranda tree, its blossoms dropping onto the roof like purple snow. Time had curled the porch boards and stripped the paint, but someone still loved the place. Wind chimes tolled gently in the salt breeze, and a faded quilt hung out to dry on the line in the side yard.

I knocked twice, expecting the screen door to creak. It did.

"Mista Marlow," came a voice as weathered as the porch. "I been wonderin' when you was gonna' come." Her smile was sun-warmed and full of secrets as she opened the door.

I removed my hat and stepped inside.

Mama Dawson was small and thin. A knitted shawl hung over her shoulders and down to her knees. She didn't walk so much as glide with a rhythm all her own, her cane carved from driftwood and worn smooth from use. Her back bent to one side, and her pace was slow, but her eyes, yellowed with age, still caught the light like polished amber. She wore a bright print dress in reds and oranges, bold
~~~

against her deep brown skin, and a lemon-colored scarf that sat like a crown wrapped around her white hair.

The inside of the house looked lived in. Not cluttered, exactly, but full. Every surface told a story. Woven baskets, carved wooden birds, jars of seeds, dried flowers hanging from the rafters like sleeping bats. It smelled like liniment, lemon balm, and something more mysterious.

She eased into a rocking chair with a groan and patted the cushion across from her. “Now tell me, chile, what a man like you want wid’ a ole woman like me?”

“I’m looking into the history of a little cottage on the island back in 1890. I was told you might know something about it.”

She nodded slowly. “Ahhh, dat I do, boy. I work der. I was der when dem Carlisles come down from New York. Miss Maddie, she was de cook. Me, I clean up. We was all Bahamian folk, fresh an’ wide-eye. Palm Beach weren’t nothin’ den, jus’ sand, palmetto, an’ big talk ‘bout de railroad. But dat cottage? She de first one built fancy.”

“What do you remember most?” I asked.

Her eyes glazed, memory pulling her far. “De smell o’ salt an’ sugar-bread. Dat Maddie, she cooks good. And, I can still hear de sound o’ silver dancin’ on china plates.”

“I heard Miss Maddie had a daughter,” I said gently.

Her fingers twitched over her shawl. “Sherry, but people called her Sharon.”

So, Hattie and Bella of Sea Gull Cottage were really Maddie and Sherry or Sharon of Sea Grape Cottage.

“Was there ever talk of trouble? With the family? Anything that might’ve caused whispers?”

She rocked once. Twice. “Whisperin’ always come when a girl got skin like sweet molasses an’ eyes like de flame o’ sunset. But trouble? Trouble ain’t come on its own.

Trouble get made." She rose with a soft grunt and turned toward the back. "Lemme fix you some tea, eh? You look like a man who don't say no to an old lady offerin' a cup."

She left me alone in the front room, and the moment she disappeared behind the archway to the kitchen, the quiet pressed in.

I stood. The house had a soul, no question. And like most souls, it had corners that didn't show at first glance. That's when I saw the shelf. Tucked half behind a faded lace curtain was a curious little arrangement. Feathers. Tiny bones. Bottles corked and sealed with wax, full of cloudy oils or what appeared to be dirt. Dried snake skins. Beads. And there, half hidden among the shells and stones, was a small cloth figure in a dark fabric suit, carefully sewn. There was something about the face. Something familiar. Pins pricked its side like a pincushion. My stomach tightened.

I stepped back and settled into my rocker as the tea kettle began to hiss.

Mama Dawson returned with two mismatched mugs and handed me one.

"Smells nice. All botanical," I asked.

"Thems herbs I dry myself. Secret mix, dat one. How you tink I live so long, eh?" She gave me a laugh that was half mischief, half challenge.

I took a sip. It was good. A little sweet. A little strange. "While you were back there," I said, trying to sound casual, "I noticed your collection on the shelf."

She didn't blink. "An' did you find what you lookin' for, Mista Marlow?"

I froze slightly, but she noticed.

"Don't fret, boy. Dis house, she talk to me. Walls got ears, floorboards got mouths. I don't need no eyes to see what goin' on."

I cleared my throat. "Is that medicine work? Or something older?"

She rocked gently, her hands wrapped around her mug. "Some call it rootwork. Some say spirit craft. De old people back in my village, dey call it keepin' balance."

"Most people would call it Voodoo."

She let out a crackling laugh. "Das what de white folks call it when dey don' know what dey lookin' at."

I glanced at the doll.

She caught me. "You got sharp eye, like a bush fox, Mista Marlow."

"Is that a likeness?" I asked, motioning with my head toward the doll.

"Could be." She stood slowly and walked over to the shelf. She picked up the doll in her thin, gnarled fingers as if it were fine china. "When a man sow pain, he reap shadow. Dis here?" She shook it softly. "It remind de spirits. Remind me, too."

"You believe in that?" I asked.

"I believe in God, sure. But I don' trust Him to mind every lil' ting Himself."

That stopped me cold.

She smiled, slow and knowing. "Faith is good on Sunday. But what about Monday, when de lies come back, an' de blood been washed off de porch?"

I leaned forward. "What about Sharon?"

"Poor Maddie. She try to keep de peace. But de sea, she don't keep secrets. Not forever."

"Why was she trying to keep peace?" I asked.

Then, soft like a whisper, she said, "You ever see de ocean give back what it take, Mista Marlow?"

"Only after a storm."

Her grin came back, slow and ancient. "Den you best look for de storm, chile. Now, time for me to rest, Mista Marlow." She rose.

"Of course," I said, putting down my mug. "Thank you for seeing me."

She walked me to the door. "I see ya gain soon." She smiled and closed the door softly behind me, leaving me with more questions than I'd come in with.

My mind raced as I drove home. So, Sea Grape Cottage was real, and so were Bella and Hattie, though they had different names. But I hadn't turned up anything solid, except Mama Dawson was angry enough with someone in a suit that she was willing to call upon the spirits to remind him his debts hadn't been forgotten. Was that George Cummings or someone else? And what was the awful event that set her anger in motion?

~~~

When I stepped into the office, the place had that hollow feel it got when Betty Lou wasn't around. Her desk was empty, but she'd left me a note in her neat script: *Bad headache. Gone home to rest. See you tomorrow.*

I tossed my hat on the rack and stood there a minute, listening to the silence. Usually, this was the part where I'd ring up Constance, tell her about some angle I was working on, or hear her voice. But this case wasn't one I could discuss politely, not yet.

Still, I picked up the receiver and got the operator. "Mrs. Anderson's, please."

The line clicked and buzzed until I heard Constance's soft but slightly surprised voice. "Drake?"

"I wanted to check on you and Mrs. Anderson. How's she holding up?"
~~~

"It hasn't been easy on her. She's still shocked by her guest's death, and I can't say it's done much for my reputation. Especially since Isabella Somerset's death wasn't that long ago."

"Neither was your fault, Constance."

"I know, Drake. Still... Oh, I hear Mrs. Anderson. I've got to go. Can we talk tomorrow?"

"Sure. Tomorrow."

The line went dead with a soft click, and I set the receiver back in its cradle. I eased back in my chair. I knew George Cummings's death, so close to that of Isabella Somerset's, would gnaw at Constance since both involved a person she was working for, but it was merely a coincidence. Still, I couldn't blame her for feeling distressed.

Constance had her hands full. Betty Lou was out with a headache. And me—I was sitting here listening to the clock tick in an office that felt too still, too empty.

But Mama Dawson's words kept circling like gulls over a garbage heap. *The sea don't keep secrets. Not forever.*

More than ever, I was starting to believe the real answers weren't here in Palm Beach at all. They were across the water in the Bahamas, where the story began long before it washed up on these shores. But knowing and proving that were two different things.

What I needed were names. Real ones. I had bits and pieces—Miss Maddie, Sherry, whispers of trouble—but no surnames to pin them down.

If anyone knew who the old families were, who had come over, when, and from where, it was Willie. He'd have cousins and uncles who remembered every ship that crossed from the Bahamas to Florida and every scandal folks tried to bury.

I'd ask him in the morning.

I locked up the office. The answers were out there, waiting. I'd continue to read *Sea Grape Cottage* and be patient a little longer.

And patience was never my strong suit.

I read late into the night, skimming some pages, lingering on others, gambling that I wasn't letting anything crucial slip through my fingers. The island rose from the words, vivid and real: Kevin's first glimpse of dolphins slicing through dark water, the wet gleam of conch shells lying half buried in the sand, lazy afternoons on Lake Worth that felt borrowed from some quieter world, fish flickering like silver coins just out of reach, and storms brooding on the horizon, ready to churn treasures up from the sea.

The heat between Hattie and Kevin was building—not loud, not yet, but it pulsed under every line like a heart. A look held too long, a touch that lingered when it shouldn't have. The tension tightened like a knot waiting to slip.

The story wrapped around the island's past, but I knew more lay hidden in the pages like whispers that didn't want anyone to hear. Only by crossing the water myself would I pry them loose, and when I did, I'd have to face whatever came crawling out.

Chapter 6

Willie's newsstand caught the first light of morning like a cat stretching in a sunbeam. He was there, same as always, stacking the *Palm Beach Post* with one hand and waving to customers with the other.

"Mornin', Mister Marlow," Willie called when he spotted me coming up the walk. "You look like a man with weight on his shoulders and sand in his shoes."

"You're not far off." I tipped my hat and leaned against the counter. "I need a favor, Willie. One that calls for information on that big family tree tucked in your head."

His grin widened, showing a gap where a tooth had once lived proud and strong. "Now you're talkin' sweet. What kinda names you lookin' for?"

"Bahamians. Folks who came over around 1890. Worked in the big houses. I got first names—Miss Maddie and her daughter, Sherry. Might've worked for a family called Carlisle." I dropped my voice. "And I need last names, Willie. Real ones."

Willie scratched at his chin, eyes squinting like he was staring at a far-off sail. "Carlisle… Bahamians workin' for 'em… now that stirs up old tales my grandpappy used to mutter. Lemme think. Maddie. That'd be Madeline Rolle, most likely. She was a cook. Folks said she could make conch fritters so light they'd float off the plate."

"Rolle," I repeated, committing it to memory like gospel. "And Sherry?"

"Sherry was her daughter, Sharon Rolle. Pretty girl, they say. Got folks talkin' back then." He gave me a sharp look. "Trouble kinda talkin' if you catch me."

I caught it. Loud and clear.

"You got any others?" I pressed. "Other families tied up with the Carlisles? Or who might've been around that cottage?"

Willie leaned back, eyes half-lidded like he was sifting through old ledgers in his mind. "Of course, there was Mama Dawson. She was the maid. You might also look into Deveraux's. Or Munnings. Those families arrived around the same time. Some settled here, and some went back and forth between Nassau and the Keys. But if you want roots, Marlow, you look at the Rolles. They're thick as mangroves from here to Abaco."

Abaco. That was enough to set my wheels turning hard. I clapped Willie on the shoulder. "You just earned yourself a steak dinner, Willie."

He chuckled, already turning back to his papers. "Make it fish, Mister Marlow. You know I don't trust beef."

~~~

By mid-morning, I headed to the Green Turtle to find Cookie and plan our trip to the Bahamas. As I walked through the back door into the kitchen, the place was alive with the usual clatter—pots, dishes, and conversation.
~~~

Cookie spotted me, wiped his hands on a rag, and came over.

"Looks like we're heading to the Bahamas," I said. "I want to get over there and stir the pot."

He let out a breath and nodded. "Right, mate. Well, I'll need a day to shuffle things around and get the staff lined up so this place doesn't fall apart while I'm gone."

"That's fine. It'll probably be tomorrow or the next, depending on how soon I can make arrangements. Gives us time to square things up on this side."

Cookie gave a short, solid nod. "I'll be ready for some proper island sun." He grinned, the corner of his mouth twitching like he was already halfway to Nassau.

"You do know the islands and Florida have similar climates," I noted.

He shrugged. Then, with that dry twinkle in his eye, he said, "Wouldn't it be somethin' if we wound up in jail over there? Keep our record goin' strong."

I gave him a look. "If you're gunning for jail time, Cookie, you're on your own. I plan on keeping my feet on dry ground and my name off the local blotter."

He chuckled, deep and easy, and slapped my back. "We'll see how long *that* lasts, mate." He turned, tossing the rag over his shoulder, accompanied by his final remark. "I'll pack my trouble shoes, just in case."

I rolled my eyes. For once, I hoped we wouldn't land behind bars on one of our road trips, especially since this wasn't just a lead. It was the key to prying open the rest of this story. And the past wouldn't stay buried once we crossed that water.

When I left the Green Turtle and returned to the office, the heat settled around my neck like a damp towel. Betty Lou barely looked up when I walked in.

"Got a minute?" I asked.

She gave me a glance over the rim of her glasses. "You need a boat captain, don't you?"

I stopped in my tracks. "You reading minds now?"

She smiled thinly and dipped into her magic file, the one packed with names of clients, witnesses, and industry experts she accumulated while working for my attorney father.

"Your father once defended a rumrunner called Captain Shadow. He's out of that game now. At least, that's what he tells people. Runs charters, fishing mostly." She slid the card across the desk. "But, fair warning. He still drinks, and if folks get wind he's been to the Bahamas, they'll think you're making a final run before Prohibition ends. You'll get yourself pinched."

I pocketed the card. "Sounds like my kind of captain." I brushed a finger kiss across the megalodon shark tooth, my talisman, on my way out.

~~~

Captain Shadow lived up to his name. I found him slouched against a piling at the West Palm Beach docks, a dark figure with skin baked leather-brown, his hat pulled low, and a cigarette dangled from the corner of his mouth. He looked like a man who'd seen too much sea and liked it that way. The boat, *Shadow*, tied up behind him, had seen better days—paint peeling, lines frayed, and the faint scent of diesel and salt.

"Are you Captain Shadow?" I asked, keeping my tone easy.

He didn't move right away. Just flicked his eyes my way, sharp and dark. "Who's asking?"

"Drake Marlow," I said. "Frank Marlow's son. My father was an attorney here in West Palm Beach. I heard he once helped you out of a tight spot."
~~~

At that, the man straightened and squinted at me as if trying to pull up a face from twenty years back. A slow smile cracked across his weathered face. “Frank Marlow. Yeah, I remember him. Kept me out of a cell when they were sure I’d be cooling my heels in one. Good man, your old man. Real straight shooter.” He flicked the remnant of his cigarette into the water and pushed off the piling. “So, you’re his boy? How can I help?”

I glanced at the boat. “I’m working a case. Need to get over to Abaco. Quietly.”

His smile faded. “Abaco, huh?” He scratched at the stubble on his chin. “I’d love to help you, son, but times have changed. Coast Guard catches me out there? They’ll slap a smuggling charge on me just for breathing salty air and take my boat for good. And that boat—” He jerked a thumb toward the tired vessel. “She’s all I got left.”

I let my eyes linger on the boat. The sagging lines, the patched canvas over the pilot seat, the dull sheen where bright work once gleamed. “Looks like she could use a little work.”

Shadow let out a dry chuckle. “You could say that. Folks don’t charter much come the end of the season.” He fixed me with a flat stare. “So, yeah. Business is slow. But not slow enough to risk losing my boat.”

I reached into my pocket, not pulling anything out yet, just letting the movement catch his eye. “Suppose I offered you twice the going rate for a charter. Enough to patch her up and keep you in fuel for a while.”

His gaze sharpened, and I could almost hear the gears turning. He glanced at the boat, then back at me. “Twice the rate, huh? No totin’ booze or human cargo?”

I gave a slow nod. “Twice. No questions asked, no cargo but me and a friend.”

Shadow rubbed the back of his neck and let out a long breath. “Abaco’s a long haul, Marlow. Lotta eyes between here and there. But I could get you to Bimini. From there… well, getting to Abaco will be your problem.”

I stuck out my hand. “Bimini’ll do.”

He looked at it, then shook, his grip rough and calloused. “Midnight tomorrow,” he said. “We leave then. Slip over the Gulf Stream through the twelve-mile limit under cover of dark. Safer that way if the Coast Guard’s sniffing around. We’ll hit Bimini in daylight.”

“Midnight tomorrow,” I echoed. “Deal.”

His grin came back, thinner this time. “Your old man knew how to pick his moments. Let’s hope you do, too.”

~~~

Back at the office, Betty Lou raised a brow as I walked in.

“He bit,” I said.

“Told you money talks,” she murmured, turning back to Cummings’s book, which was open on her desk.

I walked into my office, grabbed the phone, and dialed Cookie. “Pack your sea legs, mate. We leave at midnight tomorrow. Bahamas or bust.”

Cookie let out a whoop loud enough to make me wince.

I figured I’d better squeeze in a little family time before disappearing over the horizon. I dropped into my chair, loosened my tie, and dialed my folks’ number.

Mom answered, her voice warm as ever. “Drake! What a nice surprise.”

“Hi, Mom. Thought I’d invite myself over for dinner tonight. Does that suit you and Dad?”

“Of course it does! We’d be delighted. Will Constance be joining you?”
~~~

"I'll give her a ring and find out."

"We'll set an extra place just in case," she said, already sounding brighter.

I thanked her and hung up, then dialed Constance at Mrs. Anderson's. She answered, her voice edged with the strain of a busy day.

"Constance, it's me. Any chance you're free for dinner at my folks' place tonight?"

She sighed. "I'm sorry, Drake. I can't make it."

I glanced at the calendar and rubbed the back of my neck. "I just wanted to see you before I go."

"Go? Where?"

"Cookie and I are heading to the Bahamas tomorrow. Just for a couple of days. Following up on the case."

Her voice softened. "Well…if you want to stop by Mrs. Crippen's boarding house later, I'll be there."

"I'll see you tonight then."

We hung up, and I wasted no time dialing Alan Cummings's residence. The maid picked up and summoned him.

"Cummings here."

"Hello, Mr. Cummings, this is Drake Marlow. I called to give you a quick update."

"Go ahead."

"I've done some preliminary research and have a promising lead. I'm heading out of town to chase it down and should have something more concrete in a couple of days."

There was a moment of silence. "Good to hear, Marlow. Keep me posted."

"Will do."

I hung up and leaned back in my chair, staring at the ceiling. One more dinner with the folks, a quick word with

Constance, and then it was just Cookie, me, and the vast blue sea late tomorrow night.

~~~

Dinner at my parents' house was a familiar comfort that made a man forget, for a moment, all the stories out there. Dad said grace, and Mom served one of my favorites—roast chicken with rosemary from her little garden.

"So, what's this case that's got you running around town?" Father asked, leaning back in his chair, one hand resting lightly on his belly. "We keep hearing things about that *Sea Grape Cottage* book. Some say it's quite the scandal, others it's realistic fiction."

I wiped my mouth with the linen napkin, buying a second before I answered. "Funny, you mention it. My case involves the book."

They exchanged glances, my mother's eyebrows arching slightly, but they didn't press. They knew the line I walked.

I reached for my water glass. "I'm heading to the Bahamas for a few days. It's connected to the case. I'll call when I get back."

Dad nodded, his curiosity tempered by years of knowing better than to dig. "Well, take care crossing the stream. The weather's been temperamental."

Mother touched my hand. "Be safe, darling. And bring back some of those little straw purses I like."

"I'll see what I can do," I said, smiling.

Later that evening, I stopped by Mrs. Crippen's. The smell of night-blooming jasmine hit me before I even knocked.

Constance met me at the door, a tired smile on her lips and her hair a little undone from the day. She studied
~~~

me for a moment, then we sat in the chairs on the front porch.

"So, how's your case coming?"

I looked away. "I'll know more when I get back."

She gave a light laugh. "Well, see if you two can keep out of trouble for once."

"We'll try," I said, leaning over and giving her a lingering kiss, a promise that I'd make it right when the dust settled.

She leaned against my shoulder. "Be careful," she murmured.

"I will be," I said.

Chapter 7

The next day moved as slowly as molasses, though I kept myself busy enough. I picked up the morning papers, *The Palm Beach Post* crowing about some senator's speech, while the *Herald* gave more ink to Miami than anything worth reading. I scanned them anyway.

At the office, Betty Lou glanced up over her spectacles as I entered. "Good morning, boss. You set with your captain?"

I nodded. "Midnight run. Should get us to Bimini by morning."

She arched a brow. "Just make sure you don't end up in a Bahamian jail."

"Cookie already suggested it. Wants to keep up our record intact."

She smirked. "Well, I'd hate to have to call the chief to bail you two out."

I caught up on a few messages, nothing urgent enough to derail my plans, then went to the Green Turtle for lunch. Cookie had the place humming along, but when he spotted me, he wiped his hands on his apron and came over. "Boat all set, mate?"

"Ready as it'll ever be. I'll pick you up here a half hour before midnight."

After lunch, I headed home. I packed light—clothes, Marvin with extra shells, a notebook, and the kind of cash that made a man nervous to carry. Yet, I never knew when it would come in handy when trying to pry history from those in the know. I had squared everything away by evening and had to wait for the clock to crawl toward midnight.

At half past eleven, I swung by the Green Turtle again. Cookie was locking up, his bag slung over his shoulder, and his grin wide. "Adventure calls, mate."

"Let's hope it doesn't call too loud."

We drove through the dark streets, past locked shops and sleeping houses, until we reached the dock where Captain Shadow tied his boat. The moon cast enough silver on the water to make the scene peaceful.

Shadow was leaning against a piling, smoking a cigarette, his silhouette as rough as his name.

"Captain Shadow," I called. "This is Cookie."

The captain gave me a once-over and nodded. "Long as he doesn't get seasick, we'll get along fine."

We climbed aboard, and Shadow cast off lines with the ease of a man who'd done this a hundred times. The engine coughed to life, and soon, we were slipping away from the dock, the lights of Palm Beach shrinking behind us.

Once we hit open water, Shadow loosened up, regaling us with stories that smelled of salt and old liquor. He told us about the days when he ran crates of rum from Nassau to Florida. Picking it up on the floating docks in Nausau, then dodging the Coast Guard like a fox outpacing hounds.

"Wasn't just the law we had to watch for," he said, voice low over the engine's hum. "Pirates, too. American lads who figured rumrunners were ripe pickings. Lost two shipments that way. One bunch even took my engine belt and left me adrift."

Cookie chuckled. "Cheeky devils."

Shadow pointed off the port side, where distant lights bobbed on the horizon. "That's a Coast Guard cutter. Stays clear at this range, but if they get curious…" He let the thought hang.

Then he leaned in, voice dropping. "Found a seaplane once, stuck in the mangroves off Andros. Pilot'd been shot in the leg by Coasties. Seventeen, that kid. Barely more than a babe. Said he was flying hooch back for Al Capone and got spotted leaving Biscayne Bay. Took a slug and crash-landed in the trees."

Cookie let out a low whistle. "Seventeen."

Shadow spat overboard. "That's the game. High stakes, no rules."

After that, the sea stretched dark and quiet. Cookie and I tried to catch some sleep below deck, rocked by the rhythm of the waves. The rest of the trip passed without trouble.

When the first hints of morning painted the sky pink and gold, we saw the low shape of Bimini rise from the water. Shadow eased us in and dropped us off at the dock.

"We're here," he grunted. "Bimini."

I stretched the stiffness from my back and looked at Cookie.

He gave me a wide grin like a kid at the circus. "Welcome to the islands, mate."

~~~

The minute my shoes hit the dock at Bimini, I caught a noseful of the island, salt air laced with the sharp
~~~

tang of drying fish and the sweeter fragrance of frangipani blooms drifting in from somewhere inland. The sea slapped at the pilings in a lazy rhythm, and the sun, still fresh in the sky, cast everything in molten gold.

The dock itself was busy even at this early hour. Barefoot boys in frayed shirts darted past, hauling wicker baskets heavy with spiny lobsters and snapper, their laughter sharp and high like gull calls. A woman in a faded dress balanced a crate of pineapples on her head with effortless grace, her hips swaying in time with the calypso tune floating from a radio somewhere, scratchy and distant.

Cookie stepped down beside me, sniffed the air, and grinned. “Smells like my kinda place, mate.”

Beyond the dock, a scatter of low, wooden buildings huddled along the waterfront painted in sun-bleached pastels, sea green and coral pink, their shutters thrown open to catch the breeze. Signs hand-lettered in peeling paint advertised “Cold Kalik Beer,” “Fresh Conch,” and “Boat Hire.” The island’s streets were more like wide sandy paths where bicycles and donkeys shared space with old Fords that had seen better days.

A pair of men sat at a small table, playing a game of bones, dominoes slapped hard against the tabletop. They gave us the once-over as we passed, their eyes sharp but not unfriendly. One tipped his straw hat in greeting. I nodded back.

The sun was climbing now, turning the ocean to blue fire and bringing out the color of the painted hulls of the fishing boats bobbing at anchor. A fisherman in a broad straw hat stood knee-deep in the shallows, tossing a cast net with practiced grace, the weights splashing down in a silver circle.

A rooster let out a ragged crow somewhere inland, answered by a chorus of dogs and a goat’s bleat. The smells shifted with the breeze. From seaweed and brine to woodsmoke and frying dough, underneath it all came the faint reek of kerosene from the fishing skiffs' sputtering engines.

Cookie elbowed me lightly. "Now, this is more like it."

I had to admit, there was something raw and honest about the island. But I wasn't here for the scenery. I scanned the shoreline, taking mental notes. Somewhere amid all this color and clatter was the lead I needed. And I aimed to find it.

~~~

The sign was hand-painted, and the letters were uneven but clear enough: *BOAT HIRE.* It swung lazily in the sea breeze, creaking on rusted chains. Beneath it, a man was throwing back the shutters of his shack. Tall, lean, with skin like oiled mahogany and a face creased by years of sun and salt, he lit a cigarette, the smoke curling around his head.

I stepped up, Cookie at my elbow. "Are you the man to talk to about getting to Abaco?" I asked.

The fellow paused and sized me up through narrow eyes. He took a drag, then blew the smoke out slowly. "Who be askin', eh?" His voice rolled easy but rough, like waves scraping the shore.

"Name's Marlow. Looking to hire passage. Me and my partner here." I thumbed toward Cookie, who gave him a friendly nod. "I got cash, and I hear you folks know the way better than anyone."

The man's gaze flicked between us, then he shrugged. "Could be. But Abaco, now… dat ain't 'round no corner, y'know. Long run, plenty of fuel. And de sea, she got her moods, man." He tapped the ash off his cigarette. "Price gonna be steep, hear me?"
~~~

"How steep?" I asked, folding my arms.

He named a number that made Cookie let out a low whistle. I didn't flinch, just countered with something lower, enough to show I wasn't green but fair enough to keep him talking. We went back and forth, numbers dancing like minnows until he finally grunted.

I jerked my chin toward the plane bobbing in the harbor. "What's the story with the seaplane?"

The boatman spat into the sand. "Dat one? Belong to Jimmy de Flyer. Used to run rum for de Nassau boys. Now, he carry folk who can pay. Faster dan my boat, for sure." He gave me a sideways grin. "But faster don't mean cheap, y'see."

That perked me up. I thanked him and promised to return if we planned to go by boat.

Cookie and I headed for the shore, where the plane rocked gently. The pilot, a sun-browned man with sharp eyes and a wiry frame, was checking the engine, his hands black with grease.

I stepped up. "You, Jimmy?"

The pilot straightened and wiped his hands on a rag. His grin was sharp, teeth white against his tanned face. "That'd be me, old chap." His voice carried the clipped, easy confidence of an Englishman who'd seen his share of skies. "What's on your mind?"

"Name's Marlow. I'm looking to get to Marsh Harbour on Great Abaco Island. Heard you might be faster than a boat."

Jimmy sized me up with a pilot's quick eye. "Faster, absolutely. But speed comes at a price, friend. Can't cheat the miles, eh?"

I glanced at Cookie, then back at him. "We pay fair. What's your price?"

Jimmy named a sum that made Cookie's eyebrows jump. I chewed it over, thinking about the time saved. Finally, I nodded. "You got yourself a deal. When do we leave?"

Jimmy glanced at the sky. "Give me an hour to fuel her up and check the plugs. We'll be airborne by then. You two ever flown before?" He grinned like he already knew the answer.

Cookie let out a slow whistle. "Not on one of these crates, mate."

Jimmy's grin widened. "Then you're in for a treat. Bring your bags—and hold tight when we lift off. She's got a mind of her own on the water."

My stomach growled on cue. "How about breakfast? Anywhere close by?"

Jimmy jabbed a thumb down the road. "Rosie's place, a yellow shack with green shutters. Tell her Jimmy Albury sent you. She'll fill you up right."

"Appreciate it," I said.

Cookie was already grinning. "If it's got fish and rum, I'm in."

We left Jimmy to ready his craft and followed the sandy path. The morning sun climbed higher, and the island came alive. Chickens darted under porches, a woman swept her stoop with a palm broom, and kids kicked dust as they chased a tin can on a string.

Rosie's wasn't hard to spot—yellow paint peeling, but cheerful, green shutters flung wide. Inside, the smell hit me first: frying fish, sweet plantains, and goat pepper sauce sharp enough to wake the dead.

Rosie herself, broad-shouldered and smiling, set us up. Cracked conch fried golden, johnnycakes hot off the griddle, and a heap of pigeon peas and rice. The fish tasted like it had jumped straight from sea to pan.

Cookie tore in like a man starved. "Now this is travelin' right, mate."

I couldn't argue. I ate and listened to dominoes clatter. A scratchy steel drum tune hummed from a radio in the corner.

When we finished, bellies full, we tossed Rosie a few extra coins and headed back. Jimmy reviewed his mental checklist, his sleeves rolled up, and the plane gleaming dull silver under the sun. On its side, I spotted a faded roundel: Royal Flying Corps.

"You flew in the war?" I asked.

Jimmy straightened, a flicker of pride in his sharp blue eyes. "RFC, 1917. Over the Somme. Jimmy Albury, at your service." He extended a hand.

I shook it firmly. "Drake Marlow. American forces, Meuse-Argonne. My friend here—"

"Cookie Koa," the Aussie said, gripping Jimmy's hand. "Gallipoli, then France. That's where me and this bloke met." He jerked his head at me.

Jimmy laughed short, nodding slowly. "Well, now. Comrades in arms, eh? No matter the flag. Didn't reckon I'd be ferrying Yanks and Aussies in these parts, but I'll shave a bit off the price for brothers who've smelled the same mud and cordite."

Cookie gave him a wide grin. "Now you're speakin' my language, mate."

Jimmy jerked his thumb toward the plane. "Load up, gents. Marsh Harbour, if the winds stay friendly. Hundred miles east with clear skies today. You'll see the banks like few ever do."

We climbed aboard, mingling with the smell of oil and sea salt. The passenger seats, just behind the cockpit, were wide open to the view. Jimmy settled in, hands dancing over controls like a former radio man.

"Hold tight, boys," he called back. "She's got spirit on takeoff, but once we're up, we're free as birds."

The engine roared, rattling my teeth. The plane surged, skimmed the waves, and then lifted. Below, the water turned sapphire, then turquoise, sand ribbons winding between cays like pale threads.

Cookie leaned over, shouting above the growl. "Not bad for a flyin' crate, eh, mate?"

Chapter 8

The hum of the engine settled into a steady drone, and after a while, even Cookie went quiet, just staring out at the shifting colors below. Reefs of coral gleamed pale against the darker sea, and here and there, I caught the flash of a shark's shadow or the white churn of a fishing boat miles out.

Jimmy glanced back, his cap tilted against the wind that sneaked through the seams. "Making good time," he said. "Marsh Harbour'll show up on the nose in another twenty minutes or so. You'll see the lighthouse first. Red and white stripes. Can't miss it."

Cookie craned his neck, eager as a schoolboy. "This the bit they call the Sea of Abaco?"

Jimmy grinned. "Aye, that's right. Protected waters, smooth as glass most days. Pretty, but shallow. It'll catch you unawares if you're not minding your keel."

I nodded, feeling the sun creeping in warm through the glass, the steady thrum of the engine settling somewhere deep in my chest. After days of chasing shadows, the open sky felt almost clean.

"How's the landing?" I asked.

Jimmy just flashed that easy grin again. "Little bump and splash, but she'll sit down gentle. I've done it blind in the rain in the rum days. This'll be nothing."

Ahead, the thin line of land was beginning to rise out of the blue haze. I spotted the faint candy-stripe twist of the lighthouse standing sentinel.

Cookie slapped my arm. "There she is, mate. The Great Abaco Island."

I sat up straighter. Time to leave the sky behind and get back to work.

The seaplane touched down smoother than I expected, skimming the sheltered waters before Jimmy eased her to the wooden jetty like he was parking a bicycle. Spray fanned out, and the smell of salt and mangrove drifted in through the open windows.

Cookie let out a breath. "Well, we're still in one piece. I'll call that a win."

Jimmy hopped down from the plane to the float to the dock, tying off the line with practiced ease. We climbed out, boots thumping on the sun-warmed planks.

I shook his hand. "Appreciate the lift, Jimmy. What's the best way to reach you when we're ready to head back?"

He flashed a grin. "Simple enough. See the harbor master in town. He'll put through a call on the wireless. I keep an ear on the set most days."

Cookie adjusted his hat against the glare. "And if the weather turns sour?"

Jimmy shrugged. "Then you wait till it clears. This ain't Miami, gents. Skies rule the schedule out here." He winked. "But I'll come fetch you, never fear. Cheerio!"

We thanked him again, and he casually saluted before returning to his plane, already checking lines and gauges like a man who trusted habit over luck.

Ahead, a shack with a tin roof stood under a crooked coconut palm. A painted sign read: ***GOVERNMENT CUSTOMS & IMMIGRATION***. A man stepped out as we approached—tall, dark-skinned, wearing a short-sleeved khaki shirt with brass buttons and creased shorts that exposed his knees above polished boots. A faded British crown insignia dominated his pocket.

"Identification, gentlemen," he said crisply, his accent precise but softened at the edges— island-born but trained in the Queen's English.

We handed over our driver's licenses. He scanned them, wrote down our names, and returned them to us. Then asked, "Your bags, please."

We set our bags down on the counter, and he casually looked through them.

"You're all clear. Business or pleasure on Abaco, sirs?"

"A bit of both," I said smoothly. "We're looking for someone who knows the history of the people here. Family lines, settlements. That sort of thing."

His eyes narrowed, weighing me. Then he jerked his chin inland. "You'll be wanting the Methodist chapel. Reverend Hall's the man you seek. Knows every soul on this island and the stories that go with them. Been here his whole life."

"Where do we find him?" I asked.

"Follow the main road till you reach the market square. The church sits back on the rise. White walls, red roof. Can't miss it."

Cookie tipped his hat. "Appreciate it, mate."

The attendant gave a curt nod. “Mind your manners with the Reverend. He’s respected here.”

We thanked him and shouldered our bags, the heat pressing down as we set off toward the heart of Marsh Harbour. The town had narrow streets lined with clapboard houses, many of which had stucco walls surrounding them. Purple and pink bougainvillea peaked over the top as if to see who was passing by.

By the time we reached the church, Cookie and I were both fanning ourselves with our hats and wiping sweat off our brows like men who’d crossed a desert instead of a town square. The heat clung to us, thick as molasses, and even Cookie, born under a sun hotter than this, looked wilted around the edges.

We stepped inside the Abaco Methodist Church, and the change was like stepping into a cool well. The shutters were wide open to catch the breeze, and the whitewashed walls seemed to push back against the heat. We found a pew near the back and sat down, both of us sighing like old men. My shirt stuck to my back, and Cookie muttered something about the Bahamas giving Australia a run for its money.

Before long, a man appeared from a side door near the pulpit. He was about forty, with a strong build that said he worked more with his hands than with books. His shirt was open at the collar, sleeves rolled to the elbow, and his stride had the easy confidence of someone at home in his place.

He gave us a warm smile as he approached. “Good day to you, gentlemen. Welcome to Abaco Methodist Church. I’m Reverend Hall. What brings you out in this heat?”

I stood and offered my hand, which he took with a firm, dry grip. “Name’s Drake Marlow. This is my partner, Cookie Koa. We’re looking to learn a little about the island's history and its people. Thought maybe someone like yourself could point us in the right direction."

Reverend Hall's smile didn't fade, but I caught a flicker of curiosity in his eyes. "History, is it? Well, now, you've come to the right place, Mr. Marlow. Folks often forget, but the church has long memories." He gestured toward the front pews. "Why don't you come sit where there's a bit more breeze and tell me just what kind of history you're after?"

Cookie and I exchanged a glance and followed him forward, glad for any seat that might shave off a degree or two.

We followed Reverend Hall down the aisle, the wood planks creaking under our shoes. The front pew caught more of the cross breeze, and when I sat, I felt the breeze against my face.

Hall sat sideways on the edge of the next pew, arms resting loose on his knees. "So," he said, giving us both a look that invited truth, "what kind of history are we speaking of, Mr. Marlow? Church records? Old settlers?"

I cleared my throat and adjusted my hat in my lap. "We're tracing some family connections. Old ties between folks from here and folks who ended up in Palm Beach, Florida. It could date back to the 1890s, possibly earlier. We're trying to understand the movement of Bahamian families who might have crossed over, settled, or mixed in ways that got forgotten over time."

Cookie added, wiping his neck with a handkerchief, "We heard that Abaco's got some of the oldest families with ties to both sides of the water. We're hopin' to find someone to help us fill in the blanks."

Reverend Hall leaned back a little, his eyes thoughtful now. "Ah. That sort of history." He tapped his fingers once against the wood, then nodded slowly. "You're right, plenty of that here. Families came and went, and ties got tangled up in the crossings along with some stories that folks don't much speak of anymore." His gaze sharpened. "Is this for your knowledge, or are you digging for something larger?"

I met his eye. "A little of both. We hope to set the record straight on a matter that has been causing trouble back home. Nothing official, just trying to get to the truth before folks start drawing their own conclusions."

Hall studied me, then gave a slight nod. "Well, Mr. Marlow, you've come to the right place. The church keeps records. And old folks here still remember the stories their parents told them." He stood. "Let's start in the back, where we keep the books. If what you're looking for is written down, we'll find it."

Cookie grunted as he pushed to his feet. "Now you're talking, Reverend."

I stood, too, feeling that familiar prickle along my neck, the sense that we were about to find what we were looking for.

Reverend Hall led us to a side room, cooler and dimmer, lined wall to wall with shelves that bowed under the weight of old ledgers and hand-bound books. The air smelled of dust and a faint trace of old wood polish.

"These here," he said, pulling down a heavy volume and laying it on the table with a soft thud, "are the church registers—baptisms, marriages, deaths. Some go back nearly a hundred years."

He flipped the pages carefully, the paper thin and yellowed at the edges. "Families who left for Florida are noted here, too, when they transferred their letters of membership. You'll want to look for entries from the 1880s and 1890s when folks started heading to Florida to work in the fields and on the railroads."

His finger traced a line of elegant, looping script. "Names are listed by head of household, then kin. And here—" he tapped a narrow column "—this shows where they resettled if they sent word back."

Cookie leaned in close, squinting. "Blimey, this is like reading chicken scratch."

Hall chuckled, straightening. "Takes a little getting used to. I can help you get started."

I glanced at Cookie, then back at the Reverend. "The surname we're tracing is Rolle. Seems to pop up in the line we're following."

The Reverend chuckled lightly, leading us toward a tall wooden cabinet stacked with worn ledger books. "Yes, not surprising. Rolle is a common name here among the Black Bahamian community. It traces back to the Loyalist days. The Rolle family, whites from England, settled here with their slaves after the American Revolution. When emancipation came, many freedmen retained their names. Most inhabitants of these islands descended from a mix of British settlers and enslaved Africans. The story's written right here in these books if you know how to read them."

The jangle of the telephone cut him off. He glanced toward the door. "Pardon me a moment, gentlemen. That'll be the clinic callin'."

He left them with the open book, the wooden door swinging shut behind him.

Cookie wiped at his brow again, muttering, "Nice fella. But I got a feelin' this is gonna take all afternoon."

I leaned over the pages, eyes scanning the names. Somewhere in these cramped lines was what we came for.

Cookie and I sat again at the table, the heavy books spread open like ancient maps. The church was quiet now, except for the distant murmur of the Reverend's voice on the phone.

I pulled out my notepad and flipped to a clean page. "All right, Cookie, let's keep this straight. We're looking for Madeline Rolle first—she'd have been in her thirties around 1890, which puts her birth somewhere around 1856. Her daughter, Sherry, was sixteen when she worked at Sea Grape Cottage, so she would have been born around 1873. If we pin down Sherry's birth, we might trace where they moved."

Cookie nodded, wiping his hands on his trousers before carefully turning the brittle pages. "Got it. I'll start with this volume from the 1850s. Look for Madeline first."

I opened the big ledger marked 1870-1880 and ran my finger down the neat columns. Names, dates, and parents listed in tight, cursive script. The paper smelled faintly of mildew and ink, but the entries were clear enough to read. Births, baptisms, sometimes a small note— "moved to Nassau," or "deceased," written in the margins.

Cookie grunted as he squinted at a page. "Some of these names repeat a lot. Lotta Rolles here, like the Reverend said. Gonna take a sharp eye."

"Just stick with Rolle and look for a Madeline born around '56," I muttered, eyes scanning as I flipped ahead to 1873. "I'll handle the daughter."

We both settled into a rhythm, the soft rustle of pages and the occasional tap of my pencil on the notepad the only sounds in the still church. Outside, I could hear the distant hum of cicadas rising in the afternoon heat.

By the time the light slanting through the high windows turned golden, my back felt like it had aged ten years, and my stomach had started chewing on itself. Cookie took a sharp breath and tapped the page with one thick finger.

"Here she is, mate. Madeline Rolle. Born in 1856, just like we figured. And look, departure was noted in 1889. Says she left for Florida."

I leaned in, blinking the fuzz out of my eyes. Sure enough, there it was in neat, faded ink. It felt like the first crack in a door we'd been pounding on all day.

Just then, Reverend Hall's footsteps echoed back into the room. He glanced at the dimming light and smiled apologetically. "Gentlemen, I hate to interrupt, but I must lock up the church now. You're welcome to return in the morning and continue your search."

Cookie stretched and groaned. "Guess we lost track of lunch, huh?"

I stood and slipped my notepad back into my pocket, but something made me hesitate. We were close, and waiting until tomorrow gnawed at me. I turned to Reverend Hall.

"Reverend, before we go, do you happen to recall anyone by the name Madeline Rolle? Or her daughter, Sherry? They would've left for Florida some years back, but maybe someone in the community knew them."

Hall paused, his keys jangling lightly in his hand. His brow furrowed as he considered.

Reverend Hall's eyes narrowed like he was sifting through his memory. "Madeline Rolle, you say? And a daughter, Sherry?" He tapped the keys against his palm, thoughtful now. "I can't say I knew them personally, that would've been before my time. But the Rolle name… well, that's an old one around here. Many moved to Florida and the United States during the late 1800s. Some sought work. Others… well, times were changing."

He glanced back at the shelves of ledgers, then at me. "If Madeline left in 1890, as the record says, she'd have been part of that wave. As for Sherry…" He paused again.

"I do recall hearing older folks mention a young Sherry Rolle who left the island with her mother. A pretty girl, they'd say. Spirited. There was some talk—" He caught himself, clearing his throat. "But island talk is like the tide. Comes and goes."

That got my attention. I stepped in a little closer. "Talk about what, Reverend?"

Hall gave me a measuring look. "Just that she returned here later that year with her mother and then left again after about six months. Folks wondered why. Could be nothing more than gossip. But if you're digging through family histories, sometimes the gossip tells you where to look."

Cookie muttered, "Ain't that the truth."

I nodded. "Appreciate that, Reverend. That might save us a day's work."

Hall smiled faintly. "Glad to help. Now, you come back tomorrow, and I'll have the books ready when you arrive."

I caught the Reverend before he could turn the lock.

"One more thing, Reverend," I said, tucking my notebook back in my pocket. "We'll need a place to stay the night and someplace that serves a decent meal wouldn't hurt, either. Any recommendations?"

Hall's stern face softened just a notch. "You'll want to try Miss Genevieve's. It's a small hotel just off Queen's Road. Nothing fancy, but clean and comfortable. She's been hosting visitors longer than I've been here." He hooked his thumb toward the west. "And if you're hungry, her kitchen serves supper till sundown. Good Bahamian cooking. You won't go hungry."

Cookie brightened. "Now you're speaking my language, Reverend."

"Tell her Reverend Hall sent you."

"Much obliged," I said, tipping my hat. "We'll be back first thing tomorrow."

Hall nodded and opened the door wide. "I'll have the ledgers waiting. You, gentlemen, take care walking. Sun's still sharp out there."

We stepped out into the heat again, but with the promise of a meal and a bed, it didn't feel quite as hot.

~~~

We left our bags at the front desk of the hotel and slipped into the restaurant, which was a simple place with plaster walls and ceiling fans doing their best to cool the place down. Cookie and I found a table near the window to pretend there was a breeze. We ordered conch fritters, fried fish, and a bottle of local rum to take the edge off the long day.

But Cookie didn't stop at a couple of drinks. By the time our plates were empty, he was well past two.

"I tell ya, mate," Cookie said, thumping his glass down and holding up his hand, thumb and forefinger a half inch apart. "We're *this close* to crackin' it. We found Madeline, and we'll find Sherry, too, mark my words. What's in those books no one here wants us to find?"

I stiffened and glanced around. Sure enough, some locals at the other tables had gone quiet. One man in a short-sleeved shirt and suspenders leaned back in his chair, giving us a slow look. Another muttered something under his breath.

I leaned in, my voice low. "Lower your voice, Cookie. We're guests here, not bounty hunters. And we don't need to go shouting names around."

But Cookie was on a roll. He pointed a finger at no one in particular. "What kinda dirt y'all hidin' about Madeline and Sherry Rolle?"
~~~

Chair legs scraped as the man in suspenders stood. "You best watch that tongue, mister," he said, voice clipped with that Bahamian lilt but edged hard. "Ain't no dirt here, only folks who don't fancy strangers stirrin' things up."

I stood, too, hands out. "Let's not make this a thing. My friend had too much to drink, that's all. We'll be on our way."

But Cookie pushed back his chair, swaying. "I wanna know what ya scared of, mate?"

The man in suspenders stepped forward, shoulders squared. I grabbed Cookie's arm to haul him back, but Cookie flailed, trying to shake me off, and his elbow clipped the man square in the jaw.

The man lunged, knocking over a chair. In an instant, the restaurant erupted: fists flew, chairs toppled, and shouts rose sharply over the clatter. Cookie took the brunt of the brawl—eye, cheek, stomach—while I ducked a swinging arm and cursed under my breath. So much for a quiet dinner.

Two more men grabbed us before I could drag Cookie out of there. I twisted free long enough to see two uniformed constables pushing through the crowd, a whistle shrilling.

"That's enough! All of you, enough!" the constable barked. His eyes landed on Cookie. And me. "You two. You're coming with me."

I let out a long breath and raised my hands. "Terrific," I muttered. "Vacation's going great so far."

~~~

The jail cell smelled like sweat, and the cot was little more than a wooden bench with a thin blanket. I sat on the edge, rubbing my temples while Cookie snored softly against the wall, one shoe off and his hat tipped over his face. We remained that way the rest of the night.
~~~

Morning light slanted through the barred window by the time we revived enough to face the constable. Cookie's face was swollen and bruised, and dried blood smeared his forehead from a small gash.

"Last time you pulled this stunt, I called Chief Borman from the Orlando PD, and he got us out by breakfast." I glanced at Cookie, who didn't stir, but I knew he was listening. "This is the Bahamas. Something tells me Borman's badge doesn't carry much weight here."

Cookie groaned and shifted. "We're still alive?"

"Alive, but not exactly thriving," I said, leaning back against the wall. "Congratulations, you've officially started an international incident with your mouth and elbow."

Cookie didn't respond, trying to keep a low profile.

A constable entered the jail and stood outside our cell. I stood, dusted off my soiled and wrinkled jacket, and put on my best professional face.

"Look, we're sorry about the ruckus," I said. "We're here on legitimate business. We were researching some historical family records at the Methodist Church with Reverend Hall yesterday. If you let me, I can call Florida and prove it."

The constable, a stocky man with wary eyes, folded his arms. "I'll be checking with the Reverend myself."

Half an hour later, Reverend Hall appeared at our cell, looking more tired than angry. "Morning, gents," Hall said with a thin smile. "I told the constable you were at the church, and your research was aboveboard, though I can't vouch for your friend's drinking habits."

The constable sighed and unlocked the door. "You can go, but there's a fine. A hefty one. Pay it, and keep your noses clean from now on."

I handed over the cash without arguing, swallowing the bitter taste. Reverend Hall lightly clapped us on the shoulders as we gathered our things.

"I suggest you wrap up your work quickly and return to Florida before you stir up any more... situations," he said, giving Cookie a pointed look. "And I'll add, turning to the Lord might help you avoid these troubles in the future."

Cookie nodded.

We returned to the hotel, gathered our things, and left. The sun was already beating down hard by the time we walked back to the church, hopeful we could at least finish what we started with the books. When we entered the church library, our breaths caught. The table where we'd left the ledgers was bare.

My heart sank. "Where are they? "Would those thugs have taken them?"

Reverend Hall, who had followed us in, looked troubled. "I don't know. I left them here last night, as I always do. Someone must've moved them. I assure you, no one would destroy church records. They'll turn up once the men involved have calmed down. But for now, it seems the ledgers have disappeared.

I glared at Cookie. "You just had to run your mouth. All the time, money, and effort to get this close, and now we're back at square one because you couldn't hold your liquor."

Cookie looked genuinely stricken. "I know, mate. I was feelin' good, and I didn't think. I'm sorry."

I let out a long, slow breath, fists clenched at my sides. "Sorry doesn't find the books," I said through tight teeth.

Hall stepped in before things got uglier. "Give it time. They'll turn up. No one's burning history. But for now, perhaps you should head home."

"Yeah. We're done here," I said, nodding stiffly.

I shook Reverend Hall's hand, thanking him for his efforts, and left the church in silence, Cookie several steps behind me. The walk to the harbor master's office felt longer than it was. I barely looked at Cookie as I stepped up to the desk.

"We need to get a message to Jimmy. Tell him we're ready to head back as soon as possible."

We grabbed a bite at Rosie's while we waited for Jimmy. By late afternoon, his seaplane skimmed over the turquoise waters and glided up to the dock. He climbed out, his cap tilted back, and a knowing smirk tugging at his mouth.

"Heard you boys managed to make a name for yourselves over here," Jimmy said, helping us aboard. "Didn't take long."

I climbed in without meeting his eye. "Just get us out of here, Jimmy. And I need a favor. Can you take us straight back to Florida instead of Bimini?"

Jimmy shrugged, settling into the pilot's seat. "Florida it is. You're lucky I like you, Marlow."

Cookie slumped in his seat, looking like yesterday's bad news. He didn't say much on the ride back; he kept his eyes on the floorboards and muttered about being sorry.

The flight was bumpy. I barely said a word the whole way, staring at the endless sea, my mind fixated on every inch of ground we'd lost.

When we finally taxied to the Palm Beach dock, Jimmy cut the engine and turned in his seat. Safe and sound. Try to stay outta Bahamian jails from now on, yeah?" he said with a grin.

I forced a tired smile, paid him, and hauled Cookie out of the seat with a stern look. "Come on. I'm dropping you off at the Green Turtle."

The car ride was as quiet as the flight had been. When we reached the restaurant, I didn't bother with a speech and jerked my thumb toward the door. "Get out and sleep it off. And stay outta my hair for a while."

Cookie nodded, eyes down. "Yeah. I got it, mate. I messed things up."

I waited until the door closed before driving off. Anger was still there, but exhaustion took precedence. By the time I got home, the sun had set, painting the sky with the last purples of the evening. I tossed my keys on the table, peeled off my jacket, and sank onto the bed.

My eyelids were heavy, but my brain wouldn't quit spinning. The names, the missing ledgers, the money wasted. All of it tangled up in a knot behind my eyes.

I let out a breath and brought my lids down.

Tomorrow, I'd figure out my next move.

But tonight. I needed to sleep.

Chapter 9

Willie was already waving the morning paper at me when I stepped up to his stand the next morning, my shoes still carrying the sand of yesterday's trouble.

"Mr. Marlow," he said, voice tight. "I know you've been outta town, but you need to read this. Now."

I took the *Post* from him, unfolded it, and my stomach turned to stone. **CHIEF BORMAN CONFIRMS GEORGE CUMMINGS MURDERED**, the headline blared in fat black letters. No details yet, Max reported, just whispers that Chief Borman was keeping details close. No suspects. No motive. Simply that someone had killed the best-selling author of *Sea Grape Cottage*.

The case had just turned from complicated to deadly.

I muttered my thanks to Willie, still staring at the front page like the article might rewrite itself if I looked hard enough. Then, I folded the paper under my arm and headed straight for the office.

When I pushed through the door, I caught sight of Betty Lou behind my desk, talking to none other than Alan Cummings. She looked up, startled to see me.

Alan was sitting in front of her, but when he spotted me, he stood. “Mr. Marlow, I hope you don’t mind. I came without an appointment. Betty Lou was kind enough to hear me out while you were away.”

“Don’t get up from my chair,” I told Betty Lou, forcing a tired grin. “I’ll take the guest seat this time.” I dropped into the vacant chair across from Alan, folding my arms. “I just got back from Abaco. There’s definitely a secret buried there, something worth killing over. But I had to leave before I could dig it out.”

“Then go back,” Alan said, his voice tight with urgency. “Whatever it costs. I want this done, Mr. Marlow. I want to make sure my name is cleared before they confirm my appointment. I can’t have this hanging over me.” He reached into his coat and slapped another check down on the desk. “Please. And keep me informed.”

I gave him a short nod. “Will do.”

He stood, buttoned his jacket, and left without another word.

When the door closed behind him, Betty Lou looked at me, one eyebrow arched. “Why’d you leave so fast? What happened in Abaco?”

I ran a hand down my face and let out a breath. “You don’t wanna know, but I’ll tell you anyway.”

I leaned forward on the desk. “We found the church. Found the ledgers, and we were this close to cracking something wide open.” I showed her the tiny gap between my thumb and index finger. “But Cookie... well, he got into the rum at the hotel that night and started running his mouth about what we were digging into. Locals didn’t take kindly to that. Next thing I know, there’s fists flying, chairs tipping, and we're both cooling our heels in a Bahamian jail cell."

Betty Lou chuckled, shaking her head. "Figures. That man can't walk into trouble without tripping over it first." She gave me a wry look. "This makes what… the third time you've been locked up together? Tallahassee, Orlando, and now the Bahamas? I oughta get you boys matching stripes."

I grunted. "It isn't funny. Not this time. I can't go back there. They made it clear. The Reverend smoothed things over, but if I push my luck, I might end up in a cell they forget to unlock."

She tapped her pencil against her notebook and looked thoughtful. "Why not tell Joe? Have *him* call over there. Explain what you're doing. If the Abaco chief gets a call from a Florida police chief, he may give you the green light to return and finish what you started. Make it official."

I sat back and let that roll around in my head. She had a point. Borman might play ball if he thought it'd keep a bigger scandal from landing on his doorstep.

"Yeah," I muttered. "Maybe I will ask the chief. I'll pay him a little visit and get the lay of the land on George Cummings's murder while I'm at it. See if he's got anything he's not putting in the papers yet."

Betty Lou crossed her arms and gave me that look. The one that said *you know you're already knee-deep into this case, so stop pretending you're not.*

"Didn't want to wade into waters this deep," I sighed. "But now, I've got no choice. George is dead. Alan's panicked. And if somebody killed over this, they won't stop until they're sure no one else can talk."

"That's the spirit!" said Betty Lou.

I stood and grabbed my hat.

~~~
~~~

I stepped into the lobby of the police station and spotted Holcomb leaning against the front desk, jawing with the desk sergeant. He grinned and pushed off the counter. Ever since the case of stolen jewels at The Breakers, he and I had patched up our relationship, and now it was refreshing to be peers instead of adversaries.

"Well, if it isn't Marlow. What brings you around this morning?" he said in a friendly voice.

I shook his hand. "Oh, just following up on a case. What about you? What's got you busy these days?"

Holcomb chuckled. "The George Cummings case."

I raised a brow. "Funny, that's the one I'm working on, too."

We both laughed, the sound a little too loud in the quiet lobby.

Holcomb clapped me on the shoulder. "Well, I guess we'd better talk, huh? Swap notes before we trip over each other."

"Sounds like a plan."

We headed together down the hall to Chief Borman's office. The chief looked up from a stack of papers, his face sour until he saw us both standing there. "This looks dangerous. Marlow and Holcomb in the same room." He motioned us in. "What's this about?"

I eased into the chair opposite his desk. "Chief, I'd like to know what you've got so far on George Cummings. The papers aren't saying much."

Borman's eyes narrowed. "Before we get into that, Marlow, maybe you'd better explain your connection to Cummings. Why are you so interested?"

So I told him. About the son, Alan. About the book, the investigation, the trip to Abaco, and the murder hanging over everything like a storm cloud.

Borman leaned back, hands laced over his belly. Holcomb shot me a look that said he was filing it all away.

I cleared my throat. "And there's one more thing. I need a favor. I need to return to Abaco and finish my research, but I ran into a little local trouble last time. I'd appreciate it if you'd phone the Superintendent of Police over there and clear the way for me."

Borman's mouth twitched. "Local trouble, huh? You mean that little scuffle Cookie started? I heard about it. Landed you in their jail, right?"

Holcomb started grinning.

I sighed. "Yeah. That. Look, I need a couple of days so I can finish the job."

Borman leaned forward. "Tell you what. I'll make the call. But maybe I ought to send Holcomb with you this time. Keep you out of the lock-up."

Holcomb and I looked at each other and grinned like old partners in crime.

"I can live with that," I said. "I know a pilot who can get us over there. Give me a few days to tie up things here and arrange the pickup with Jimmy."

Borman nodded. "Fine. You boys behave yourselves over there this time. I don't want to get more calls from the British authorities."

Holcomb slapped his knee. "Who, us?"

With the two of us, this case just went from deep water to shark-infested.

~~~

I picked Constance up just as the sky turned pink over Palm Beach. She looked lovely, as always, but her smile told me she still felt raw about what happened to Cummings. I couldn't blame her.
~~~

Over dinner, I tried to ease the weight between us. I asked, "So what's next for you now that the big event's over? No more grand galas to organize?"

She gave a small, rueful smile. "I'll stay through my commitment. Another ten days or so. Then, it's back to the diner at Woolworths. I was looking forward to the event, but I can't say I mind having more time to myself."

I smiled at that, then leaned back in my chair. "Well, you won't have to hear about Palm Beach high society for a while. By the way, I'm heading back to Abaco. Got unfinished business, and this time, I'm bringing company. Holcomb's coming along for the ride."

That got a laugh out of her. "Holcomb? To keep you out of trouble, I suppose."

"Something like that," I said, grinning into my coffee cup.

But the smile faded when I realized we'd been sitting there the whole evening, and Cookie hadn't come out from the kitchen to say his usual hello. Granted, I understood why, but he never missed a chance to greet his customers.

As Constance gathered her purse, I lingered, my eyes drifting toward the double swing doors that led to the kitchen.

"I'm just going to say hello to Cookie before we go," I told her. She smiled and nodded.

I pushed through the doors and stepped into the warmth and clatter of the kitchen. Pots steamed, a line cook barked an order, and the smell of butter and garlic hit me like a familiar wave.

But no Cookie.

One of the younger fellows at the prep table spotted me and straightened, wiping his hands on a towel. "Hey, Mr. Marlow. You looking for Cookie?"

"Yeah. Tell him I'm here. Figured he'd want to say hello."

The kid blinked. "He hasn't been in since he left."

That made me pause. "What do you mean? We got back from the islands yesterday evening. He should've been back today."

The kid shook his head. "No, sir. We thought maybe he was still over there with you."

My mouth went dry. "Thanks," I muttered, turning back toward the dining room.

Cookie hadn't come back. And I hadn't noticed.

I drove Constance home and kissed her goodnight outside Mrs. Crippen's boarding house. She lingered a little longer this time, which I took as a sign that maybe I hadn't completely landed myself in the doghouse for taking off again.

Her kiss still warmed my lips as I descended the steps, but my heart was entirely elsewhere as I pointed Celia II toward Cookie's apartment.

I had a bad feeling I wouldn't like what I found.

After driving to his apartment, I knocked on his door. Nothing. I knocked again. The door stayed shut, and the apartment behind it was quiet.

I was about to give it one more when I heard footsteps coming down the hall. A man in his shirtsleeves, hair mussed like he'd called it an early night, ambled toward me.

"Evening," he said, giving me a curious look.

"Evening," I answered. "You know Cookie? Lives right here."

He chuckled softly. "Course I do. He's my neighbor." He thumbed toward the door across from Cookie's.

I shifted my stance. “Have you seen him in the last couple of days?”

The neighbor scratched his head. “No, can’t say I have. The last time we talked was a few days back. He was heading out with his suitcase.” He paused. “But… now that you mention it, I did hear something last night. Late. Some thumping, like furniture moving or something. I just rolled over and went back to sleep. Figured it was none of my business.”

My stomach turned. “Didn’t sound like voices? No shouting?” I asked.

He shook his head. “Nah. Just noise. Might’ve been nothing.”

Might’ve been. But my mind was already running through a dozen darker explanations, each worse than the last. The last thing I’d said to Cookie before we got back was sharper than it should’ve been and echoed in my head like a record needle stuck in a groove.

I thanked the neighbor and turned back to the door. Still locked. Still quiet.

Chapter10

I spent the next two days trying to find Cookie and lining everything up for the trip. No one had seen or heard from him. With nowhere else to look, I continued with plans to return to Abaco, stopping by Chief Borman's office to ask him to keep an eye out for Cookie and to confirm he'd rung the Superintendent in Abaco. I wanted to make sure that Holcomb was officially cleared to travel. Then, it was a matter of meeting Jimmy at the Palm Beach dock when the tide made for the smoothest takeoff.

Holcomb and I stood on the dock by the water's edge, our bags slung over our shoulders, as Jimmy's seaplane came in low, its pontoons skimming the surface. The engine's steady drone faded to a hush as he taxied in.

"Afternoon, gents," Jimmy called, climbing out and wiping his hands. He glanced past us, eyebrows lifting. "Didn't expect to fly Cookie back to Abaco so soon."

Holcomb and I exchanged stunned looks. I stepped forward. "Cookie's in Abaco?"

Jimmy nodded. “Aye. He booked a passage back two days ago. He said something about unfinished research and that he needed to clear his name after the trouble he stirred up last time.”

My heart thumped. “Cookie told you that?”

“Swore he had to vindicate himself,” Jimmy said. “I warned him it’d be dangerous with locals still talking about that brawl. But he was determined.”

Holcomb shook his head slowly. “That man’s got a death wish.”

I squared my shoulders. “Or courage, but right now, I don’t know which one.” I turned back to Jimmy. “All right. Let’s get to Abaco before Cookie decides to pull another stunt.”

Jimmy grinned and helped us aboard. As the plane lifted into the sky, I felt that familiar knot in my gut.

Holcomb and I chatted about what we’d do once we landed, and a few hours later, the floatplane’s pontoons kissed the sea with a soft slap. Moments later, Jimmy guided us up onto the weathered dock.

The sun beat down like it had a score to settle as we disembarked. Even Holcomb, who usually wore his discomfort like armor, tugged at his collar.

Jimmy hopped out first, tying us off. “Remember to contact the harbor master when you want to return.”

“Thanks,” I said, handing over the payment.

Holcomb and I shook his hand and headed toward the immigration shack.

Our first stop was the Methodist Church. Reverend Hall greeted us, shaking my hand firmly. “Mr. Marlow, and—?”

“Detective Holcomb, Palm Beach Police,” Holcomb said, showing his badge.

Reverend Hall's brow rose. "Well, I'm surprised to see you again so soon. Especially after Mr. Cookie spent the whole day here yesterday. He found what you were after, I believe."

"So the ledgers showed up?" I asked.

"Right after you two left the island," he said.

"Do you know what Cookie found?" I asked.

"I'm not sure, but he sure left in a hurry."

My stomach dropped a notch. "You haven't seen him since?"

"No, sir. That was yesterday afternoon. Said he had what he needed."

I glanced at Holcomb, then back at Hall. "Did he say where he was going next?"

"No, he didn't. But he looked determined, Mr. Marlow. Burdened, if I may say so, but also happy."

Outside, the sun seemed even hotter. Holcomb muttered, "Let's go to the station."

At the Abaco police station, Superintendent Fisher ushered us into his cramped office, a ceiling fan doing little more than stirring the heavy air.

"Chief Borman called ahead," the Superintendent said, nodding at Holcomb. "Asked for clearance for you boys to poke around."

Holcomb set his hands on the desk. "Superintendent, there's a complication. Mr. Marlow's friend, a civilian named Cookie, who was working with him here, came back without our knowledge. He's now missing. Reverend Hall says he hasn't seen him since late yesterday afternoon."

Superintendent Fisher's face tightened. "Yes, I remember him with Mr. Marlow. Blond fella, blue eyes? Sticks out like a pelican in a henhouse around here. I heard he was asking questions again. Didn't know he'd gone missing."

I leaned in. "We're hoping you can help us find him. If he's in trouble, we're already late."

The Superintendent nodded slowly. "We'll put the word out and check the hospital."

Holcomb's jaw tensed. "Good. Start there."

I caught my reflection in the Superintendent's dusty window as we turned to leave, my face drawn tight around the eyes. Cookie was out there somewhere, and my last words to him were sharp enough to cut. I wasn't about to let those be the last he ever heard.

Our next stop was the restaurant where the trouble started.

The place hadn't changed much since the last time Cookie and I turned over a few tables. The same faded awning flapped in the breeze, the same cracked tile underfoot as Holcomb and I stepped inside. The smell of frying fish clung to the walls.

We found a table near the back where we could see the door and sat down. Holcomb leaned back in his chair, eyes scanning the room like he was casing the joint.

The waitress, a thin woman with sharp cheekbones and tired eyes, came over. Her glance flickered from me to Holcomb and back again. She handed us menus without a smile. "Morning, fellas. What can I get you?"

I set the menu aside. "You seen my friend? Blond fella, blue eyes. Name's Cookie. Might've come through here in the last day or so."

Her eyes darted sideways, then back. "Might have," she said, voice low. "But I can't talk here."

Holcomb's mouth twitched. "We'll have the fried snapper and two coffees," he said, not missing a beat.

She nodded quickly and left, but I caught the way her head turned as if she was checking to see who might be listening.

Holcomb leaned in. “Bartender’s been watching us since we walked in,” he muttered. “And now he’s on the phone.”

I turned my head just enough to catch the man behind the bar, receiver clutched to his ear, his beady little eyes cutting our way.

“Looks like we rattled a cage,” I said under my breath.

We kept eating, playing it casual, but my stomach wasn’t interested in fish anymore. Holcomb shoveled in the food like any other day, but I saw the stiffness in his shoulders.

Near the end of the meal, the door creaked open, and in walked double trouble.

Two of them. The same bruisers from last time, the tall one with the busted nose and his stocky partner with the scar down his cheek. Both stopped when they spotted us and then shared a look that made my skin tighten.

Holcomb set down his fork and wiped his mouth with deliberate calm. “Well, Drake,” he said softly, “looks like we’re about to have dessert.”

The tall one cracked his knuckles as he started toward our table, his partner behind him, eyes dark and watchful. Holcomb shifted just enough that his coat fell open, flashing the badge clipped inside. That slowed them down, but not by much.

“Look who’s crawlin’ back,” the tall one said, voice thick with that rolling island lilt. “You got nerve, mon. Big nerve.”

I leaned back in my chair, calm on the outside. “You boys here for the lunch special, or you looking to finish what you started?”

Scarface bared his teeth in something that wasn’t a smile. “You talk too much, white boy.”

Holcomb let his coat fall back just a little more, the badge plain now. “Sit down. We got questions.”

The two men looked at each other, weighing their odds. Scarface’s tongue flicked over his lips. “Ain’t got notin’ for you.”

The bartender muttered something sharp in Bahamian Creole from behind the counter. The waitress was gone. She slipped into the back the minute the air turned heavy.

I pushed my plate away and stood slowly, hands open. “We’re looking for a friend. Blond fella. Came through here yesterday. You boys know something. I’d hate to think you left him worse off than last time.”

That hit home. The tall one’s eyes flickered.

Holcomb saw it, too. He stood, big and solid. “We can call the Superintendent Fisher right now. Bring the whole station down here. You want that?”

Scarface’s face stayed tight, but the tall one shifted his weight, uneasy now. “Ain’t us touch him dis time,” he muttered. “Ain’t our problem.”

Holcomb’s voice dropped low, like a distant roll of thunder. “Then whose problem is it?”

The tall one’s glance darted to the back door. Scarface stayed locked on me. His jaw clenched so hard I could see the muscle jump.

To our left, a chair scraped the floor. The bartender hung up the phone. And I had a bad feeling whoever he’d called wasn’t bringing flowers.

I stepped in close, my voice like ice. “Where is he? Because if he’s lying somewhere bleeding out, I swear to you—”

Holcomb’s hand clamped on my shoulder.

I stopped. Barely.

The tall one swallowed, his voice tight. "Check de hospital," he muttered. "He git mash up bad. Dat's all I know, mon. Swear it."

My pulse thumped hard in my ears.

Holcomb's grip stayed steady. "Hospital, huh?" Holcomb said coolly. "Guess that's our next stop."

I nodded, my heart hammering. "Yeah. And if you're lying."

The tall one raised both hands, palms out. "No lie, boss. True t'ing."

Holcomb tugged me back a step. "Let's go, Drake. Before this turns into a scene."

I threw some cash on the table, then let him steer me toward the door, but I kept my eyes on those two the whole way. The next time I came back, I wouldn't be asking so politely.

We stepped out into the harsh glare of the Bahamian sun, the door of the café swinging shut behind us with a slap like a challenge. My jaw was tight enough to crack a tooth.

Holcomb blew out a breath, his gaze following mine back toward the door. "You were two seconds from throwing the first punch."

"Yeah," I muttered. "And I'd have made sure they stayed down this time."

We stood there, unsure how to get to the hospital, when the waitress from earlier slipped out the side door, glancing around before hurrying toward us. She was a slight woman, her hair tied back with a faded scarf, eyes sharp and flicking left and right like she expected trouble to follow.

"You lookin' for your friend, the tall one with the funny talk?" she asked, keeping her voice low.

I turned to her fast. "Yeah. Cookie. You seen him?"

She nodded, lips pressed tight. "He came back yesterday, looked real tired. Heard he went up to the church again. But later, word is he ran into trouble. Bad kind."

Holcomb stepped in, serious and steady. "We need to find him. Fast. You know where the hospital is?"

Her eyes flicked over to the café door, then back to us. "Ain't far. I can show you. But we best go now, before them boys get ideas."

I didn't need more convincing. "Lead the way."

We set off down the dusty street at a sharp clip, the heat pressing down but not enough to slow the thud of my heart. Holcomb kept glancing over his shoulder, making sure no one was tailing us.

As we walked, the waitress kept her voice low. "I didn't see the fight, but I heard it. Folks say two rough boys caught him outside the docks last night. Said somethin' about him pokin' where he shouldn't."

My gut twisted. "He come in the restaurant afterward?"

She shook her head. "No, sir. Ain't seen him since. Heard somebody carted him to the hospital, though. That's where we goin' now."

Holcomb grunted. "Sounds like they meant to finish what they started."

I didn't answer. I was too busy chewing over the last words I'd snapped at Cookie before this whole mess. They rang in my ears now, sour and sharp.

We rounded the corner, the whitewashed walls of the small hospital coming into view. It wasn't much, more like a clinic, but it had a sign and a promise of care.

The waitress pointed. "There. That's where you'll find him, if he's still breathin'."

I pressed a couple of bills into her hand. She looked startled, then tucked them away fast and nodded. "Hope your friend's alright."

Holcomb and I didn't waste time. We headed up the steps and through the door, the smell of antiseptic slapping us in the face. The nurse at the desk gave us a flat look, her mouth a thin line when Holcomb flashed his badge.

"We're looking for a man brought in yesterday," Holcomb said. "White, tall, blond hair, blue eyes. Australian accent."

Recognition sparked in her eyes. "He's here. Came in late last night. Bad shape." She eyed us warily. "You family?"

"Friends," I said, voice rough. "Close enough."

She hesitated, then nodded toward the corridor. "Room four. But, he's pretty busted up. Doc says no visitors, but… maybe for a minute."

I was already moving, Holcomb close behind.

Room four's door was cracked open. The stink of disinfectant hit first, then the sight of Cookie.

I stopped cold.

He was in bed like a man who'd lost a fight with a freight train. One eye swollen shut, his face a roadmap of bruises, his leg thick with bandages and rigged up in a sling. His skin, usually tanned and full of life, looked sallow against the white sheets.

Holcomb muttered an expletive.

I swallowed hard, guilt hitting me like a gut punch. He was lying there, broken because he'd tried to fix the mess I'd dragged him into.

"Cookie," I rasped.

His good eye cracked open, glazed but alive. When he saw me, he managed a crooked, painful grin. "Drake… took ya long enough, mate."

I stepped closer. “What happened to you, pal?”

He tried a chuckle. It turned into a wince. “Turns out… I ain’t much of a scrapper.” He coughed weakly. “Found what we needed… ledger… but they found me after.”

Holcomb crossed his arms, face like stone. “You’re lucky to be breathing.”

Cookie’s eye drifted to him, then back to me. “Yeah. Lucky.” His gaze turned heavy. “Sorry, Drake. I had to make it right… after all the trouble I caused.”

I grabbed his hand, careful but firm. “Forget that. You rest. We’ll handle it now.”

His fingers twitched weakly around mine. “Files… Reverend Hall’s got ‘em… ledger… You finish this… clear it up.”

“I will,” I said, my throat raw. “You got my word.”

Holcomb put a hand on my shoulder. “Let’s let him rest. We’ve got work to do.”

Cookie’s eye was already slipping shut again.

I stood there, watching his chest rise and fall, the guilt gnawing a hole right through me.

Holcomb tugged me back. “Come on, Drake.”

I let him steer me out, but my mind was already burning.

First stop: Reverend Hall.

Second stop: finding those goons and making them wish they’d never laid hands on my best friend.

We left the hospital with Cookie’s battered face burned into my brain. Neither of us said much as we hoofed it back to the police station, the dust rising around our shoes in little angry puffs.

Superintendent Fisher was at his desk when we came in, going over some paperwork. He looked up, and his eyes narrowed. “Find your man?” he asked.

Holcomb stepped forward. “Yeah. In the hospital. Bad shape. Broken leg, face all beat up. Looks like someone took a grudge too far.”

Fisher’s face went still for a beat. Then he pushed back from the desk. “Hospital, eh? Who did it?”

“We were hoping you’d help us find out,” I said. “But first, I need to place a call. To Chief Borman back in Palm Beach.”

Fisher grunted. “Long distance, huh? Ain’t cheap, but I reckon this warrants it.” He turned and barked through the open door. “Eloise! Get me the operator. We’re patching through to Florida. Chief of Police, Palm Beach.”

I caught Holcomb’s eye. He gave a single nod. We both knew this was about to get more official.

A few minutes later, Fisher waved me over and handed me the heavy black receiver. “You’re on, Marlow.”

The line crackled and hissed like frying bacon before Borman’s voice came through, tinny but sharp. “Marlow? You find him?”

“Yeah, Chief. Found Cookie in the Marsh Harbour hospital. Looks like someone worked him over good. Broken leg, face is a mess. He’s conscious but not fit to talk much yet.”

A pause. I could almost hear Borman’s blood pressure rising through the line. “Put Fisher on.”

I covered the mouthpiece and glanced at the Superintendent. “He wants a word.”

Fisher took the receiver. “Superintendent Fisher here… Yes, sir… I understand… Absolutely, sir. I’ll see to it personally… Yes, my men will be on it within the hour.”

When he hung up, he didn’t sit back down. He straightened his belt and barked at the two uniformed officers lingering near the front desk. “You two. Get out there. Start at the Harbour View Restaurant. Find out who’s been running their mouth about that foreigner getting beat up. I want names before sundown."

They snapped to it like hounds cut loose.

Fisher grabbed his cap off the peg. "You two still got business at the church?"

Holcomb nodded. "We do. Some records we need to finish going through."

"Right," Fisher said. "I'll drive you. Quicker that way. And when I get back, I'm gonna find out exactly who thought they could rough up a visitor on my watch."

We followed him out, the tropical sun blazing overhead. As the engine of the British-made Morris Oxford police car with its brass bell coughed to life and we headed down the rutted road, I felt a small knot of satisfaction tighten in my gut. At least now the dogs were loose, and someone would answer for Cookie.

Superintendent Fisher let us out in front of the church, the brakes on his car squealing as he hurriedly pulled away. Holcomb and I stood there, the sun pressing down like a heavy hand, before we spotted Reverend Hall off to the side, trimming back a wild hedge with a pair of rusty clippers.

He looked up, squinting against the light. "Back again so soon, Mr. Marlow?"

I stepped forward. "We wanted to talk to you about Cookie. He's in the hospital badly beaten."

Hall's face fell, clippers lowering to his side. "Good heavens. That poor boy. He spent the whole day here yesterday, working through the ledgers like a man possessed."

Holcomb glanced at me. "We need to see those books. Maybe find what he found."

Hall nodded and gestured for us to follow. "Come on, then. They're still in the library where he left them."

Inside, the church was cooler, shadows stretching long in the open hallway. Hall led us to the little library. A small stack of worn ledgers sat on the table, their covers cracked, and corners curled from years of handling.

"There they are," Hall said quietly. "Just as he left them."

I stepped over and ran a hand along the top one, feeling the dry leather under my palm. "Reverend, do you know who took these books the first time?"

Hall shook his head, frowning. "No, sir. I found them on the porch the next morning. No note, no explanation. I figured whoever borrowed them had second thoughts."

Holcomb muttered, "Or got spooked."

I kept my eyes on the ledgers. "Whoever took them knew they were important. And whoever put them back might've known trouble was coming."

Hall shifted uneasily, his hands gripping the clippers again. "Mr. Marlow, I don't like to think that kind of business is stirring here in Marsh Harbour. But hearing what's happened to that young man... Well, it troubles me greatly."

Holcomb crossed his arms. "We're going to get to the bottom of it, Reverend. That's a promise."

I nodded, already flipping open the first ledger, my eyes scanning for whatever it was that got Cookie nearly killed.

Chapter 11

Holcomb leaned in as I flipped through the brittle pages. The ledgers were neat, with looping cursive that made me work for every word. Inked into those lines was the whole life of Marsh Harbour.

I turned a page, then another, my finger pausing over a familiar name. "Here," I murmured. "Madeline Rolle. Returned from Palm Beach, Florida, in October 1890. With her daughter, Sharon."

Holcomb straightened. "That's our window."

Reverend Hall hovered behind us, peering over my shoulder. "That's right. Families coming and going back then."

I kept going, my heart beating a little faster. Six months. I needed to find something in that stretch. Baptisms, births... My hand stilled again as my eyes landed on it.

"Here it is," I said, voice tightening. "Sharon Rolle. Daughter of Madeline Rolle. Event recorded March 1891."

Holcomb's brow furrowed. "Event?"

I read slower this time, making sure I wasn't seeing ghosts. "Birth of female child, Jasmine. Mother: Sharon Rolle. Father:—"

I blinked. The line was blank. Or rather, not blank. There was a single note scrawled where the father's name should've gone.

Holcomb leaned in. "What's it say?"

I swallowed. "Sea Grape Cottage."

He let out a low whistle. "Not a name. A place."

Hall made a slight sound behind us. "That's unusual. Father's name should always be listed, unless—"

"Unless somebody wanted to keep it quiet," I finished for him, my stomach sinking. "Sea Grape Cottage. That's the house where they worked in Palm Beach. That's the title of George Cummings's novel. In the book, the young boy Kevin spent a month there in the summer of 1890, where he met the Bahamian cook's daughter, Hattie."

Holcomb massaged his neck. "So whoever was at that cottage…"

"Is the father," I said flatly. "Or at least that's how they covered it up."

I turned another page, but the trail went cold after that. No name, no follow-up. Just that one damning clue left behind like a frayed end.

Holcomb stepped back, letting out a slow breath. "Well, now we know why Cookie nearly got himself killed. He found this. And somebody doesn't want it getting out."

"We're getting closer. Too close for somebody's comfort. I think George Cummings knew who the father was, and that's what got him killed."

Hall looked pale now, his hands wringing the handles of those clippers. "Mr. Marlow, I pray you know what you're doing. This is old business, but dangerous business, still."

I gave him a look that was more tired than reassuring. "Reverend, I never know where the trail leads. But I keep going anyway."

Holcomb nodded. "Let's write down that record. Then we pay Cookie another visit. He might remember more, assuming he's awake."

I closed the ledger gently, but my mind was already racing. Willie mentioned two other names that might be connected to Rolle.

"Pastor Hall, you know anyone named Deveaux or Munning who might be relatives of Maddie and Sherry?" I asked, wanting to find someone local to speak with. "They'd need to be old enough to remember the birth forty-three years ago, or, perhaps, deliver the baby. Maybe someone in their 70s who's a midwife?"

Reverend Hall rubbed his chin, eyes narrowing in thought. "Deveaux, now… that name rings a bell. Old family here in Marsh Harbour. As for Munning, it could be connected, though I haven't heard that name in some years." He shifted his weight, the pruning shears still hanging from one hand. "But if you're asking about midwives from back then, folks still mention only one name, Miss Lila Darville. She was the midwife for nearly everyone back in those days. She has passed on, but her granddaughter, Hester Darville Rudy, still lives on the edge of town. Keeps to herself mostly."

Holcomb straightened. "Worth a visit."

Hall nodded. "She'd be your best bet. Miss Hester was just a child when her gran delivered half the babies in Marsh Harbour, but folks say she's got all her gran's old records packed away. And if anyone knows the old family ties around here, it'd be her."

I felt that flicker in my gut, the same flicker I got when a thread started to show itself. I looked at Holcomb.

"Let's write down Cookie's record, like you said. Then we visit Miss Hester. Might be time we get ahead of whoever's trying to keep this quiet."

Holcomb gave a short nod, already pulling out his notebook.

Hall gestured toward the door. "I'll leave you to your work, gentlemen. But be careful. Digging into old bones around here, you're bound to stir up more than just memories."

I gave him a thin smile. "Seems like we already have."

Holcomb and I stepped out of the church into the late evening, our heads still buzzing with the weight of that old ledger. My stomach reminded me that I needed food.

"Let's head to Rosie's," I said, adjusting my hat against the sun. "I think better on a full stomach."

Holcomb grunted his agreement. "And I could use something cold. This Bahamian sun is no joke."

We made the walk in silence, chewing on the same question: Who that baby girl had grown up to be? Rosie's place was busy when we entered, the smell of frying conch and sweet bread hanging in the air. We took a table near the window and ordered fried snapper, plantains, and two icy bottles of Kalik beer.

Half an hour later, with our plates clean and the edge off our nerves, I paid the tab and left a tip. "Time we find a driver. I don't fancy walking all over Marsh Harbour in this heat."

Outside, we didn't have to look far. A stocky fellow was leaning against a faded Austin 12/4 with flaking paint and tires worn slick from too many miles. He watched us with the patience of a man who knew visitors would eventually come looking.

"Afternoon," I said, tipping my hat. "We're looking for someone who can take us to see Miss Hester."

At the mention of her name, his face broke into a grin that showed a gap where his front tooth used to be. "Miss Hester, eh? Lawd, now there's a lady! Her granny, Miss Lila Darville? She deliver half my folks. Even my baby brother, she catch him when she was ninety-five, can you believe it? She brought babies into this world longer than most folks been alive."

Holcomb gave a little chuckle. "Sounds like she's a legend around here."

"That she is, boss. That she is." The driver affectionately slapped the side of his car. "Name's Amos. I'll take you to her, no trouble. But I tell you now, she don't suffer fools, so mind your manners, eh?"

I nodded, already liking Amos's straight talk and the gleam in his eye. "We're just looking to ask a few questions. Nothing more."

"Good then," Amos said, swinging open the back door of his smallish car. "Hop in, gentlemen. Miss Hester don't live far, but the road's rough. Hold on to your hats."

Holcomb and I climbed in, the car creaking under our weight, and the seat so cramped that our thighs touched. As Amos started the engine with a coughing roar, I caught Holcomb's eye in the rearview mirror.

"Let's hope Miss Hester remembers more than just babies," I muttered.

Holcomb gave a thin smile. "I bet she remembers everything."

Amos turned the wheel and guided the car out of the busy part of Marsh Harbour, the tires kicking up dust as we rattled along the narrow road.

"Used to be, this whole island was pines and coppice," Amos said, glancing at us in the rearview mirror.

"Foreigner folks come in and build, but out here..." He jerked his chin at the stretch of land ahead. "This still the real Abaco."

We passed clusters of pastel cottages with tin roofs that caught the sun like mirrors. Chickens darted across the road, and kids played barefoot in the shade of broad tamarind trees. Beyond that, the road narrowed, flanked by tangled bushes and patches of scrub pine. The air smelled faintly of salt and something sweet. Maybe wild guava ripening in the thickets.

Amos kept talking as the town fell behind us. "Miss Hester, she don't come into town much no more. Folks go to her. She live quiet now, but back when I was a boy, she was everywhere like her granny—deliverin' babies, settin' bones, even mixin' up bush medicine when folks got the fever. Ain't many like her left."

The houses thinned out until there was nothing but open land, the horizon low and flat with flashes of sea in the distance. Finally, Amos slowed the car and pointed with his thumb. "That's her place up yonder. Little white house with blue shutters. You want me to wait?"

I turned to Holcomb, who shrugged. "Might take a while, might not."

I looked back at Amos. "If you see us wave from the porch, that means she's agreed to see us. Come back in half an hour."

Amos grinned and tipped his cap. "Alright then. You give me that wave when you ready, and I'll wait by the dock road."

We got out and crunched up the sandy path toward the porch. The house was small but neat, paint weathered but fresh enough, shutters thrown open to let the breeze in. A stand of sea grapes grew thick along one side, their big, round leaves rustling softly.

The screen door creaked open before we could knock. Miss Hester stood there, lean and straight despite her years, her dark skin etched with fine lines and her eyes sharp as a hawk's.

"You two the ones come asking after old times?" Her voice was rough but steady.

Holcomb and I glanced at each other. Word sure did travel fast on this island.

"Yes, ma'am," I said, touching my hat and introducing myself and Holcomb. "We sure would appreciate a word with you."

She squinted at us a moment, then nodded once. "Come on in, then."

I waved to Amos, who gave us a salute from his car before driving on.

Holcomb and I stepped inside, the door closing behind us with a soft thump. The cool dimness of her little sitting room wrapped around us, smelling faintly of bay rum and old wood.

Miss Hester's eyes narrowed as I mentioned the Rolle women. "Maddie and Sherry, you say? That goin' back a ways." She rubbed her hands on her apron, her mouth working side to side like she was turning over stones in her mind.

Holcomb and I waited. The air in the little house felt tighter by the second.

"My grandmother, she was the midwife here back then," Hester finally said. "Passed on near twenty year ago, but I kept her old books. Couldn't bring myself to throw 'em out."

I leaned forward. "We'd be grateful to have a look, Miss Hester. It's important."

Her eyes flicked between us, weighing the risk. "Folks been pokin' at that old business again? Ain't no good come from stirrin' ashes. But… if it helps someone." She gave a little grunt and disappeared through a back door.

We heard boxes dragging, a muffled curse, and then the soft thump of papers shifting. After a while, she returned with a cracked leather ledger, brittle at the edges.

"These here's birth records in my granny's hand," she muttered, flipping through. Her finger paused. "Here. October, 1890."

Holcomb and I crowded closer. The entry was faded but clear enough.

Mother: Sharon Rolle.

Female child born alive, light-skinned, with port-wine mark on left collarbone.

Father:

Notes: Connection to Sea Grape Cottage.

I felt Holcomb stiffen beside me. I tapped the line with my finger. "No given name. Just Rolle as the surname?"

Miss Hester nodded grimly. "That's how they did when things was meant to stay quiet. My granny said this child… light like a conch shell, and marked plain as day. Big patch, red as wine, right here—" She tapped her left collarbone. "Couldn't hide it easy."

Holcomb cleared his throat. "Sea Grape Cottage… that was where Maddie and Sharon worked?"

"Yes, sir," Miss Hester said, her voice lowering. "Folks knew that house. People come, stay some weeks, leave things behind they didn't want to claim. Some whispered it was a young man who came to stay or his daddy. Others said it was Mr. Carlisle, the owner. But no one dared say outright. After that baby came, them Rolle women left quickly. I hear the Carlisles left not long after. Trouble was brewin', they said."

I closed the ledger gently. "No name for the baby. Just that she was light and marked."

"That's all," Miss Hester said, watching me carefully. "But folk would remember that mark. 'Specially on someone born from mixed blood. It showed plain."

Holcomb looked at me, and I could feel the gears turning in his head like mine. A Rolle girl, light-skinned, with a birthmark like that. If she were still alive and in the Palm Beach area, that mark would be the thread that could unravel everything.

We thanked Miss Hester and went outside to wait for Amos. The sun hit like a hammer, but my mind was too busy to feel the heat. Holcomb pulled a handkerchief from his pocket and mopped his neck.

"Light-skinned with a mark on her collarbone," he muttered, his gaze distant. "Forty-three years old now, give or take. Could be living under any name."

"But that birthmark. That's the key. You can change a name, change your hair, but you can't change something like that. Not easily."

Holcomb grunted. "And if she's been passing as white all these years, she'd have every reason to keep that covered. But somebody local might remember. A girl like that doesn't go unnoticed."

I tried to picture it. A woman in Florida, maybe Palm Beach, maybe somewhere else along the coast. Light enough to pass. Born of scandal and quietly shuffled away from her island beginnings. But carrying that mark like a brand.

And if she had children… I glanced sideways at Holcomb. "If she had kids, Holcomb, that mark might've passed along. Not always, but sometimes."

His eyes flicked to me, sharp now. "So you're thinking this isn't just about finding her. It's about finding her line. The whole blood trail."

I nodded. "And every step of it ties back to Sea Grape Cottage. And to George Cumming's family, one way or another. We just don't know which man left the mess behind."

Holcomb folded his arms. "So what's your move?"

"We go back to Cookie to see if that beating jogged anything loose. Then, one of us heads back to Florida. Start asking quiet questions about any woman born into the Rolle family who is light-skinned and has a port-wine stain just below the collarbone. Someone's seen it."

"And the other of us?" Holcomb asked.

"Stays here to make sure Fisher arrests those hoodlums and gets Cookie home when he's able."

Holcomb gave a low whistle. "Dangerous game, Marlow. Especially if the wrong people figure out what you're after."

I gave him a thin smile. "Yeah. But I've already got my toe in the crocodile's mouth. Might as well see if I can pull the teeth out before it snaps shut."

Holcomb nodded. "Since you have no official capacity, and I do, I'll stay here and oversee Fisher's investigation and check in on Cookie. I'll get Jimmy to fly us back when Cookie's able. A couple of days, I should think. He won't be walking on his own yet, but with crutches, I'm sure he'll hobble good enough."

"Sounds like a plan," I said. "One more round with Cookie, then Fisher. After that, I want a stiff drink and a bed that doesn't rock like Jimmy's seaplane."

Holcomb gave a dry chuckle. "Enjoy that while you can. Once you get back to Palm Beach and start sniffing around, things'll heat up fast."

I gave him a sideways glance. "Wouldn't be the first time I've danced too close to the fire."

"Yeah, well, this time, the flames have powerful names. You'll need to watch yourself, Marlow."

"Always do."

~~~

The seaplane touched down on the Intracoastal with a hiss and a bounce, spray kicking up against the floats as Jimmy eased her in like he was setting down a feather. I stepped onto the dock, the Florida sun hitting me like an old friend. After the stink of bruises and trouble in Marsh Harbour, even the sticky Palm Beach air felt like a relief.

Jimmy hopped out after me, wiping his hands on a rag. "So, what's the word, Marlow? Am I heading back solo, or do I wait around?"

"You'll be making another run in a couple of days," I said, adjusting my hat and tugging the brim against the glare. "Holcomb's staying behind to wrap things up with Fisher. Cookie's banged up bad, but once he can hobble, they'll return with you."

Jimmy gave a low whistle. "Heard that fella took quite a pounding."

"Yeah," I said, jaw tight. "And somebody's going to answer for it."

Jimmy squinted at me as if he could see the storm cloud forming behind my eyes. "You just say when, and I'll have the plane gassed and ready."

I clapped him on the shoulder. "Holcomb will let you know. Meantime, keep your ear to the water. Things are moving fast, and I have a few stones to turn over before this gets any messier."

Jimmy grinned, already turning back toward the plane. "Ain't it always messy with you, Marlow?"
~~~

I didn't answer. Just set my sights on town and started walking to Celia II. There were questions to ask and pots to stir, and somewhere in this sunny paradise, there was a woman with a name I didn't know and a birthmark someone had noticed and, perhaps, whispered about.

I planned to be listening.

Chapter 12

By the time I pushed through the door marked *Marlow Investigations*, the ceiling fan was turning lazy circles, and Betty Lou was perched at her desk, looking cool as a cucumber in the morning heat. She glanced up, and the smile that flickered across her face told me I'd been gone too long for her liking.

"Well, well," she said, setting her coffee down. "Look what the tide washed back in. You're a day early or three late, depending on who's been asking."

I dropped my hat on the coat rack and loosened my tie. "Pour yourself another cup, Betty Lou. This one's gonna fill up a whole file drawer before we're through."

She grabbed her steno pad without another word and followed me into my office, already flipping to a fresh page.

I started from the top with Holcomb and me landing in Marsh Harbour, the trip to the church, the missing ledgers that suddenly turned up again, and Cookie's near-death beating. Her shorthand scratched steadily, eyes flicking up occasionally when the details got dark.

When I got to the part about Sharon Rolle and the baby girl, light-skinned with a port-wine stain just below the collarbone, Betty Lou's pencil stilled. "That's what you're looking for here? A woman who might not even know her own story?"

"That's the shape of it," I said, running a hand through my hair. "And somewhere between 1891 and 1933, that child grew up and became someone with a name that ain't Rolle. I'm betting someone's seen that birthmark in a dress shop, swimming pool, or someplace."

Betty Lou gave a low whistle and got back to scribbling. She dropped the pad and flexed her fingers when I finally leaned back. "That's a whole mess and a half, boss. I'll type this up for the file. Should be ready in an hour."

"Good. I'm heading over to see the chief. He needs the straight version before this story starts walking around town."

She smirked. "Tell Joe I'm keeping track of all your troubles and making a copy for him. Also, I'll have dinner ready when he gets home, and we can review any details to make sure they're accurate in case someone writes a book about all of this one day."

"If they do, make sure they spell your name correctly. You'll be the only one making me look respectable."

She waved me off, already rolling a fresh sheet into the typewriter, the clack of keys following me out the door.

~~

The Palm Beach police station had the same cracked linoleum and squeaky front door that announced every visitor. I nodded at the desk officer, who barely looked up from his paperwork, and made my way down the hall to Chief Borman's office.

His door was open, and he was behind his desk, sleeves rolled up and glasses perched low on his nose as he scanned a report. When he saw me, he set the paper down and leaned back in his chair.

"Well, Marlow," he said, voice dry as dust. "Figured I'd be seeing you sooner or later. Word travels even from the Bahamas. Come in and shut the door."

I stepped in and closed it behind me. The room smelled faintly of old cigars and strong coffee.

Borman eyed me like a man sizing up the weight of bad news. "Let's have it. I assume this is about Cookie getting worked over down there. Fisher wired me. He says he's already got men on it."

"It's more than that," I said, settling into the chair across from him. "Holcomb's still there to ensure the investigation is thorough, and Cookie gets out of there when he can travel. Aside from that, what we stumbled into might tie back to some old business that certain people don't want dragged into the daylight. The kind that crosses borders and stirs up names best left buried. It's directly tied to George Cummings's murder."

His jaw tightened just a fraction, enough to tell me I had his attention now. "You think this is going to spill over here?" he asked.

I nodded. "Already has. I'll be sniffing around town looking for a woman in her mid-forties, light-skinned, with a port-wine stain under her left collarbone. Born a Rolle, though I doubt she goes by that name now. And depending on who her father was, things could get politically sticky quickly."

Borman took a long breath and leaned forward, forearms braced on the desk. "You planning to keep this quiet?"

"As quietly as I can," I said. "But if the wrong people catch wind while I'm asking around, they might get nervous."

Borman grunted. "And I suppose you want me to keep my ears open. See if any of those nervous types start twitching."

"Wouldn't hurt," I said. "And I'd appreciate it if you'd lean on your boys to let me know if anyone new has been asking questions around town or sniffing at the same trail."

He nodded once. "All right. But Marlow—" his gaze sharpened, "if this turns into a political stink, don't expect me to stand between you and the fire. I'll help, but I'm not getting this department burned for you."

"Wouldn't ask you to," I said. "Just want a heads-up before the flames get too high."

Borman sighed and rubbed the bridge of his nose. "Fine. Keep me posted. And Marlow, watch your back on this one. It's got that smell."

"Yeah," I said, rising from the chair. "Oh, Betty Lou said she'll have dinner waiting when you get home, and she'll give you a copy of the notes for your file. You can discuss them over dinner." I grinned.

His lips twitched in something close to a smile. "Get outta here."

I tipped my hat and left, the weight of what came next settling on my shoulders like a storm cloud.

The office felt still as Betty Lou must've stepped out for a late lunch. I loosened my tie, settled into my chair, and reached for the phone. First things first.

The line clicked, then rang twice before my mother answered, her voice warm and familiar. "Hello?"

"Hi, Mom. It's me."

"Drake! We were starting to wonder if you'd fallen off the edge of the earth. Are you all right?"

"Fine. Just got back from the islands. Listen, I want to come by for dinner and bring Constance if that's all right."

"Of course, it's all right! We'll be thrilled to see you both. Six o'clock?"

"Perfect. See you then." I almost heard her smile through the receiver as she told me she'd make my favorite roast. I hung up feeling a little more grounded.

The next call was Alan Cummings. The line buzzed long before he picked up, his voice sounding thinner, worn at the edges. "Marlow? You back?"

"Just touched down. I'm getting close, Mr. Cummings. Close enough to smell the truth but not yet close enough to grab."

There was a pause. I heard him sigh. "I appreciate the update. I'm headed up to Philadelphia tomorrow, taking my father's body home. The funeral's in three days. After that, I'll be back. I want to be there when you crack this open."

"You will be," I said. "Safe trip. And my condolences again."

"Thanks, Marlow."

I set the phone down, feeling the weight of the noose tightening around this case. No room for mistakes now.

My last call was to Constance, her voice edged with something like worry. "Drake? Finally. I was getting worried."

"Yeah, I know. It wasn't easy to get a line where I was. Listen, how about dinner tonight? My folks are cooking, and we're to be there by six o'clock."

There was a moment of silence, then her tone softened. "All right. Yes, I'd like that."

"I'll pick you up. And I'll tell you all about my island adventure over dinner."

"You'd better," she said, but there was a smile in her voice this time. "See you later."

I hung up, leaned back, and let out a breath. Phone calls made. Now, I had to get through the evening without tipping my hand too much. Because if what I suspected was true, things were about to heat up.

~~~

I pulled Celia II to a stop before Mrs. Crippen's at six sharp. Constance stepped out the door just as I killed the engine. The porch light caught the soft gold in her hair, and when she saw me, she folded her arms, giving me that look—half relief, half exasperation.

"You do know there's such a thing as sending a wire, don't you?" she said as she descended the steps.

I managed a crooked smile. "Yeah, but where's the drama in that?"

She slid into the passenger seat, smoothing her skirt as she settled in. "Well, you've certainly stirred up enough of that lately. Abaco, of all places. I hope you're planning to start talking, Drake Marlow."

I put the car in gear and eased us away from the curb. "Over dinner," I promised. "With a plate of my mother's roast in front of me, I might even give you the long version."

Constance arched a brow, but she didn't press. The evening breeze slipped through the open windows, carrying the salt tang from the inlet. We rode like that for a while, the tires humming against the road and the unspoken questions hanging between us.

When we turned onto the familiar street leading to my parents' house, she glanced over, softer now. "I'm glad you're back in one piece."
~~~

I cut a glance at her and gave her hand a squeeze on the seat between us. "Me too, sweetheart. Me too."

The house came into view, the porch light glowing like a beacon, and the smell of something rich and familiar wafting through the screen door.

My mother met us at the door with a smile that was all relief and a little reprimand tucked in the corners. "Drake Marlow, you had me half ready to send your father after you with a boat," she said, pulling me into a hug that smelled of lavender.

"Wouldn't put it past him," I muttered into her shoulder before stepping back and letting Constance in.

Constance got the warmer greeting, a kiss on the cheek, and an approving look that said my mother said I'd finally come to my senses where she was concerned.

Dad was in his chair in the parlor, pipe in hand, but he set it aside when he saw me. "About time you showed up. Come in, sit down. Your mother's been cooking enough for an army."

We settled around the dining table, the roast beef steaming, potatoes golden and crisp, and a gravy boat that looked like it hadn't left its post since 1920. For a while, the conversation stayed safe, my father grumbling about the price of oranges and the heat that wouldn't let up even though summer wasn't here yet.

But Constance wasn't going to let me off the hook that easily. "So," she said, slicing neatly into her meat, "are you going to tell us why you disappeared to the Bahamas? Or do we have to read about it in the papers later?"

I set my fork down, wiped my mouth, and eased back. "You know I was working a case tied to George Cummings's death. Only, it's gotten a little deeper than we first thought."

Dad grunted. "Deeper how?"

"Deep enough that people are getting beaten up for asking the wrong questions." I caught Constance's sharp look and added, "Not me. Cookie. He's laid up now in the Marsh Harbour hospital, but he'll pull through."

"Cookie! Not again!" Mother reached for her glass of water.

"And?" Constance prompted.

"And I'm close to the real secret behind that book. Close enough to smell it but not close enough to name names. Yet." I let my gaze travel between them. "But it's bad. Bad enough that the people behind it are willing to kill to keep it buried."

The table went quiet, the only sound the tick of the grandfather clock in the living room.

Dad's voice was low when he spoke. "That kind of business can swallow a man whole, son."

"I know." I picked up my fork again, but my appetite had cooled. "I'm heading back into the thick of it tomorrow. Got leads here in Palm Beach that might finally crack it open."

Constance's fingers brushed my wrist under the table, light but firm. A reminder I wasn't as bulletproof as I liked to think.

We left my parents with the promise of returning soon. I drove her home, and we stood on the porch.

"Next week will be my last at Mrs. Anderson's, until next season, that is," she said.

"Well, I'm sorry it had to end with George's murder. I'm working hard to figure out why it happened, but it appears somewhat tangled." I kissed her softly.

"Aren't all your cases, Mr. Marlow?" Constance said with a laugh.

"I guess you're right. I'll call you tomorrow. Let's go out on a proper date this weekend. You up for that?" I took her hands and gazed into her aqua eyes expectantly.

"That would be nice," she said.

We kissed, and I returned to the bungalow, figuring if I was going to unravel this mystery, I needed to find out what happened at *Sea Grape Cottage*.

I snuggled into bed and flipped through several chapters that continued to hint at a mutual attraction between Hattie and Kevin. Nothing overt until I found this:

The moon was a silver coin tossed high into the sky that night, and Hattie's eyes glittered like polished stones when she turned to Kevin. "Come on," she whispered, her voice filled with secrets. "Let's go to the lighthouse. The sea ain't never looked prettier than under a full moon."

Kevin had already sneaked out and met Hattie in the garden, unbeknownst to his parents. He glanced back toward the sleeping house, with its windows open to let in the night breeze. His heart beat from guilt and expectation loud enough, he was sure, to wake them all. But Hattie's fingers were warm around his wrist, tugging, insisting.

"Come on, boy," she whispered again, and this time, he followed.

Barefoot, they ran down the narrow path to the moonlit beach, their laughter cutting through the rush of the waves. Kevin had never run like that before, like he was weightless and belonged to nothing and no one. Hattie's long, muscled legs glided over the sand, and her curly hair flew behind her like a banner. When she splashed into the shallow surf, he followed, clothes and all.

They tumbled together into the water, laughing until they couldn't breathe. The salt stung his lips, but he hardly noticed when he looked up and saw her face so close to his.

Her smile faltered just a little, and so did his. The world slowed. The waves forgot to crash.

He kissed her. Bold and clumsy, yes, but full of something he couldn't name. She stiffened at first, then kissed him back, soft, lingering, and salty.

But then she gasped and pulled away, water dripping from her chin. "No," she murmured. "Not like this."

Before Kevin could speak, she was off again, scrambling through the waves onto the beach and sprinting up the sand toward the dark shape of the lighthouse.

He chased her, his heart hammering for reasons that had nothing to do with the running now. She disappeared through the door. He followed. Up and up they climbed, the wooden steps creaking beneath their feet until they burst out at the top and stood on the narrow catwalk that circled the light. The wind blew sharp and cool against their wet skin.

Below them, the ocean stretched wide and silver, the moonlight dancing on every ripple. Hattie leaned against the railing, breathing hard, her face turned to the sky.

Kevin stepped closer, reached out, and found her hand. She didn't pull away.

Their second kiss was slower, deeper, and when they parted, they stood there gasping, foreheads pressed together like they were afraid to let go. Kevin's hands caressed her face, then moved down her neck. Her shoulders. And below.

George went on to describe Kevin and Hattie's intimacy with a disarming tenderness and how their hearts pounded in uncertain rhythm, caught somewhere between fear and longing. He spoke of the warmth that bloomed between them, the breathless hush of discovery, and the trembling edges of youth where exhilaration met restraint. It was everything two young souls might feel when the world fell away, and all that remained was the nearness of the other, along with the wonder, the ache, and the unspoken promise of something forever changed.

When their intimacy ended, Hattie shuddered and pulled back as if shaking off a dream. "It can't be," she whispered. "Not ever."

She abruptly stood, dressed, and fled down the stairs, her footsteps fading into the dark.

Kevin stood there, trembling, feeling like the boy he was and the man he'd just become.

He found her again down by the dunes, on her knees in the sand. She dug with her hands, fast and desperate, until her fingers struck something solid.

Two gold coins, worn and dulled by time, glinted in the moonlight.

She brushed the sand away and pressed one into Kevin's palm, closing his fingers tight around it. "This is our promise," she said, her voice shaking. "No matter what, we don't speak of this. Ever."

He swallowed hard and nodded. The coin felt heavy and cold against his skin.

Their secret. Sealed in gold.

I pulled out the drawer on the bedside table and lifted a box. The doubloon lay inside on a bed of white cotton. Lifting the coin, its gold caught the light the way the passage described.

A promise, huh?

If the coin was so precious to him, why did George Cummings, if he was Kevin, hide his little treasure in the hem of the curtain like it was a weight?

I had the gnawing feeling that there was more to this story. More secret rendezvous, more desperate moments, more heat. I flipped the pages. I was not disappointed.

Then came the ending.

The sun cast a golden hue over Sea Grape Cottage as the Hadleys prepared to depart. The staff loaded their trunks onto the wagon while the gentle murmur of the sea provided a melancholic background to the farewells.

Mr. and Mrs. Hadley exchanged pleasantries with the Travers, expressing gratitude for their hospitality. The staff stood nearby, respectful yet attentive.

Hattie stood slightly apart, her eyes searching for Kevin. When their gazes met, time seemed to pause. In that silent exchange, they acknowledged the depth of their summer together, a connection that had transformed them both. The lighthouse, their secret rendezvous, the whispered promises. All now memories to be cherished and concealed.

Kevin reached into his pocket, fingers brushing against the gold coin, a tangible reminder of their bond. As he climbed aboard the wagon, he cast one final glance at Hattie, a silent vow passing between them: the secret of their summer would remain theirs alone.

As the wagon pulled away, Kevin held the coin tightly. Sea Grape Cottage faded into the horizon, but the memories etched there would remain vivid, a testament to a summer that changed everything.

A shiver pulsed through me as I looked up from the book. If George had been Kevin, he would have been the father of the baby girl with the wine-colored birthmark born to Sharon in Marsh Harbour. Was that the secret George was about to reveal at the book signing? Had the girl been there? Was he planning to introduce her as his daughter? If so, no wonder his son would have wanted it kept a secret.

I needed to find the girl. The one with the mark. She was the only one who knew the truth.

Chapter 13

The morning sun over Palm Beach was sharp after spending the night immersed in *Sea Grape Cottage*. I handed Willie the change, took the morning *Post* and *Herald* off his hands, and scanned through the pages without reading. Nothing new—a little news, a little society gossip, and a reminder that election season was heating up like the summer sidewalks.

Betty Lou already had the coffee going and her fingers poised over her notepad as I slipped inside the office,

"Anything break overnight?" I asked, tossing the paper on her desk.

"Nothing but the usual nonsense," she said. "You're early. Thought you'd sleep in after feeding your folks all that detective business."

I grunted and poured myself a cup. "Didn't sleep much. Finished the book."

She raised a brow. "Quite the story, huh? No wonder everyone's talking about the book. With George out of the picture, no one will ever know the truth unless you can run down that other angle."

"The girl," I said. "The one with the birthmark. I'm thinking maybe Constance can help point me to her. She's got eyes and ears in places I don't."

Betty Lou jotted a note for the file, then looked up. "Good luck with that. Society secrets run deep around here."

I gave her a half-smile. "Yeah, but sometimes they trip over their shoes."

By the time I stepped out into the heat, I already had Mrs. Anderson's estate in my sights. Constance would be there, probably up to her ears in phone calls. I was counting on her to have caught sight of someone the rest of Palm Beach preferred to forget.

The maid invited me in and directed me to Constance's office. She looked up from a stack of correspondence as I stepped through the doorway. She blinked in surprise.

"Well, this is unexpected," she said, setting down the folder she'd been filing away. "I can't remember the last time you came to *my* office. Usually, it's me dropping by yours."

I closed the door behind me and crossed the room. Constance's desk was neat as ever, papers stacked in precise columns, the telephone tucked neatly against its cord. No nonsense. Just like her.

"I wouldn't barge in unless it were important," I said. "It ties back to this case with the Cummings family."

Her brow furrowed, and she leaned back slightly in her chair. "The manuscript… the scandal… and the murder. Of course. What is it?"

I dropped into the chair across from her, lowering my voice. "I'm looking for someone. A woman. I only have one detail. She's got a wine-colored birthmark somewhere near the left collarbone. Big enough to be noticeable."

Constance's eyes sharpened. "And you think she's local?"

"More than that. She might be connected to everything swirling around this mess. I know it's a long shot, but with all the fittings and parties you handle for Mrs. Anderson, I figured you'd have seen more faces than I have."

She tapped her fingers against the edge of her desk, thinking. "You know… There *was* someone. A seamstress. She's a young colored woman who worked on Mrs. Anderson's gown for the book event."

My pulse quickened. "Go on."

"She was quiet. Kept mostly to herself, but I noticed she wore a scarf around her neck when she came for Mrs. Anderson's fitting. Odd choice, considering the heat."

My eyes widened. "That could be her, trying to cover the mark. How old was she?"

"In her twenties, I should think, but too young to be George's daughter."

"Maybe a granddaughter?" I offered.

Constance nodded slowly. "Could be. I didn't get a name, but I can check the vendor records. Mrs. Anderson's dressmaker would know. Give me a day or two."

I stood, heart thudding a little faster. "You're a lifesaver."

She arched a brow. "Drake, I'm your fiancé. It comes with the territory, especially in your line of work."

That stopped me cold, and I gave her a lopsided grin. "Fair point."

But even as I left her office, my mind was already racing. A seamstress with something to hide. The lighthouse scene flashed in my head, and that doubloon in my pocket suddenly felt heavy.

~~~
~~~

I stepped into Chief Borman's office looking for an update on George Cummings's murder. Borman looked up from his desk, squinting over his reading glasses.

The chief grunted, pushing a folder across the desk. "Autopsy report on George Cummings. Figured you'd want a look."

There was nothing I didn't already know except confirmation on the poison in the water--strychnine.

"Seems to confirm my hunch," I said, then changed the subject. "You got anything new on Holcomb and Cookie?"

Borman's mouth twitched into something close to a smile. "The Bahamian authorities scooped up the thugs involved. They're sitting in Marsh Harbour jail now. Holcomb's fine. Your pal Jimmy radioed in. He's bringing Holcomb and Cookie back. They should be landing around four this afternoon. They'll need transportation."

I rose, taking a copy of the report with me. "I'll go meet them at the dock, make sure they get in safely. Thanks, Chief."

Borman grunted again. "Just keep me posted, Marlow. This case of yours is starting to sprawl."

I gave him a two-finger salute and left.

The sun hung low, casting golden streaks across the water as I leaned against a piling, eyes scanning the horizon. The distant hum of an approaching engine grew louder, and soon, Jimmy's seaplane came into view, skimming the water before settling near the dock.

As the plane taxied closer, I stepped forward, watching the door open, and Jimmy stepped out to secure the aircraft. "Safe and sound," he said, wrapping the line around the dock cleat.

"Thanks," I said, shaking his hand.

Holcomb emerged, followed by Cookie, whose face was still a mess as he maneuvered cautiously on crutches. I moved quickly to assist.

"Easy there, Cookie," I said, offering an arm.

Cookie grinned wryly. "Don't fuss over me, mate. I've managed worse."

Holcomb chuckled. "He's been saying that the whole flight."

Once they were all on the dock, I turned to Holcomb. "Let's get you to the station. Chief Borman's expecting you."

Holcomb recounted the events in the car. "The Bahamian authorities were cooperative. We identified the thugs, and Fisher is handling the charges. They're in Marsh Harbour jail now. We'll return for the court case unless they plead guilty."

I nodded. "Good work. Let's hope they save us the trip."

After dropping Holcomb at the station, I drove Cookie to his apartment. He wouldn't let me help him and tried to navigate the steps himself. He stumbled, and I caught him.

"That's it," I said firmly. "You're coming with me to my parents' house. They'll take good care of you."

Cookie protested. "Blimey, Drake. I can manage. Just help me inside."

I shook my head. "No arguments. You're staying with my folks."

As usual, my parents welcomed Cookie warmly. My mother, ever the caretaker, immediately began preparing the den for Cookie. "We'll set up a bed here so you don't have to climb stairs," she said.

Cookie looked around, touched by the hospitality. "Thank you, Mrs. Marlow. I appreciate it."

I watched the scene, a mix of gratitude and unresolved feelings swirling inside me. I knew I needed to address the strain in our relationship. We'd been friends since the war, and I didn't want the guilt we both felt to fester between us.

Dinner at my parents' place was a familiar affair. My father offered grace, and the clink of silverware against china, the soft murmur of conversation, and the comforting aroma of home-cooked food filled the evening. Cookie sat across from me, his crutches leaning against the wall, his plate piled high.

"You sure you don't need anything else, Cookie?" my mother asked, her eyes filled with concern.

"I'm fine, ma'am. This is more than enough," he replied, offering a grateful smile. "Next time you're at the Green Turtle, dinner's on me."

"That would be a treat," said Mom.

After dinner, the house settled into a comforting hush. Cookie propped himself up in the living room, his leg on an ottoman and his crutches leaning against the arm of the chair. I brought in two glasses of bourbon, handing one to him as I took the seat opposite.

"Cookie," I began, my voice hesitant, "I've been meaning to talk to you."

He looked up, his eyes meeting mine, but he said nothing.

I took a deep breath. "I know things are strained between us, and I hate that it's come to this."

He nodded slowly. "Look, mate, I started this when I opened my yap after getting drunk. No excuses on my part."

I felt a lump form in my throat. "But you tried to make up for it, and you did by finding a vital piece of the puzzle."

"Yeah?"

"Yeah," I said. "What we know is that Sharon had a daughter. No name, but we think she's here in Palm Beach. Once I find her, this puzzle will come together like your cooking. So you see, what was once negative is now positive."

Cookie smiled. "Well, I guess I'm good for something."

"Good for lots of things, my friend. And besides, we kept our record going. That says something."

A small smile tugged at the corners of his mouth. "You mean our night in the Marsh Harbour pokey?"

"Uh-huh," I said.

"Well, mate, at least we're consistent."

We both laughed, the tension easing between us.

I leaned back, sipping my bourbon. "I'm glad you're here, Cookie."

He nodded, his eyes reflecting a mix of relief and gratitude. "Me too, mate. Me too."

~~~

I decided to revisit Mama Dawson the next morning. I needed answers and hoped she could provide them.

The sun filtered through the swaying palms as I approached Mama Dawson's porch. The familiar creak of the wooden steps under my feet brought back memories of our previous conversations. She sat in an old wooden rocking chair, a glass of sweet tea in hand, her eyes scanning the horizon as if searching for answers in the sea breeze.

"Morning, Mama Dawson," I greeted, tipping my hat.

She looked up, a warm smile spreading across her face. "Well, if it isn't Detective Marlow. Come on up and sit a spell."
~~~

I settled into the chair beside her, the wood cool against my back. "I've been digging into the past and doing a pretty good job of piecing together the story of Maddie and her daughter Sharon."

Her eyes narrowed slightly. "Dat so?"

"I went to Marsh Harbour, found Pastor Hall at the Methodist Church, and looked in the ledgers. They pointed me to the record of Sharon delivering a daughter in 1891."

She raised an eyebrow. "You work fast, Detective."

"Time isn't always on our side," I replied. "I also talked to the midwife who delivered the baby. Seems she had a distinctive birthmark on her left collarbone. What was the child like? Do you know her name?"

Mama Dawson's gaze drifted to the horizon. "Shush," she said, bringing her knarled index finger to her pursed lips. "Some things are be best left unsaid. Names have power, and this one carries weight."

I leaned forward. "I'm trying to help, to understand. Is this girl George's daughter?"

She sighed. "You're treading on dangerous ground, Detective. George paid the price for telling his story. You might pay for digging too deep."

"Are you saying my life is in danger?"

She met my eyes. "There are forces beyond law and reason at play. Be careful. That's all I can say."

"Thank you for the warning," I said, acknowledging she probably wouldn't say anymore. As I stood and walked away, the breeze carried her final words to me. "Some secrets are meant to stay buried."

And some were meant to be unearthed.

I returned to the office, still chewing on Mama Dawson's warning. The phone rang early afternoon.

"It's Constance," said Betty Lou through the intercom.

"I've got a name for you," Constance said. "Lisa Dandy. She lives out on Sweetbay Lane."

I jotted it down. "I'll go pay her a visit."

There was a pause. "No, Drake. That wouldn't be appropriate. A white man showing up alone in the Negro section? Folks will talk. But your mother and I can go. It would look natural enough for white ladies to visit a seamstress."

I ran a hand down my face. "All right. Here's what I want to know..."

The familiar scent of lemon polish in the entryway greeted me later that evening when I found myself again at my parents' house. Mother and Constance were waiting in the living room, their faces tight with something unspoken.

"Well?" I said.

"We drove to Sweetbay Lane, a modest street, where the little homes were tidy and the yards lined with marigolds and hibiscus, but nothing fancy," said Mom. She glanced at Constance, then nodded for her to speak.

"We went this afternoon," Constance began, her voice steady. "We brought some fabric swatches to make it seem natural. Lisa met us at the door. She wasn't wearing a scarf today, but I noticed when she got nervous, she'd touch her collarbone, like she was hiding something there."

Mother made a slight noise in her throat. "She's a lovely girl. Polite. Runs a little sewing shop right from her home. Several young women were inside, all working, machines buzzing, fabric everywhere. Like a little beehive."

Constance leaned forward. "I told her I worked for Mrs. Anderson, who spoke highly of her work. That seemed to put her at ease. I asked how she'd learned to design garments and sew so well. And that's when I saw it." She looked directly at me. "She has a birthmark. Wine-colored.

It blends with her skin, but only when the light hits just right."

I felt something cold settle in my stomach.

"She said she had been adopted as a baby," Constance went on. "Her parents were Aubree and Samuel Dandy. Both are gone now. But here's the part that stopped us cold, Drake." She swallowed. "She said a local attorney arranged the adoption. A man named Frank Marlow."

The room went silent. I heard the ticking of the grandfather clock like a drumbeat.

Mother's voice was soft. "Your father never spoke of this, Drake. Never."

I let out a slow breath. "Did Lisa say anything else?"

Constance nodded. "She thinks of the Dandys as her real parents. She knows nothing else, or if she does, she didn't say. We stayed a little longer. I even hinted that she could make a wedding dress for me to keep things light." She leaned back. "But Drake, your hunch was right. There's more to this than we guessed. And your father's name being involved..."

I rubbed my thumb against my jaw, feeling the roughness there. "Thanks," I said quietly. "You both did good."

But inside, my mind was spinning.

Lisa Dandy.

Birthmark.

Adoption.

Frank Marlow.

Pieces shifted in ways I wasn't ready for.

I sat through dinner with Constance, Cookie, and my parents, pushing food around my plate, my appetite dulled by the weight of unanswered questions. The conversation flowed around me, but I barely registered it, my mind fixated on the name Lisa Dandy and its implications.

After the meal, I turned to my Dad. "Can we talk in your office?"

Dad nodded, leading the way to his den, a room lined with bookshelves and the scent of old law books. Once inside, I closed the door behind us. He sat behind his desk. I took a chair in front.

"How can I help you, son?" he asked in his usual helpful manner.

"I need to ask you about Lisa Dandy," I began, my tone measured.

Dad's expression tightened. "I'm not comfortable discussing past clients. You know that."

I leaned forward, my gaze steady. "This isn't just about a client. It's about the truth. I need to understand what's going on."

Dad sighed, rubbing his temples. "Some things are better left in the past, son."

I studied Dad's face, noting the lines etched deeper by the years. His evasiveness only fueled my determination. "You've talked about the people you've represented in the past. Nothing intimate, of course. Why not this one?"

"This one's different. I swore to secrecy." Dad's tone was firm.

"Alright," I said, standing. "I understand your position, and I hope you'll understand mine. My client hired me to get to the truth. My obligation to him is to do just that. If you can't or won't help me, that's fine, but know I'll get there one way or the other."

Dad looked up sharply, concern in his eyes. But he said nothing. I left the room, the silence between us heavier than any words.

I wouldn't ask him again, but I had two people who knew a lot about folks in this town—Willie and Betty Lou.

Tomorrow, I hoped to uncover the truths Dad refused to share.

Chapter 14

I spotted Willie at his usual post at the newsstand, selling papers to the locals. I picked up my copies, exchanged a few coins, and lingered near the stacks until the morning rush thinned out.

When the lull came, I leaned in. "Willie, have you ever heard of a couple named Aubree and Samuel Dandy? Had a daughter named Lisa?"

Willie paused, tucking a stray paper under his arm. His eyes narrowed thoughtfully. "Sure, I knew the Dandys. Good folks. Aubree was a dressmaker. One of the best with a needle. Samuel worked down at the railroad, a steady hand, never missing a shift. As far as anyone knew, they couldn't have children. Then, one day, word was they were adoptin' a baby girl. The whole neighborhood was joyous for 'em."

I nodded slowly. "Any idea where the child came from?"

Willie scratched his chin. "I heard it was arranged real quiet-like. Actually…" He gave me a pointed look. "I believe it was your father who helped them with the adoption papers. You might want to ask him about that."

I gave a half-smile, playing it light. "Yeah, I'll talk to him later. Just wanted to get the lay of the land first, you know, from someone from their side of town."

Willie shrugged. "As far as I know, no one ever said who the real parents were. Folks figured it was someone local, but that's just talk. I do know that the Dandys raised that girl like she were their own. Tragedy struck when Aubree and Samuel got killed in that train wreck some years back. Ever since then, Lisa's been holding down the fort. Took up her mama's trade. She's a good worker and a real lovely person. Quiet, keeps to herself mostly."

I clapped Willie on the shoulder. "Appreciate it. You've been a big help."

"Any time, Mr. Marlow," Willie said, giving me his signature two-finger salute before passing a paper to another customer.

With that, I folded my papers under my arm and headed toward the office, my mind already turning over this new piece of the puzzle.

I stepped into the office, a familiar song playing on the radio in the background. Betty Lou was at her desk, humming along with the tune and typing away with her usual precision.

"Betty Lou," I said, "could you join me in my office? I need you to take some notes for a file."

She nodded, grabbed her notepad and pencil, and followed me in.

As I began dictating, I noticed a subtle shift in her demeanor. Her pen hesitated, and she seemed unusually tense.

"Is everything alright?" I asked, pausing mid-sentence.

She looked up, her eyes meeting mine with a hint of unease. "I remember the Dandy adoption," she said softly.

That caught my attention. "You do?"

She nodded. "Your father usually involved me in client matters, but this time was different. He handled everything himself and kept the file locked in his office. I was only involved when the Dandys came in to sign the adoption papers. I never even saw the child."

I leaned back, absorbing her words. "What happened to the file?"

"After the adoption, your father took everything home," she said, her voice barely above a whisper. "I think he might have burned it. He never spoke of the adoption again."

I sat in silence, the weight of her revelation settling over me. This case was more complex than anticipated, and my father's secrecy deepened the mystery.

"Thank you, Betty Lou," I said finally. "You've been very helpful."

She gave a nod and returned to her desk, leaving me with my thoughts and a growing sense of unease about the implications of what I'd just learned.

I leaned back in my chair, frustration mounting. Then, like a bolt of lightning, it hit me. Betty Lou's "magic file." She kept meticulous records in the form of index cards on every person my father had encountered during his years as an attorney, anyone connected to his cases. If there were a lead to find, it would be in that file box.

If I asked Betty Lou outright, chances were good I'd get the same line my father gave me—*"I swore to secrecy."* That phrase still carried the chill of a locked door slammed in my face. I didn't need another one. Better to sidestep the question and go digging on my own. It wasn't the way we usually operated, but rules had a funny way of bending when the stakes rose high enough. And right now, the circumstances left me with little choice but to pry open the file myself.

I glanced at the clock. Once Betty Lou left for the day, I would delve into that file to see if I could find anything that would point me in the right direction.

The day's light faded into the warm hues of late afternoon while I sat at my desk, biding my time until closing.

Betty Lou approached with her purse and offered a gentle smile. "Goodnight, boss," she said.

"Goodnight, Betty Lou. See you tomorrow," I replied.

A hush settled over the office as the door clicked shut behind her. I waited a few moments, ensuring she was well on her way home, before rising from my chair. The only sound was the soft creak of the floorboards beneath my feet.

I went to Betty Lou's desk, where the "magic file" resided—a long metal box stuffed with index cards, each meticulously cataloged. Sliding the drawer open, I carefully lifted the box and placed it on the desk. Its weight was physical and symbolic, heavy with the secrets of the past.

As I opened the lid, the file revealed neatly arranged cards, each tabbed and labeled. My fingers hovered over them, uncertain where to begin. I was searching for a thread, a clue that would lead me back to 1891 or 1892, the time when the adoption of the child with the wine-colored birthmark took place.

I began to sift through the cards, looking for names, dates, and anything that might connect to that period. The cards whispered stories as I flipped through them, tales of lives intersecting with the law, some mundane, others tragic.

Then, a card caught my eye. The date 1891 stood out. I pulled it from the box and read the details: a young couple seeking counsel. No mention of a child, but the fact that it didn't have any additional information felt off.

I continued to search, finding another card from 1892. This one referenced an adoption, with the date relatively close to the previous card's. The ink had faded with time, but I could still make out the names Aubree and Samuel Dandy, verifying what I already knew.

Those were the only two cards I found related to the case, yet fragments of information helped to form a tapestry woven from forgotten lives and hidden truths.

With the file cards slipped back into their slots, I closed the file box, placed it back into Betty Lou's desk drawer, and walked into my office. The path ahead was uncertain, but I was determined to follow the trail wherever it led.

I stepped into my office. The room was quiet, the only sound coming from the soft ticking of the wall clock. I approached the blackboard, its surface clean and ready. Picking up a piece of chalk, I began to jot down the fragments of information I had gathered:

- Sharon impregnated
- Baby girl delivered in Marsh Harbour
- Wine-colored birthmark on left clavicle
- Child returned to Palm Beach, whereabouts unknown
- Sharon's supposed daughter Lisa is a seamstress adopted by Aubree and Samuel Dandy
- Adoption arranged by Frank Marlow in secret
- A couple visited Dad shortly before the adoption. Lisa's birth parents?

- Gold doubloon found in hem of curtain. Same kind as in the book. Why hide the coin?
- Those involved want the past left alone, except for Alan Cummings.
- Is George the father?

I stepped back, contemplating the web of connections. So far, everything pointed to George Cummings being the father—the account in his book, the gold doubloon. But without conclusive proof, it remained speculation. I needed to update Alan and share what I'd uncovered so far.

The phone felt cool against my ear as I leaned back in my chair, the day's discoveries swirling in my mind. I dialed Alan's number, each ring echoing the weight of the secrets I'd uncovered.

"Hello?" Alan's voice came through, steady and familiar.

"Alan, it's Drake." I tried to keep my tone even. "I've been digging into your case. There's more to it than we thought."

A pause. "Go on."

"Not over the phone. Can we meet? Tomorrow morning, perhaps?"

He hesitated, then said, "Come by at ten. We'll talk then."

"Thanks, Alan. See you tomorrow."

I hung up, the click of the receiver sounding final. The pieces were aligning, but the picture remained incomplete. Tomorrow, perhaps, clarity would come.

After a few moments, I picked up the receiver again and dialed my parents. A couple of rings later, Mom answered. "Hello?" she said, her voice full of warmth.

"Hi, Mom. It's me. Just checking in to see how Cookie's doing?"

She chuckled softly. “Oh, he’s as restless as ever. Keeps insisting he’s ready to get back to the restaurant, crutches and all.”

“Really? Is he managing okay on them?”

“Surprisingly well. He’s even going up and down the stairs without much trouble. He says he’s ready to climb the steps to his apartment, too.”

I smiled, picturing Cookie’s determination. “That’s good to hear. Listen, I have a client meeting at ten tomorrow, but after that, I’ll swing by and take him to the restaurant.”

“He’ll be thrilled, honey.”

“And after his shift, I’ll ensure he gets back up the stairs and into his apartment safely.”

“Thank you, Drake.”

“Of course, Mom. See you tomorrow.”

I hung up, relieved knowing Cookie was on the mend and eager to return to his routine. Tomorrow would be a busy day, but helping him return to the restaurant felt like a step toward normalcy.

The sun dipped low, casting golden hues across the sky as I left the office. The beach beckoned, always a place where the rhythmic crash of waves often helped me untangle the knots of complex cases. I changed in the bungalow, then walked the two blocks to the beach and strolled along the shoreline, the cool water lapping at my feet, each step grounding me, offering clarity.

After a while, I tossed my towel onto the sand and dove into the surf, letting the saltwater envelop me, washing away the day’s tension. Swimming always brought a sense of renewal, a momentary escape from the weight of unanswered questions.

Returning to the bungalow, I showered and settled into my favorite chair. I picked up *Sea Grape Cottage*, flipping through its pages again. The narrative was familiar, yet I searched for any detail I might have previously overlooked. So far, nothing new surfaced. But I made a mental note to ask Betty Lou about it in the morning, sure she had finished the book by now.

The evening air grew cooler, and I closed the book, placing it on the side table. The mysteries remained, but the sea had offered solace for now, and tomorrow held the promise of new insights.

Chapter 15

I opened the front door of the office, carrying the morning papers, the ink still fresh enough to leave smudges on my fingers. The bell gave its usual jingle as I stepped inside.

Betty Lou was standing in front of the blackboard in my office, arms folded, her head tipped slightly to one side. Her gaze traced the chalk lines I'd scrawled there last night. When she heard me come in, she didn't turn right away. She lifted one hand and pointed to a particular entry.

"This part here," she said, tapping her finger against the line that read: A c*ouple visited Dad close to the time of the adoption. Lisa's birth parents?* "Where'd this come from, Drake? Everything else fits, but this. I don't remember you mentioning it before."

I hesitated, my mouth going dry like I'd been chewing cotton. "I—" I started, then let out a breath. No point in dodging. "I found it in your file box. You'd already gone for the day, and I didn't want to bother you at home. The idea hit me after you left, so I looked myself."

She turned then, giving me the full weight of those steady eyes. "You could've asked me, you know. After all, it's my box. My system. I'd have helped you."

I shifted the papers in my hands, feeling like a schoolboy caught with a hand in the cookie jar. "I didn't think you'd mind since you weren't here. And—well—the idea just came to me suddenly, and I didn't want to lose the thought."

Her eyes narrowed, not quite buying it. "Drake, I know the story's not exactly straight. Just next time, respect me enough to let me do my job. Please don't go through my things without asking."

I nodded, feeling the weight of her quiet disappointment more than if she'd raised her voice. "You're right, Betty Lou. I promise. Won't happen again."

That seemed to smooth the lines on her brow a little. She stepped back from the blackboard, letting out a breath.

"Have you finished the book yet?" I asked, steering the conversation onto safer ground.

She gave a nod. "Yes, last night. Read straight through to the end."

"Anything else jump out at you? Some detail I missed that might give us a lead?"

She thought, then shook her head. "No, nothing that would help. It's all pretty much lined up with what you've already got here." She gestured at the blackboard again.

I nodded, filing that away. "I've got a meeting with Alan this morning at ten sharp at his place. After that, I'll take Cookie to the Green Turtle. He's itching to get back to work."

Her face brightened at that. "That's wonderful news. I'm sure he's been chomping at the bit to get out of the house."

I smiled, feeling some of the earlier tension lift. “Yeah, it’ll do him good to get back to work.”

“I’ll be back after the meeting. Hold down the fort, will you?”

She gave me a little salute. “Always do, boss.”

I grabbed my hat and stepped back into the sunlight, my mind already shifting gears for the conversation ahead. The Cummings residence reflected the grandeur of a sophisticated estate, as evidenced by its meticulous landscaping and stately architecture.

The maid greeted me promptly, leading me through the polished corridors to the living room. Inside, a woman in a muslin gardening apron stood arranging flowers in a vase. She turned to me with a warm smile. “You must be Mr. Marlow. I’m Eleanor Cummings, Alan’s wife.”

Her dark eyes met mine, and I couldn’t help but notice how fair her skin was, or her fine features framed by dark curly hair. My mouth turned to cotton when she turned around to face me. The gold coin pendant dangling from her neck, the markings unmistakable, matched the doubloon in the curtain hem.

“That’s an intriguing pendant, Mrs. Cummings. May I ask about its origin?”

She touched it gently, a hint of nostalgia in her expression.

“It’s a doubloon my birth mother left me. It’s the only keepsake I have from her. She gave me up for adoption shortly after I was born.”

A surge of adrenaline coursed through me. Not the exhilarating kind, but a jolt of realization. Could this coin be connected to Sharon? If so, that would mean Eleanor was George’s daughter. Alan married his sister!

My head reeled, and I could hardly speak, but managed to eke out, "Do you know anything about your adoptive parents?"

"They were from Ohio but spent winters in Palm Beach. They adopted me during one of their stays and took me back to Ohio, where I grew up."

Before I could process this revelation further, Alan entered the room. Eleanor removed her apron, revealing a wine-colored birthmark on her clavicle. The same as Lisa's.

My mind swirled with the implications. I needed time to piece this together.

"Alan, I apologize," I said, "but I feel unwell. Can we reschedule our meeting?"

"You do look a bit pale. Call me when you're feeling better," he said, showing me to the door.

Sweat poured off me as I left, the weight of the implications of this discovery pressing heavily on me, like someone was standing on my chest. I needed to discuss this with someone, so I rushed back to the office.

Betty Lou looked up from her desk as I stepped inside Marlow Investigations. Her eyes narrowed as she took in my appearance. "Drake, you look like you've seen a ghost."

I managed a weak smile. "Feels like I have."

She followed me into my office, concern etched on her face. I closed the door behind us and sank into my chair.

"I met with Alan Cummings this morning. His wife, Eleanor, greeted me. She wore a gold doubloon around her neck, the same kind George had. She said it was the only thing her birth mother left her before giving her up for adoption."

Betty Lou's eyes widened. "That's quite a coincidence."

"It gets more complicated. Eleanor mentioned her adoptive parents were from Ohio, but adopted her in Palm Beach. Then Alan walked in, and as Eleanor removed her apron, I saw a wine-colored birthmark on her clavicle."

Betty Lou sat down slowly, processing the information. "If Eleanor is George's daughter, and he didn't know it, then neither did Eleanor or Alan. George wouldn't have let his son marry his daughter. And then there's Lisa. Could she be Eleanor's child?"

"Eleanor is white, Lisa is a Negro," I said.

Betty Lou nodded thoughtfully. "Yeah, but remember Willie's nephew Joshua? He passed for white when his father was white and his mother colored. Negroes come in all shades."

That was true. Joshua had light skin with fine features and passed for white despite having a colored mother. But I also knew neither his life nor his mother's was easy, and he finally left home at fifteen to fit in elsewhere.

"If Lisa is Eleanor's daughter, she and Alan might be the couple who put her up for adoption, since keeping her would have been scandalous." I sat back, contemplating the implications.

"Maybe it's time to talk to Mama Dawson again," said Betty Lou. "Lay out everything we've found and see if she can fill in the gaps."

I nodded. "She's been around long enough to know the town's secrets. Maybe she can help us make sense of this. Lord knows it's getting too complicated for me."

Betty Lou touched my shoulder reassuringly as I prepared to leave. "We'll get to the bottom of this, Drake. One step at a time."

I nodded, grateful for her support. This case was a tangled mess, but with Betty Lou's help, I was determined to find the answers.

~~~

Mama Dawson blinked at me as I stepped into her parlor. "Back again so soon, Detective Marlow?" she said, folding her arms. "I told you last time, best leave old ghosts be."

"I need your help, Mama Dawson. I found something. Something big."

She sighed and gestured for me to take a chair. "Go on then."

I sat and set my hat on my knee. Then, I laid it out—Eleanor, the doubloon, the birthmark.

Her lips pressed thin, and she shook her head, clucking her tongue. "I warned you, chile. Some stones best left unturned."

"I can't do that," I said. "My client's expecting the truth."

Mama Dawson's eyes flashed. "And you think you got the truth, boy? You don't know the half."

I leaned forward. "Then tell me. What really happened?"

She was quiet for a long time, staring out the window like she was watching the past crawl by. When she spoke, her voice was low and heavy.

"George and Sharon… de had feelings, sure. Met out at dat old lighthouse, like Cumming's book say. But dey didn't lie together. Not like folks think. She ran down dem stairs, scared of what might happen if dey cross dat line. George stayed behind, wrestling wit his own heart."

Her fingers twisted in her lap. "When he come down, he saw her. Some white man wit a knife, dragging her into de woods. George followed, but he was just a boy, scared stiff. He saw dat man take her to a shack and force himself on her. Knife at her throat."

I swallowed hard. The room felt colder.
~~~

"George wanted to help, but fear froze 'em. When he finally worked up de courage, he grabbed a jagged piece of coral rock. Went in and hit de man. Cracked his skull. Killed 'em right there."

I let out a deep breath.

"De took a few gold coins off the table from a pile of doubloons before dey left. Sharon gave one to George, a symbol dat was their secret now. The man who hurt her, and George, who stopped him. They never saw each other again. George left the next day, carrying dat weight."

I sat there blinking, as if the account Mama Dawson revealed was fiction.

Mama Dawson's eyes found mine. "Dat's the truth, Mr. Marlow. Not the story folks been whispering all these years."

"So, when Maddie found Sharon pregnant, she took her and returned to Marsh Harbour, where she had the baby. The child was light-skinned with a wine-colored birthmark on her clavicle," I said, my voice sounding hollow even to my ears as I pieced it together aloud.

Mama Dawson let out a soft, almost mournful hum deep in her throat. "Dey took dat child back to Palm Beach, put her up for adoption. Child lookin' white, dey figured she'd have a better life if someone from Palm Beach took her in. And dat's what happened."

"You mean Eleanor's parents," I said, my stomach knotting as the pieces clicked into place, each one heavier than the last.

Mama Dawson nodded slowly, her eyes not quite meeting mine. "Mmm-hmm."

I leaned in, my voice dropping. "Who was the man who forced himself on Sharon? Was he local?"

She pressed her lips together, the lines in her face deepening. "I don't know his name, but he had a son. Folks say dat boy grew up swearin' he'd find de one who killed his daddy and make him pay."

My pulse quickened. "Is that who killed George Cummings?" I asked, my voice sharper than I intended.

Mama Dawson gave a slow shrug, her shoulders rising and falling like heavy stones. "Maybe. Grudges like dat don't die easy."

I let out a breath and braced myself. "So... what about Lisa? Whose daughter is she?"

That got her. Mama Dawson's hands, worn and strong, started wringing like she was trying to squeeze water from a dry cloth. Her dark eyes flashed, and she lifted a crooked finger, shaking it at me like a warning bell. "Now, you gettin' into another pile of worms, Mr. Marlow. One dat don't wanna be stirred."

"I need to know everything," I insisted, my voice tight. "All of it."

She shook her head, already pushing herself up from her chair with a groan. "Dat can wait. Now, I go nap."

And just like that, she shuffled from the room, her skirts whispering against the floor, leaving me sitting there with more questions than I'd walked in with and the kind of answers that felt like they might sink me if I chased them any deeper.

I got up, the creak of the old chair loud in the sudden silence, and let myself out.

The afternoon sun did little to warm the chill within me. The truth she unveiled was far from what I had anticipated, and it reframed everything I thought I knew.

George and Sharon's relationship, once thought to be a romantic liaison, was instead marked by tragedy and violence. George's act of bravery, intervening to save Sharon, had been buried under years of silence and misconception. The gold doubloon, symbolizing their shared secret, now held new significance.

As I walked back to my car, my mind raced. If Eleanor possessed a similar doubloon, could it be connected to that fateful night? And what about Lisa? The puzzle pieces were shifting, and I needed to re-examine everything in light of this new information.

Returning to the office, I found Betty Lou engrossed in her work. She looked up, concern etched on her face. "You look like she told you something you didn't want to hear."

I nodded, taking a seat opposite her. "Mama Dawson told me the real story." I recounted the events as she described them, watching Betty Lou's expression shift from shock to contemplation.

"So, George didn't have relations with Sharon and wasn't Eleanor's father. Instead, he saved Sharon."

I nodded. "So she says. But something seemed off."

"Like?"

I shook my head. "I can't quite put my finger on it."

"And Eleanor's doubloon..."

"Could be from the same stash they took from the shack."

We sat in silence as the implications settled in. What Mama Dawson told me was more complex than we had imagined, and the path ahead was uncertain.

"We'll need to tread carefully, Drake."

I agreed. "The past has a way of resurfacing, and we need to be ready for whatever comes next. But one thing's for sure. If the rapest's son knew George Cummings was the one who killed his father, he had a strong motive to murder George. And, if he's still in the area, I intend to find him."

I looked at the wall clock and smacked my palm to my head. Way past the time I should have been at my parents' house to pick up Cookie. I rushed out the door and headed over the bridge to West Palm Beach.

Cookie was seated in the living room, his crutches nearby, his fingers drumming on the armrest when I arrived,

"Ready to head to the Green Turtle?" I asked.

Cookie grinned, his eyes lighting up. "Been waitin' all day, mate."

"I'm sorry, Cookie. The day got away from me," I said.

I kissed Mom goodbye and helped Cookie into the car, making sure I secured the crutches in the back seat. Light conversation flowed between us on the drive to the Green Turtle, the tension of recent events momentarily forgotten.

Upon arrival, I assisted Cookie out of the car and handed him the crutches. "I'll be back at 10:00 p.m. to pick you up and take you back to your apartment.

Cookie nodded. "Thanks, mate. I appreciate it."

As Cookie made his way into the restaurant, I watched for a moment before turning back and heading for the office to try to catch Constance at Mrs. Anderson's before she got on the bus for home.

I made it into the office just as Betty Lou slipped her purse strap over her shoulder, ready to call it a day. "How's Cookie?" she asked, pausing in the doorway with the concern and fondness she always showed for the Aussie chef.

"Better than I expected. He's back at the restaurant, stirring things up already. I'll swing by later and take him home."

She tilted her head, thinking. "If you don't mind my coming in late tomorrow, I can pick him up and drop him off at the Green Turtle. Save you a trip and let you keep chasing down killers and scandals."

I leaned in and kissed her cheek, which I didn't do often, but she earned it tonight. "You're a lifesaver."

Her smile warmed the whole room. "Good night, boss. Don't get into too much trouble."

"Too late," I muttered as she disappeared down the hall.

I rushed into my office, the door clicking shut behind me, and grabbed the receiver. My fingers spun the dial for Mrs. Anderson's home, hoping I wasn't too late.

"Mrs. Anderson's residence," came the clipped voice on the other end.

"Constance, is that you?"

"Drake? Yes, I'm still here."

"How would you like a drive home? Maybe dinner along the way?"

There was a pause, and then her soft laugh floated through the line. "Best offer I've had all day. I'll meet you out front in ten minutes."

Constance slid into the passenger seat, her perfume subtle but unmistakable. I drove us across the bridge into West Palm. We stopped at a little Italian place tucked between a women's apparel shop and a shoe store on Clematis, where the sauce was homemade, and the owner knew everyone's name.

Inside, the red-checkered tablecloths and flickering candles gave everything a warm glow. Constance placed her napkin in her lap and leaned in. "How was today? Anything to report?"

I laid it out for her—the doubloon, Eleanor's birthmark, Mama Dawson's confession— every tangled thread. She listened without interrupting, her eyes growing wider with every twist.

"Good heavens, Drake." She breathed. "That's one story where fact is stranger than fiction."

"Indeed," I said, sipping the last of my tea. "Now I'm on the hunt for the man's son. He had a motive to kill George. If it wasn't him, then I'm back to square one. But my gut says I'm on the right trail."

She reached across the table and touched my hand, her fingers warm and soothing. "Your instincts have always led you in the right direction."

We lingered over dessert, not wanting to break the spell, but eventually, I drove her back to Mrs. Crippen's. Several soft kisses later, I bid her goodnight on the dimly lit porch.

I drove home with the window down, the night air welcomed against my skin. Back at the bungalow, I barely made it through the door before I collapsed into bed, the day's revelations still tumbling through my mind as sleep finally pulled me under.

Chapter 16

I blinked as the light from the morning sun found its way through the blinds and warmed my face, but there'd be no lazy start today. Mama Dawson's words still echoed in my head, tumbling like stones in a rushing river. They'd upended everything I thought I knew about this case, each revelation tying up loose ends. George, Sharon, the man in the shack... and somewhere in that tangled web, a son with a grudge, possibly strong enough to kill.

I swung my legs over the side of the bed and shuffled to the kitchen. The gurgle and hiss of the percolator were a small comfort even though the rich aroma of coffee filled the air. I wrapped my hands around the warm mug and took a long sip, letting the bitterness wake me. My thoughts, though, were anything but settled. The nameless son, raised on vengeance, might be the missing link between George Cummings's past sins and his present fate.

Duty, I reminded myself. To my client. To justice. And to the code I carried within—finding the truth.

Betty Lou was on Cookie detail this morning, meaning I'd have the office to myself. That suited me just fine. I stopped by Willie's on the way in. We swapped greetings, the kind that said everything and nothing, and I grabbed the morning papers.

When I reached the office, I brewed another pot of coffee, purely out of habit, then pulled the Cummings file from my desk drawer and cracked it open, flipping through each page like a pastor looking for the perfect scripture to preach on Sunday.

Everyone's recollections blurred together, except for one detail that stuck out like a missing tooth: the man with the reddish hair and a limp. Neither Mrs. Anderson nor Constance could name him, but both remembered how agitated George had been after his visit. And then there was the doubloon in the hem of the curtain. Was it being hidden from the mysterious man?

Could he be a local? Someone who wintered here, blending in with the seasonal crowd? Whoever he was, I had to find him. The key lay in the past, maybe even back to 1891. A death certificate, a coroner's report, a newspaper article, anything that would give me the name of the man killed in that shack. And once I had that, I could trace the son.

I smiled to myself. If anyone could dig up a forty-three-year-old ghost, it was Max, the best bloodhound on the *Post's* payroll. Lucky for me, she was always game for a story when the stakes were high enough.

My empty coffee cup landed with a thud as I placed the porcelain mug on my desk. I stood, adjusted my suspenders, and reached for my hat on the way out. Time to visit Max.

~~~
~~~

The newsroom bustled as I stepped into the *Palm Beach Post*, the familiar clatter of typewriters and ringing phones enveloping me. Max sat at the rear of the newsroom, forcing me to navigate through the maze of desks. Her fingers danced over her typewriter keys with practiced precision as I approached.

"Max, got a moment?" I called out above the racket.

Max looked up, surprise flickering across her face. "Drake? You haven't come to see me since the article on The Breakers jewel heist. What's the occasion? Cummings's murder?"

I offered a playful grin. "Just couldn't stay away from your award-winning prose."

She chuckled, setting her work aside. "Flattery will get you everywhere, but I suspect you're here for more than compliments."

"Guilty as charged," I admitted. "I need your help digging into a case."

Max leaned back, intrigued. "I'm listening."

"Back in 1891, there was a murder in Palm Beach. A man was killed in a shack by the lighthouse. I need to know his name."

Her eyebrows shot up. "1891? That's over four decades ago! What's the angle?"

I leaned in, lowering my voice. "Let's just say the past has a way of influencing the present."

She studied me for a moment before nodding. "Alright, I'll see what I can find. But you owe me a story."

"Same term as all the others," I said, followed by a stern look.

Max rolled her eyes. "Alright. I don't print anything until I get your okay."

"Deal," I said, extending my hand.

I felt I was on the move again as Max returned to her typing, her nose twitching with the promise of another sensational story. It wouldn't be long now before the pieces fell into place.

~~~

The Palm Beach Police Department seemed subdued as I checked in with the desk officer and navigated the corridors until I reached Detective Holcomb's desk.

"Morning, Holcomb," I greeted.

Holcomb looked up, a hint of surprise on his face. "Marlow."

"Thought I'd give you an update on Cookie. He's back barking orders at the Green Turtle."

Holcomb chuckled. "Good to hear."

"I also wanted to check in on the Cummings case. Any leads?"

Holcomb's expression darkened, his jaw tightening as he leaned in slightly. "Not much," he said quietly. "We know it was strychnine—no question about that. We tracked down the waiter who placed the glass on the shelf. Middle-aged guy. Shaken. He swore up and down he didn't put anything in it. The problem is that the podium saw a lot of traffic before the crowd filed in. Mrs. Anderson, Alan Cummings, George himself, George's agent, half a dozen servers, and the setup crew. We've spoken to every one of them. Nothing solid. No real leads."

I hesitated, then said, "Mind if I get a copy of those you spoke with?"

"Sure," said Holcomb. "You got anything to add?"

"Maybe. Can we discuss this further in the chief's office?"

Moments later, we sat in Borman's modest office, the door closed behind us.
~~~

"I appreciate you both taking the time," I began. "I've come across some information that might be relevant to the case."

Borman leaned forward, intrigued. "Go on."

I recounted the details I'd learned from Mama Dawson about the incident in 1891, the man killed in the shack, and the possibility of a son seeking revenge. "It's a long shot," I admitted, "but if this man's son is still around, he might have had a motive to kill Cummings."

Holcomb rubbed his chin thoughtfully. "That's quite a theory."

"I know it's speculative," I said, "but I wanted to keep you in the loop. If I find anything concrete, I'll get you involved."

Borman nodded, his look like steel. "Yes, you will."

A mix of apprehension and determination swirled in my head as I left the station. I needed Max to come through. Otherwise, I'd have to start over.

~~~

Betty Lou was back in the office as I entered. She looked up from her desk, a warm smile on her face.

"How's Cookie?" I asked, setting my hat on the coat rack.

"He's doing just fine," she replied. "Settled in at the Green Turtle without a hitch."

Relief flowed through me. "I'll take Cookie home at night if you can pick him up in the mornings until he can drive again or make other arrangements. I'm sure the effort will come with a free meal now and then." I wiggled my eyebrows.

"Consider it done," she said, chuckling and jotting a note to herself.

I walked into my office and added the man with the reddish hair and limp to the case list on the blackboard. The
~~~

phone rang as I was about to sit down and contemplate my next move.

"It's Max," said Betty Lou through the intercom.

My heart raced as I lunged for the phone. "Max. Tell me you've got something."

"You might want to come down and see for yourself, Detective. And bring lunch. I'm starving," she said before hanging up.

"I'm heading down to the *Post*," I said to Betty Lou as I breezed through her office, heading for the door. "Please phone Woolworths and have them make two tuna sandwiches with chips and a couple of cookies. I'll pick them up on my way." I grabbed my hat and brushed a finger kiss on the megalodon tooth for luck.

Betty Lou hated it when I did that and clucked her tongue behind me.

~~~

I entered the *Palm Beach Post* carrying two brown paper bags from Woolworths.

Max met me in the lobby, her eyes alight with excitement. "You brought lunch," she said, eyeing the bags.

"That was the deal. Sustenance for our dive into the rustic archives."

She led me through the maze of corridors to the archives, where the musty odor of old newsprint assaulted me, and rows of filing cabinets and stacks of newspapers awaited. We settled at a large wooden table with several papers already stacked on top. The single bulb dangling overhead cast a bright glow over the table.

"So, what did you find?" I asked, handing her the lunch.

She opened the bag and took out its contents, neatly spreading the sandwich, chips, and cookies on a napkin.

"Max," I huffed, eager to see what she'd found.
~~~

"Hold your horses, Detective. I'm getting there," she said, hungrily taking a bite of her sandwich.

I let her chew and swallow, even though I couldn't wait to get into the meat of what the newspapers had to say.

"I found an article from 1891 in *The Tropical Sun*, South Florida's first paper, that started in June of the same year as the murder. The article is pretty rough. I guess they didn't have many seasoned reports back then. Anyway, someone murdered a man in a shack in Palm Beach." She slid the brittle in front of me, yellowed pages of the decades-old weekly publication, a double sheet of newsprint filled with ads and articles. The headline read: *"Mysterious Death in Seaside Shack in Palm Beach."*

I leaned in to read the faded text. "This matches the story Mama Dawson told me."

"Who's Mama Dawson?" she asked.

"Another time, Max," I said, hoping she wouldn't follow up on the lead I'd just carelessly exposed.

We spent the next hour poring over articles that continued to follow the death, piecing together the details as they unfolded. The victim was a drifter with no known family. Someone killed him by bashing his head with a large coral rock found at the scene. The rock contained blood and hair, assumed to be the victim's. A knife was also found, but it appeared unused. There were no suspects. The articles described the man's clothes and features, hoping someone could identify him. One feature stood out above the rest—red hair.

Two items glared at me after reading the articles: the victim's hair color matched that of the man who visited George, and "no known family," the only information that didn't match Mama Dawson's narrative.

"And here's what the *Miami Metropolis* says about the crime," she said, sliding other papers on top of *The*

Tropical Sun. "These mostly regurgitate what *The Tropical Sun* says. Still, we might find something more substantial since they were rival papers, even though they both served the area back when Palm Beach was part of Dade County."

We read all the articles we could find regarding the murder, but no new information emerged.

"This is great information," I said, finishing my chips, "but I need a name. I need to know the man's name." I forcibly crumpled the wrapping on my sandwich and chips and threw them into the empty bag in frustration.

"Local knowledge versus official records," said Max calmly, a smug look on her face.

"What?" I asked.

Max cleared her throat. "Information from your source might stem from community knowledge or oral history not captured in official reports. This divergence can mean the difference between finding the truth and only going on what you read."

I pulled back, surprised by her explanation. Pastor Hall has said something similar when Cookie and I were in the Bahamas. "Citing a lesson you learned from your editor?"

Max gazed at me intently. "Citing a lesson I learned as a reporter."

"Hmm," I said. "Come on, I'll walk you back."

We left the archive and its musty scent behind and returned to the lobby.

"Thanks for lunch," said Max, heading to the newsroom.

"Anytime. Thanks for the search and the advice."

She grinned before slipping through the swinging doors into the newsroom.

Of course, Max was right. Oral history contains lots of truths that never make it to print. Maybe the victim hadn't been a drifter after all. Maybe he lived here, but his family didn't want anything to do with him, so they never came forward. But wouldn't someone else have known him? Especially with that red hair? The trick was finding the person who knew the man's name.

Chapter 17

I approached Willie's newsstand, the headlines shouting the day's events. Ever the sentinel, Willie looked up from his perch behind the counter. "Morning, Mr. Marlow."

"Morning, Willie." I nodded, scanning the array of publications. "I have a question for you."

"Shoot," he said, handing me my papers.

"Have you ever seen a man around here with red hair and a limp?" I exchanged the papers for payment.

Willie leaned back, scratching his head thoughtfully. "Red hair and a limp. Can't say that I have. Not a common combination."

"No, it's not. Maybe the man came by only occasionally."

He shook his head slowly. "Sorry, Mr. Marlow. If someone like that had come around, I'd remember."

"Alright, thanks anyway." I turned for the office, the man's name still elusive.

The familiar scent of coffee and the latest tune on the radio greeted me. Betty Lou was at her desk, typing away and humming along with the hit tune, "Smoke Gets In Your Eyes" by Paul Whiteman and his orchestra.

"Morning, Betty Lou."

"Morning, boss."

"I just came from Willie's. No luck on the red-haired man with a limp." I placed my hat on the coat rack.

She paused, considering. "Have you thought about checking with the hospital? If the man has a limp, a doctor might have treated him."

"Good point, Sherlock. Do you have any contacts there?"

Betty Lou smiled, reaching into her drawer. "Let me consult my magic file." She pulled out her long, metal card file and flipped through the cards. "Here we go. Nurse Evelyn Thompson in the records department." She wrote down the name for me. "She's been there for years and knows the archives inside and out. She'll probably recognize your last name."

"Perfect. Thanks." I hadn't been in the office ten minutes when I turned, grabbed my hat, and walked out, lead in hand.

~~~

The scent of antiseptic and the distant hum of activity greeted me as I entered the hospital's main lobby. I offered a polite smile as I approached the reception desk. "Good morning. Could you direct me to the Records Department?"

The receptionist nodded, pointing down a corridor. "Certainly. Head down that hallway, take the third left, and you'll find it at the end."

"Thank you."
~~~

The corridors stretched before me, and I finally arrived at a door labeled "Records Department." Rows of shelves inside stretched before me, filled with files. Behind a desk sat a woman whose nameplate read "Nurse Evelyn Thompson."

"Excuse me, Nurse Thompson?"

She looked up, adjusting her glasses. "Yes?"

"I'm Drake Marlow of Marlow Investigations. I need to ask you a few questions."

Her eyes widened slightly. "Marlow? As in the detective? I've read about you in the *Post*."

I chuckled. "Yes, ma'am. I'm working on a case and was hoping you could assist me."

"I'll do my best."

"I'm trying to locate a man with red hair and a limp. I believe one of the doctors here might have treated him."

Nurse Thompson bit her lip, glancing at the vast array of files. "Without a name, it's like finding a needle in a haystack. I wouldn't even know where to start."

"I understand. Is there another way to narrow it down?"

She pondered for a moment. "Perhaps if we knew which physician treated him, we could check their patient records."

"Do you have any in mind?"

"Dr. Trenton and Dr. Fox are our physicians with orthopedic experience. Let me check if either is on duty today." She picked up the phone and dialed a number. "Yes, this is Nurse Thompson. Is Dr. Trenton available?" A pause. "Great. Could you tell him that Drake Marlow is here to inquire about a patient?"

She turned to me after hanging up. "Dr. Trenton is on duty and can see you now. He's in the emergency room, just this side of the nurse's station in the north wing."

"Thank you, Nurse Thompson. You've been very helpful." With a nod, I strode to the designated place, hopeful that this lead would bring me closer to the truth.

Dr. Trenton hunched over a stack of charts in a small office by the emergency registration desk. He looked up as I knocked.

"Dr. Trenton?"

He adjusted his glasses. "Yes?"

"I'm Drake Marlow."

Recognition flickered in his eyes. "Ah, the detective. What brings you here?"

"I'm trying to locate a man. I don't have a name, but he has red hair and walks with a limp."

He leaned back, eyes narrowing in thought. "Red hair and a limp..." After a moment, he nodded slowly. "I treated a man like that years ago. He had a nasty break from a construction accident. I believe he broke it while working on rebuilding The Breakers. The bone never healed properly."

"Do you remember when that was?"

He rubbed his chin. "At least seven or eight years ago. He was a rough character, hung around the seedier parts of the county, as I recall."

"Any chance you remember his name?"

He shook his head. "I'm afraid not."

"Thank you, Doctor."

Since arresting this guy would require a sworn officer, it was best to have one present. I returned to the Records Department and phoned Holcomb. "I might have a lead. Can you join me in the Records Department at the hospital?"

Holcomb arrived a half-hour later, his usual no-nonsense demeanor in place. I introduced him to Nurse Thompson, who greeted him with a polite nod.

"What are we looking for?" he asked, getting straight to the point.

"Dr. Trenton treated a male patient with a broken leg about seven or eight years ago. If the child were one year old when his father died, he'd have been twenty-six years old when treated. But he could have been older. Let's pull all of his records from 1925 to 1928."

Nurse Thompson led us to the back room, where rows of shelves held countless patient files. "These are all the files from the years in question. The files aren't coded by physician, so you'll have to look through each one. You'll see the physician's name at the bottom of the discharge page." She opened a file and pointed to the section where the doctor's name was listed.

Holcomb and I began sifting through the patient files, focusing on males treated by Dr. Trenton for leg injuries who were twenty-six years old or older.

Holcomb held up a file after about thirty minutes. "This one matches the description. Treated by Dr. Trenton for a compound fracture of the right tibia seven years ago."

I took the file and scanned the paperwork. "This could be our guy, but we need to check all the files since there could be another patient with a broken leg." I set this one aside, and we kept looking.

Another file surfaced. This man had broken his leg in a boating accident. By the time we finished, we had three males to check on. We wrote down the pertinent information, returned the files to Nurse Thompson, and left.

As we walked to the parking lot, Holcomb asked, "How do you want to treat this?"

I hesitated, thinking. "It's probably best to use your police vehicle to announce an official visit. The only information we know about the possible suspect is that he has reddish hair, walks with a limp, and someone murdered his father in a shack on Palm Beach in 1891."

"Then, our first clue to the man we're looking for is his hair color. If a man has blond or dark hair, we'll thank them for their time and be on our way. We can swing by each address now, but if the man works, he won't be home until later."

"Good thought," I said. "If none of them are home now, we can return around 7:00 p.m."

Holcomb and I climbed into his police car. Our first stop was a modest bungalow nestled among overgrown hedges. A middle-aged man answered the door, his dark hair peppered with gray.

"Good afternoon, sir," Holcomb began, flashing his badge. "We're looking into a case and wondered if we could ask you a few questions."

The man nodded cautiously. "Sure, come on in."

The living room was tidy, with the faint scent of pipe tobacco lingering.

"I understand that Dr. Trenton treated you for a broken leg some years back. How's your leg now?" I asked.

"See for yourself," said the man, walking around the room with no visible limp.

"Good as new," said Holcomb.

We thanked him for his time and moved on to the second address. This house was a two-story colonial with peeling paint and a sagging porch. No one answered our knocks, and the windows remained dark.

The third residence was a small apartment above a closed storefront. Again, no response. We left our contact information with a neighbor. With our initial visits yielding little, our stomachs reminded us it was well past lunchtime.

"Woolworths?" Holcomb suggested.

"Sounds good."

At the lunch counter, we slid onto the red vinyl stools, the aroma of grilled sandwiches and fresh coffee enveloping us. I ordered the grilled cheese and tomato soup combo, while Holcomb opted for the club sandwich with a side of coleslaw.

"I guess Constance will be back here serving soon," said Holcomb.

I nodded. "Mrs. Anderson leaves this weekend. She'll take a few days off before returning, then stay here until the season starts again in November."

"Hopefully, next year won't turn up any dead bodies. I'm sure Constance has had her fill."

"Indeed," I said as the waitress served our lunches.

"You think any of these leads will pan out?" Holcomb asked between bites.

"Hard to say," I replied. "But it's a start."

After lunch, we returned to the station to file our notes. I returned to the office, the day's encounters swirling in my mind, hoping the evening visits would shed more light on our elusive suspect.

Holcomb and I returned to the two addresses where no one had answered earlier. The first house appeared even more desolate than before—shutters closed and an overgrown lawn. It seemed abandoned.

We were about to leave at the second location, a modest apartment above a storefront, when a neighbor stepped out onto her porch. "Looking for someone?" she inquired, adjusting her glasses.

"Yes, ma'am," Holcomb replied. "We're trying to reach a man named Thomas Mallory."

She nodded. "Red usually stops by the Banyan Street Saloon before heading home. You might catch him there."

We thanked her and headed toward the saloon.

"Red?" I asked, turning toward Holcomb.

"Promising," he said.

The Banyan Street Saloon was a dimly lit establishment, its wooden floors worn from years of foot traffic. Laughter and the clinking of glasses filled the air. We chose a table in the back, ordered a couple of beers, and observed the patrons.

At the bar, a man with jet-black hair was animatedly conversing with another patron. As he spoke, he deftly flipped a gold coin between his fingers.

I nudged Holcomb and nodded toward the man. "That coin looks familiar."

Holcomb squinted. "Could be a doubloon."

"I'm going to get a closer look," I said. Rising and approaching the bar, I positioned myself nearby and struck up a conversation. "Nice coin you've got there."

He glanced at me, then at the coin. "Old family heirloom," he replied.

As he turned his head, I noticed a faint line of lighter hair at his roots—evidence of dye. His natural hair color was likely red.

"Mind if I take a closer look?" I asked.

He hesitated but handed the coin over. The coin's image matched the one George had possessed.

I nodded to Holcomb, who approached from behind. Leaning in, he whispered to the man, "I'm Detective Holcomb. We want to ask you a few questions down at the police station. Let's go."

The man's expression tightened as he looked between us and nodded. He slid off the stool, and as we escorted him to the police car, I noticed a subtle limp. We knew we didn't have enough hard evidence to arrest the man, but we did have circumstantial evidence.

At the station, I picked up the phone and dialed Mrs. Anderson's number. After a few rings, she answered.

"Mrs. Anderson, this is Drake Marlow. We've brought in a man who may have visited George before his death. Could you come to the station to see if you recognize him?"

"Of course," she replied. "Constance is still here. Do you want her to come, too?"

"Please," I answered.

"We'll be there shortly," she said.

While waiting for their arrival, Holcomb escorted Mallory into the interrogation room. Chief Borman joined Holcomb, introducing himself to Mallory. I activated the intercom and positioned myself behind the two-way mirror, listening to and observing the conversation.

Borman began, "Mr. Mallory, I'm Chief Borman. We have a few questions for you."

Mallory looked uneasy. "What's this all about?"

Borman gestured toward Mallory's hair. "Your hair, it's dyed, isn't it?"

Mallory smirked. "Yes. Is that against the law?"

"No," Borman replied, "but what are you trying to hide?"

"Nothing," Mallory said defensively.

Holcomb leaned forward. "Where were you on the night of George Cummings's murder?"

Mallory hesitated. "Who?"

Holcomb leaned in. "Come on, Mr. Mallory. We know you know who he is. You visited him at a private residence the day before someone murdered him."

Beads of sweat glistened on Mallory's forehead. "He sent me a note at work and said he had something to tell me and to come to Mrs. Anderson's house, where he's staying."

"And what did you talk about?" asked Holcomb

Mallory's eyes darted between Borman and Holcomb. "Once I got there, he didn't say anything worthwhile. He kept me there for a while, then thanked me for coming."

"And the night of Cummings's murder? That is, the night after your meeting, where were you?" asked Borman

"I... I'm sure I was at the Banyan Street Saloon. I always go there after work," recounted Mallory.

"And where is it that you work?" asked Borman.

"The Breakers. I'm a dishwasher."

"Are you saying that George Cummings sought you out, sent you a note, and asked you to come to Mrs. Anderson's home and meet him?"

"That's precisely what I'm saying. I thought it odd, but that's what happened."

"We'll check that out," Holcomb said. "Can you show us the doubloon you had at the bar? Where did you get it?"

Mallory reached into his pocket and produced the coin. "My father gave it to me. What's that got to do with anything?"

Borman's eyes narrowed. "Tell us about your father."

Mallory sighed. "He was murdered in a shack on Palm Beach in 1891. I was eight years old."

"What was his name?" asked Holcomb.

"Patrick Mallory."

Holcomb jotted down his answer. "What did he do for a living?"

"He was a fisherman, mostly. Did odd jobs when he could."

Borman leaned in. "Why was he on Palm Beach the night he died?"

"I don't know," said Mallory with a shrug. "But he often went there."

As I listened, noting each detail as they delved deeper into the mystery regarding George's death, the door opened, and Officer Jenkins escorted Mrs. Anderson and Constance into the observation area.

"Ladies, this is Mr. Mallory." I pointed to the window where they could see the chief and Holcomb interviewing a man at the table. "Please tell me if this is the man you saw visiting George Cummings. I realize his hair is darker than you might have seen. That's because it's been dyed. Try to think of his features and imagine him with reddish hair."

They looked intently through the window.

"Can you ask him to walk around?" asked Constance.

"Of course," I said. I went to the door, opened it, and beckoned to Holcomb, whispering the request. "Have Mallory walk behind the table to show his limp."

He nodded and went back inside.

Mallory stood and walked from one end of the room to the other and back with a noticeable limp.

"Yes," said Mrs. Anderson. "That's the man."

"I agree," said Constance.

"Thank you for coming down. Let me walk you out." I escorted the ladies through the hall and out the front door. "I'll call you later," I said to Constance.

I returned to the window as Holcomb asked a question we always wanted answered. "Why didn't your mother come forward to identify and claim the body?" he asked.

Mallory's gaze flicked between Borman and Holcomb. "Mom said he was a ne'er-do-well and was glad something happened to him. We didn't have the money to pay for the burial, so she said nothing. All we had were the doubloons he'd dug up on the beach." He held up one. "This is the only one left. We used the others to survive."

"Did you love your father?" asked Borman.

Mallory's head fell. When he looked up, tears spilled down his cheeks. "Yes, I loved him, despite what my mother thought of him. He used to take me fishing on Palm Beach. We'd climb up the lighthouse, look out over the ocean on a starry night, and then stay overnight in the shack. We had the best time. I missed him terribly after he died." He wiped his eyes with a handkerchief.

"Enough to harbor anger at the man who killed him?" asked Holcomb.

"Yes, of course, but I have no idea who that was. The case remains unsolved to this day. How could I kill the man who murdered my father when I don't even know who he is?"

"Excuse us," said Borman. "We'll be right back."

He and Holcomb left the interrogation room and entered the observation room, where I stood waiting. Borman's face was grim, his brow furrowed in thought. Holcomb flipped through his notepad, scanning the details they'd gathered.

"The ladies agreed that Mallory is the man they saw leaving the house after visiting Cummings the day before his murder. What do you think?" I asked, keeping my voice low.

Borman shook his head. "It's a complicated picture. The man's clearly emotional about his father, but that doesn't mean he's innocent or a murderer."

"The timeline fits," Holcomb added. "He would've been old enough to hold a grudge against Cummings."

I nodded. "And Mallory worked at The Breakers when the murder took place. That gives him opportunity.

We need to verify his employment, his alibi at the saloon, and talk to his mother."

"If she's still alive," Holcomb muttered.

"Here's my question," I said. "Do we tell Mallory what his father has been accused of and the reason for his murder? Do we tell him he has an aunt and a niece? Maybe shake him into telling the truth?"

"Not yet," said Borman. "Let's first verify his whereabouts the night of the murder and find out if his mother is still alive. We'll hold him here until you and Holcomb can run down his alibi tomorrow."

After the chief and Holcomb returned to the dimly lit interrogation room, a persistent unease gnawed at me. How could Mallory have known of George Cummings' involvement in his father's murder and, therefore, have a motive? The police had no suspects, so the newspapers remained silent about the suspect's name. By what means had Mallory pieced together enough facts to point to George Cummings as the one who killed his father? Even amidst all the whispered conversations surrounding *Sea Grape Cottage*, the story in the book remained incomplete, omitting Patrick Mallory's vicious attack on Sharon.

My intuition flared like a beacon in the fog. The common thread weaving through this tangled web involved the doubloons. George Cummings possessed one hidden in the hem of the curtain in his room. Sharon's daughter, Eleanor, hung one around her neck. And Mallory flipped one between his fingers. Each doubloon originated from the same source—Patrick Mallory. But neither the doubloons nor Thomas Mallory were talking.

Chapter 18

Holcomb joined me at my office the next morning, and we drove to The Breakers, the sun glaring down from a cloudless sky. The elegant hotel stood as stately as ever, its Renaissance Revival architecture reminiscent of the Villa Medici in Rome, a testament to its storied past since its founding in 1896 by Henry Flagler. The grand lobby, adorned with coffered ceilings and intricate frescoes, exuded timeless elegance.

Holcomb and I approached the front desk, and he flashed his badge with casual authority, which made people stand up a little straighter. "We'd like to speak with the manager," he said.

The receptionist smiled and made a quick call. Mr. Leland, a tall man, appeared from a side corridor moments later, dressed in a perfectly pressed dark suit. A clipboard peeked out beneath one arm, and his steps made no sound on the marble floor.

"Gentlemen. So good to see you again." He extended his hand. We shook. "I'm sorry it's under these circumstances, though. I think we've had enough dead bodies in the last few months to last us a lifetime."

"We understand," said Holcomb. "We're here to verify the employment of one of your staff."

"Of course, Detective Holcomb. What staff member are you here to inquire about?"

"Thomas Mallory. Dishwasher," Holcomb said.

Leland's brows lifted faintly as if the name barely registered. He flipped through a few sheets on his clipboard, his fingers moving mechanically. Then, without a word, he turned and gestured for us to follow.

We trailed him down a narrow hallway to the personnel office, a small, utilitarian space lined with wooden filing cabinets and humming with the low buzz of a ceiling fan. A massive corkboard loomed on one wall, cluttered with shift schedules, handwritten notes, and faded holiday announcements.

"What kind of information are you looking for?" Leland asked, setting his clipboard on a wooden desk.

"We need to know when Mallory clocked in and out on Wednesday last week."

Leland nodded to the personnel secretary, who creaked open a file drawer, then pulled out a manila folder. She flipped it open and thumbed through the timecards. "Here it is," she said, placing the timecard carefully on the desk. "Looks like he clocked in at 4:00 p.m. and out at 11:30 p.m. on the night in question."

Holcomb studied the card, his mouth a straight line. "Does he usually head to the Banyan Street Saloon after his shift?"

The manager gave a slight shrug, one shoulder rising in practiced detachment. "We wouldn't know. Once they clock out, their time is their own."

"Understood," I said with a nod. "By the way, have you thought about anything you missed or wanted to add to the statement you gave police the night of George Cummings's murder?"

Leland looked surprised. "No, I believe I told them everything I knew."

"Thank you for your cooperation," I said.

He nodded and gave us a professional smile.

Holcomb turned to me as we left the club. "His alibi checks out for his shift, but we'll need to confirm his presence at the saloon afterward."

"Agreed," I said. "The saloon probably doesn't open until late afternoon. Let's head to the station and see if the chief has gotten anything more out of Mallory."

Detective Holcomb and I arrived at the station to find Chief Borman in the jail, speaking with Thomas Mallory.

"Chief, a moment of your time," I said, stepping into the hallway.

Borman joined us, his expression inquisitive. "What'd you two find?"

"Looks like Mallory is telling the truth," Holcomb reported. "At least about his time at The Breakers. The personnel secretary verified that he's a dishwasher there, and his timecard showed he clocked in at 4:00 p.m. and out at 11:30 p.m. He was here and had ample opportunity to slip something into Cummings's water glass."

"We're still going to check out his alibi at the saloon," I said.

"Good work. Let me know what they say," Borman said, turning to go.

Later that afternoon, Holcomb and I went to the local saloon. The dim lighting greeted us as we entered. The bartender, a man named Bill, was wiping down the counter.

"Afternoon," Holcomb greeted, showing his badge. "Was Thomas Mallory here a week ago Wednesday? Did you see him here that night?"

"Mallory's a regular. Comes in every night around midnight after work. Can't swear I saw him or didn't. He's like furniture around here. You get so used to him, he blends into the bar," said Bill, tossing the towel over his shoulder.

"You ever seen him talking with anyone? Perhaps someone who isn't a regular?" I asked.

"Now that you mention it, I remember that on Wednesday night, he met with a man—tall, well-dressed, looked like he didn't belong in a place like this. They talked for a while, and the conversation seemed tense. The other guy left abruptly."

"Did you catch the name of the man he was meeting?" Holcomb asked.

Bill shook his head. "No, but I overheard the man mention something about a book. Seemed important."

Holcomb and I exchanged glances. We thanked Bill and returned to the car.

"That could have been George," I said as I slipped into the vehicle.

"Or Alan," added Holcomb, engaging the engine.

~~~

The office was quiet when I returned. "I've got an update for you," I said to Betty Lou, heading toward my desk.

She grabbed her notepad and pencil, following me.

Once inside, I recounted the details of our visit to The Breakers and the saloon. Betty Lou listened attentively, her pencil moving swiftly across the page. "I'll type these up and file them," she said, rising from her chair.

Left alone, I turned my attention to the blackboard, scanning the notes and reviewing the information Holcomb
~~~

and I acquired from our visit to the saloon and The Breakers. Mallory had met with a man at the saloon the night before George was killed. The man had mentioned something about a book. It could have been Alan, but how would Alan have known Mallory? Something didn't add up.

I pulled out the case file and began rereading the notes. My eyes landed on the interview with Mrs. Anderson and Constance regarding George's visitors. There it was—a potential missing link I'd overlooked.

I reached for the phone and dialed Mrs. Anderson's number, hoping to speak with Constance. The maid put me right through.

"Hello?"

"Constance, it's Drake."

"Hi," she said, her voice warm.

"I was wondering if you remember meeting Mr. Slater, George's agent."

She paused for a moment. "He came to the house and met Mr. Cummings. They both went upstairs. He was a sharp dresser in a fine suit, with a pleasant smile. But I don't recall much else. I didn't spend time with him and only saw him from the living room."

"Do you happen to know where he was staying?"

Another pause. "I think he was staying at The Breakers. But I doubt he's still there. After George's death, there'd be no reason for him to stick around."

"Thanks, Constance. That makes sense, but I wish I'd known earlier. Holcomb and I were just there."

"Sorry, Drake. You never asked."

After hanging up, I called The Breakers. To my surprise, Slater was still registered there. I grabbed my hat, slid into Celia II, and headed toward the grand hotel.

As I approached the front desk, Simon, the ever-attentive clerk, greeted me with a warm smile. "Mr.

Marlow, it's a pleasure to see you again. Will you be staying with us?"

"Not this time, Simon," I replied with a chuckle. "I think the hotel had enough excitement during my last visit."

Simon leaned in conspiratorially. "Truth be told, Mr. Marlow, it was a thrilling time. A hidden passageway, your dash through the dining room after the thief, and those hoodlums almost drowning in the pool. It was like something out of a novel."

I nodded, memories of the chaos flooding back. "I'm here to see Mr. Slater. Could you direct me to his room?"

Simon consulted the ledger. His expression shifted, and he swallowed hard. "He... He's in room 347."

"Ah, room 347," I said, the number resonating with familiarity.

As I made my way to the elevator, the scent of polished mahogany lingered. The hotel's commitment to preserving its Gilded Age grandeur was evident in every detail. I exited the third floor and walked down the familiar hall toward room 347.

"Señor Marlow," a familiar voice called out.

Turning, I saw Marta, the floor maid, her eyes lighting up. "Marta," I greeted, embracing her warmly. "It's good to see you."

"And you, Señor. The hotel hasn't been the same since you left."

"Quieter, I'm sure," I said with a grin. "Have you seen Mr. Slater in room 347?"

"Sí. Room service just delivered his lunch."

"Gracias, Marta. Take care."

She clasped my hands gently. "Hope to see you again soon, Mr. Marlow."

I continued toward room 347, the infamous suite with the concealed door in the back of the armoire leading to the secret passageway. Memories of my previous stay, filled with intrigue and peril, surfaced as I approached the door and knocked.

The door opened to reveal a distinguished man in his early fifties, impeccably dressed in a tailored suit. His brown hair, silvered at the temples, was neatly combed, and his piercing blue eyes studied me with curiosity.

"Mr. Slater?" I inquired.

"Yes," he replied.

"I'm Private Investigator Drake Marlow. I'm so glad you're still here. Alan Cummings has hired me to look into his father's death."

"A tragedy," said Slater, shaking his head. Then, his expression shifted subtly. "I thought the police were handling the matter."

"They are," I assured him. "I'm working alongside them to uncover any additional insights."

He hesitated for a moment before stepping aside. "Very well. I was just about to have lunch. Care to join me?"

"Thank you."

I entered the suite, its opulence evident in the rich mahogany furnishings and the view of the Atlantic Ocean beyond the balcony. His lunch sat on the dinette table, and a room service cart stood nearby.

As Slater picked up the phone, I noticed a notebook partially concealed beneath an afghan on the couch. The worn, leather-bound book had frayed edges from use. Several envelopes, yellowed with age, protruded from its pages. The worn initials "G.C." were embossed in gold ink on the lower corner of the notebook's cover.

"Yes, this is Mr. Slater in Room 347. Could you please send up another lunch special? Thank you. Please, have a seat, Mr. Marlow." He gestured toward the chair at the table. "I hope you don't mind if I continue."

"Certainly not," I said, settling into the chair and pulling out my notebook. "I appreciate your time. I didn't think you'd stick around after George's death."

He shook his head."I lost a good friend and client, and I hope you can find out who did this to George. But I had come a long way and had already made arrangements, so why not? This hotel is lovely, and I've never been to Florida."

"I'd like to ask you a few questions about George Cummings and his book."

Slater nodded, taking a sip from his glass of water. "Of course."

"How long have you known George?"

He talked while he ate. "About fifteen years. We met at a literary conference in New York. He was presenting a paper on maritime folklore, and his storytelling prowess immediately took me."

"And you've been his agent since then?"

"Yes. I saw great potential in George's work and offered to represent him. We've had a fruitful partnership ever since."

"How have his books been performing?"

"Quite well," he said, dabbing the corners of his mouth. "His earlier works had moderate success, but *Sea Grape Cottage* was a breakout hit. It's already become a best seller, resonating with readers in a way his previous books didn't. And that makes his earlier works sell, too."

"What do you think made *Sea Grape Cottage* such a success?"

Slater paused, his gaze drifting toward the ocean. "It was more personal, more intimate. George poured his soul into that book." He sighed. "I warned George about delving too deeply into real events. Some aspects of that story could hurt descendants who are still alive. Not to mention, revealing certain truths could have tarnished his reputation."

"And yours," I added.

Slater met my gaze. "Yes. George's success has benefited both of us. But he felt compelled to tell the story, to unearth the past, regardless of the consequences."

"How did you feel about that?"

"I wasn't happy about it, if that's what you mean." Slater took a large gulp of wine.

"Though George won't be writing any more books, isn't it true that this book, and his others, will sell many more copies now that he's been murdered? And won't you be asked to fill in for the scheduled and paid speaking engagements on his behalf?"

"All true," he said, without apology.

"Do you think Alan or his wife knew the real story?"

He hesitated. "I can't say. George was a private man. He kept his secrets close. I only knew fragments, enough to be concerned but not enough to stop him."

A knock at the door interrupted our conversation. A hotel staff member entered, placing another covered dish before me. "Your lunch, Mr. Marlow," the attendant said, setting the plate on the dinette before exiting.

I uncovered the plate to reveal a perfectly cooked steak, roasted vegetables, and a baked potato. A glass of red wine accompanied the lunch.

"Thank you," I said, as the waiter pushed the cart out the door. Turning back to Slater, I asked, "Do you know what he wanted to say at the book talk?"

"George didn't exactly say, but he indicated that I probably wouldn't like the results."

"And that bothered you?" I asked, cutting into my steak.

"Of course. George's demise, for whatever reason, would be mine, too. Once an author has a best-seller, the next book tends to have the same success. George would have made it to the top echelon of his profession, but he wouldn't leave well enough alone," said Slater, forcefully setting his fork down on his plate with a loud clink.

I ignored the noise and pressed on. "The doubloons he mentions in the book. Did you ever see George with one?"

"No, can't say I did. Is that important?"

"Could be," I said, jotting down a note. "What about Hattie? Did George ever say what happened to her? Did they ever correspond?"

"Hmm. Not that I know of, but George didn't share everything with me."

"What about any notes he might have made while writing the book? Did George ever share those with you?"

Slater poured himself another glass of wine, the clink of the bottle against the glass echoing softly in the room. "He kept a journal on every book he wrote," he said, swirling the wine thoughtfully. "But he never shared them with me."

I leaned forward, locking eyes with him. "Ever meet a man named Patrick Mallory?"

"Hmm, Patrick Mallory." Slater's brow furrowed slightly, but he maintained his composure. "Can't say it's familiar. Am I supposed to know him?"

"Well, it's possible you were seen with him at a saloon in West Palm Beach the night before George died."

Slater let out a nervous chuckle. "Whoever told you that is mistaken. I've never met this Mallory, and I certainly haven't been to that saloon."

His denial was swift, perhaps too swift. I studied him closely, noting the slight tremor in his hand as he sipped his wine.

"Well, if you recall anything else that might be pertinent, please don't hesitate to contact me," I said, laying my napkin aside.

"Of course," he replied, his expression thoughtful. "I hope you find the answers you're seeking."

"Always do," I said, ensuring my gaze punctuated my statement.

I thanked Slater for his time, handed him my business card and an appropriate amount for my lunch, and left, knowing he knew more than he was letting on. Part of the truth lay in the notebook beneath the afghan, and I was determined to see what it said.

It would be only a matter of time until Slater left town now that I had tipped my hand regarding Thomas Mallory. I headed down to the lobby and slipped into a pay phone. Dropping in a nickel, I dialed Holcomb.

"Holcomb here," came his voice after a couple of rings.

"It's Drake," I said. "I just spoke with Slater, George Cummings's agent. I asked him about meeting Mallory, but he denied it. However, I noticed a notebook on the couch partially concealed by an afghan with George's initials on the cover. I believe it contains notes from Cummings's real story about Sea Grape Cottage."

There was a brief pause on the line. "That could be crucial evidence," Holcomb replied.

"Exactly," I said. "We need to obtain that notebook officially. Can you come up here?"

"I'm on my way," he affirmed.

I hung up the receiver and stepped out of the booth, the weight of the impending confrontation pressing on my shoulders as I awaited Holcomb's arrival.

The Breakers lobby was its usual parade of white suits, clinking glassware, and the steady murmur of money. I spotted Holcomb as he came through the door, walking with that restless energy he got when something was about to break.

I joined him beneath the stained glass dome. "Slater's still up in his suite," I said, keeping my voice low. "Staff says he hasn't checked out, but he called for a bellhop. He's getting ready to move."

"That notebook," Holcomb said. "The one with George Cummings's initials on the cover. If it's here, it's our best shot at tying all this together."

I nodded. "Yeah. And if Slater's smart, he's either got it hidden or about to burn it."

I watched a porter wheel past with a silver luggage cart, then turned back to him. "You bring a warrant?"

He shook his head. "Didn't have time. And frankly, I'm not sure we need one."

I raised a brow. "That so?"

Holcomb shifted his weight, then gestured subtly toward the elevator bank. "We've got a statement from you that Slater admitted Cummings kept a journal, you saw it in Slater's room out in the open, and there's a credible risk Slater might destroy the notebook before we get back with a judge's signature. We're within our rights to go in. Plain view doctrine. Exigent circumstances."

"You planning to break the door down?"

"I'm planning to ask Mr. Leland to let us in if Slater doesn't open the door," Holcomb said. "If he is in the room, I'll ask him nicely to give the notebook to us. If he says no, we hold him until we get the paperwork. If Slater's not in the room, and the notebook's sitting in plain sight, we secure it. Either way, that journal's not going up in smoke while we stand around watching."

I glanced toward the front desk. "We're close, Holcomb. If that journal is in the room, it's the thread that unravels the whole thing."

Holcomb pulled out his badge and smoothed the lapel of his jacket. "Let's go find it before it disappears."

I knocked on room 347's door. "Mr. Slater, it's Drake Marlow. I need to speak with you again."

A moment later, Slater opened the door. "Ah, Mr. Marlow, back so soon? And who's this with you?"

"Detective Holcomb, Palm Beach Police Department," said Holcomb, displaying his badge.

"To what do I owe the pleasure, gentlemen?"

"May we come in?" I asked.

Slater stepped aside. A half-packed suitcase lay open on the bed, neckties draped over the side like they were trying to escape.

"We're here about the notebook," Holcomb said. "Belonged to George Cummings."

Slater moved to a drinking glass on the credenza and took a sip, as if that would buy him some dignity. "Ah. That old thing."

"You still have it?" I asked.

"I do," he said, motioning toward the desk. "Right there."

Sure enough, a black leather-bound notebook lay beside a fountain pen and a copy of *The Saturday Evening Post*. The initials "G.C." were stamped into the lower corner in faded gold.

"George gave it to me," Slater added a little too quickly. "Said he wanted me to have it."

Holcomb stepped forward and picked it up, flipping it open to a page filled with tight, slanted handwriting. "You have anything in writing to that effect?" he asked.

Slater stiffened. "No, but I don't see what business—"

"George Cummings is dead," Holcomb said, his voice firm. "He's not here to confirm your story. Until a judge sorts out who owns what, this notebook is potential evidence in an ongoing criminal investigation."

"You can't just take it," said Slater.

Holcomb raised an eyebrow. "Sure I can. And if you've got nothing to hide, you won't mind letting the court settle it."

I stepped in. "Where are the letters?"

"What letters?" asked Slater.

"Come on, Slater. You know what letters. The ones stuffed inside the journal's pages. Where are they?"

Slater stood there, grinning and saying nothing.

"If what's inside that notebook and the letters line up with what you've told me, it'll help your case, not hurt it. But if you were planning to slip the notebook into that suitcase and head for the county line—"

"I wasn't," Slater said quickly, holding up his hands. "I was going to leave it with my attorney."

Holcomb closed the notebook with a soft *thwap* and tucked it under his arm. "That's fine. He can read it after we do."

"The letters," I said, holding out my hand.

Slater said nothing. Just stood there, watching us like a man who realized the game was moving faster than he could shuffle the deck. Then he stepped to the suitcase, reached in, and brought out a handful of letters. He handed them to me. "That's all," he said.

"I hope you don't mind us not taking your word for it," said Holcomb. He stepped to the suitcase and sorted through its contents, coming up empty-handed.

"Told you," said Slater.

Holcomb hesitated a moment. "One more thing, Mr. Slater. You're coming with us. We've got a few more questions, and I don't like the look of that suitcase."

Slater's jaw tightened. "Am I under arrest?"

"No," Holcomb said flatly, "but you will be if you try to leave this hotel. Right now, we want to question you concerning a suspicious death and possible tampering with evidence."

I watched Slater swallow hard and glance toward the window as if he were weighing whether to make a run for it. But the fight left his eyes just as fast. "I'll get my jacket," he muttered.

We brought Slater to the station and placed him in the small, windowless interrogation room. A ceiling fan turned overhead with the lethargy of a summer afternoon.

Holcomb and I took the notebook and the bundle of letters into an adjacent office. We sat across from one another at a metal desk, flipping through page after page of George Cummings's slanted handwriting.

He'd written it all down—what happened that night at the lighthouse. Every harrowing detail matched what Mama Dawson had recounted: Hattie running down the steps, the man dragging her into the shack, the murder. Only Cummings had added one piece she hadn't known, the name of the man in the shack.

"He learned it from the Carlisles," I muttered, tapping the margin where the name was written. "Apparently, Mallory brought them fresh fish more than once. They knew his name."

Holcomb leaned back in his chair, arms folded. "Then the question is whether Slater shared the name with Alan, Eleanor, or Mallory."

"Exactly," I said. "We need to find out who knew what and when."

Holcomb stood. "Let me get Mallory out of lockup. If he recognizes Slater, we'll at least know they've met. Maybe that'll shake something loose."

We walked down the corridor to the cells, where Mallory sat on a bunk with his arms folded, eyes sunken from a night on a cot, and a conscience he hadn't quite made peace with.

Holcomb rapped on the bars. "Mr. Mallory, we've got some good news."

Mallory blinked and looked up.

"The bartender confirmed you were at the Banyan Street Saloon the night George Cummings was killed. He backed up your story."

Relief flickered across his face, but it didn't stay long.

"There's something else, though," I added. "That same bartender said you met with someone the night before. A well-dressed man. And he mentioned a book."

Mallory tensed. "I... I'd had a few drinks. I don't remember."

"Who was he?" Holcomb pressed. "What was his name?"

Mallory shook his head slowly. "It was dark. We sat near the back of the saloon. He wore a hat low over his eyes. Said said something about a book. I figured he was some writer or something." Mallory shifted in his seat, rubbing his hands together like he was trying to scrub away a memory.

"What about the book?" I asked.

"That night... the man told me he knew who killed my father," he said finally.

Holcomb and I both straightened.

"He said it was George Cummings," Mallory continued. "That he covered it up all these years. That he wrote the whole thing down in a notebook."

My voice was steady. "You realize that gives you a motive to kill Cummings."

"I know," Mallory snapped, then lowered his head. "But I didn't do it. I swear. I was in the kitchen washing dishes."

Holcomb narrowed his eyes. "Then why didn't you say anything?"

"Because I figured no one would believe me. My old man's killer, lying dead on the stage. They'd pin it on me before I opened my mouth."

I watched his face for signs of deception—a twitch, a blink, a slip of the mask. But Mallory just stared at the floor, his jaw tight.

Whether he was lying or telling the truth, one thing was clear. Slater tracked down Mallory, told him Cummings had killed his father, and knew we'd look at Mallory as the prime suspect.

Holcomb took Mallory back to the cell while I returned to the interrogation room.

Slater sat with his arms folded, a thin smile tugging at the edge of his mouth. Holcomb joined us, leaning against the wall, arms crossed. "We just spoke to Thomas Mallory."

Slater's smile twitched. "Who?"

"He recognized you," I said. "From the saloon in West Palm. Said you approached him, asked about his father."

Slater's eyes flicked between the two of us. "So? Talking to someone's not a crime."

"No, but setting them up for murder is," Holcomb said flatly. "You told Mallory that George Cummings killed his father. Got him all riled up."

"Because it's true," Slater snapped. "George admitted it in that notebook."

"And now George is dead," I said. "You knew the story, you knew where the notebook was, and you knew exactly who'd take the fall. Pretty convenient, wouldn't you say?"

Slater's expression hardened. "You think I killed George? That's rich. Maybe you ought to look harder at Mallory. He had the motive. I just gave him the truth."

"Did you?" I asked. "Or did you dangle a story before a grieving man and hope he'd lash out? You didn't need to kill George yourself. You just lit the fuse and stepped back."

Silence hung in the room, the kind that made a person feel the sweat under their collar.

Holcomb stepped forward. "Who else did you tell, Slater? Who else knows what you know?"

Slater hesitated just long enough to confirm he had told someone. His eyes shifted slightly, calculating. "I'm not saying another word," he said.

Holcomb raised an eyebrow. "This isn't a courtroom, Mr. Slater. You're not under arrest. You're here answering questions voluntarily."

Slater leaned back in his chair, arms crossed. "Still. I'd feel more comfortable not answering any more of your questions."

I gave a short laugh. "Comfort wasn't a priority the night George Cummings was poisoned."

Slater's jaw tightened.

Holcomb stepped closer, wrapping his hands around the back of the chair across from him. "Look, you're not on trial yet. But someone's going to be. Right now, you've got a chance to cooperate. If you're not the one who killed Cummings, we need names. If you are, we've got your lies already on the record."

Slater looked between us, his gaze colder now. "I've got nothing more to say."

I nodded slowly. "That's your choice. But know that every minute you stay quiet, that noose tightens. And whoever knows the truth might not be as careful with your name as you're being with theirs."

We left Slater in silence, arms folded, lips sealed.

Holcomb and I made our way down the corridor, the soles of our shoes tapping a slow, steady rhythm against the linoleum. We stepped into his office, the door clicking shut behind us.

I sank into the chair opposite his desk. "He didn't kill Cummings," I said, rubbing the bridge of my nose. "He's hiding something, sure, but it's not murder."

Holcomb nodded, lowering himself into the chair beside me rather than behind the desk. That told me he was in no mood for formality. "I agree. Then there's Mallory. He had a strong motive and the opportunity, but his alibi holds up. The timecard checks out. So, we need to look elsewhere."

Holcomb gave me a sideways glance. "We don't have enough to hold either Mallory or Slater any longer. I've got to let them go."

I stared at the blinds behind him, watching the slats flicker with the glow of streetlights beyond. "I understand. The only others Slater would've told are Alan and his wife, Eleanor. No one else had a stake in the game. No one else had anything to lose."

Holcomb ran a hand through his hair, his expression tight. “Alan’s clean-cut and climbing. Doesn’t strike me as someone who’d kill his father despite their rift.”

“Exactly,” I said. “Alan’s too invested in his career to risk throwing it all away. But Eleanor... she’s got cracks beneath the polish. Nervous fingers, quick eyes. If anyone’s likely to splinter under the pressure, it’s her.”

“You going to rattle her cage tomorrow?” asked Holcomb.

I nodded. “Hard.”

Holcomb leaned back and exhaled. “Just ensure she doesn’t slam the door shut before we get what we need.”

“Don’t worry,” I said, already picturing the look in her eyes the last time we spoke. “I think the door’s already starting to open.”

Chapter 19

The next morning, I went directly to the Cummings's house. Eleanor's maid led me to the living room, where she announced my presence. Eleanor stood by the tall arched window in a pale silk dress, staring out at the ocean like it might carry answers if she waited long enough. Sunlight slanted through gauzy drapes, painting long amber streaks across the Persian rug, and a half-filled teacup sat untouched on the coffee table.

"Mr. Marlow," she said, barely glancing over her shoulder. "Alan's out of town if that's who you hoped to find. His train doesn't come in until tomorrow."

"You're the reason I came," I said.

She didn't respond; she turned her head slightly before drifting back toward the window like a ghost tethered to some unfinished thought.

I waited a moment, letting the silence settle, giving her time to brace for what I was about to say. "It's important, ma'am. About your past."

"My past?" Eleanor murmured, her hands clasped before her.

"Yes, ma'am. If you'd like to sit down."

She moved slowly to the couch and sat with a quiet grace. I noticed the tension in her knuckles, white and strained. I took the armchair across from her and set my hat on my knee.

"The doubloon around your neck, the one your mother gave you. I came to tell you about its history."

She lifted her eyes to mine, steady but wary.

"Are you familiar with Thomas Mallory?" I asked.

"Perhaps," she said coolly, neither confirming nor denying, though her fingers curled tighter in her lap.

"Well, I've discovered some information that may be difficult to hear, but it's a story you need to know. It starts with your mother… George… and the doubloon."

I laid it out for her. Every sordid piece. George and Sharon. The lighthouse. Sharon's abduction. Patrick Mallory's dead body. The pact made in blood and silence. The gold coins passed between them like the price of guilt.

When I finished, she didn't speak. Didn't move. Her face was pale and rigid, like a porcelain mask. She took a shallow breath and rose from the couch, drifting back to the window before returning and sitting again. This time, her composure slipped. Her fingers trembled as she reached for the teacup, but didn't lift it. Her eyes had gone glassy, fixed on some far-off corner of the room.

"I was adopted," she said softly, almost like she was reminding herself. "I've always known. But no one ever said who my mother was."

"A Negro woman with a white baby?" I said gently. "It would have been a scandal both in the Bahamas and Palm Beach. Your mother gave you up to protect you. She gave you one of the doubloons… just like the one George kept."

Her gaze shot to mine, like I'd named something she'd spent her whole life denying.

I let it sit for a moment, then said, "And you and Alan… you had a child, didn't you?"

The silence that followed stretched long enough to count heartbeats. When she finally spoke, her voice cracked. "A daughter. She had… Negro features. There was no hiding it. We said she died in childbirth. But we gave her away. And paid dearly to make sure everyone stayed quiet."

"And now," I said, my voice low, "that baby, your daughter, is a woman named Lisa. She lives in West Palm Beach. She's a gifted seamstress."

Eleanor's breath left her. She clutched her stomach, like she'd been punched, her frame curling forward under the weight of it all. Her eyes filled, but the tears held, teetering on the edge. "You can't prove any of that," she said, her voice flat but quivering at the edges.

"Not everything," I admitted. "But I've got your family trait on my side."

She gazed at me curiously. "What do you mean?"

"The wine-colored birthmark on your left clavicle. Lisa has one, too."

Her eyes widened. "If anyone finds out that I'm the product of a white father and Negro mother, even though she'd been raped, or that Alan and I had a Negro child, we'd be ruined. Everything we've worked for. All of it. Gone."

"That's not what I care about," I said, watching her closely. "What I care about is how George died. You knew things no one else could have. And now that I know the past, I have to ask: what part did you play in his death?"

Her breath caught. Then she straightened, spine stiffening like someone yanking on invisible strings. "I didn't kill him."

"I don't believe you," I said flatly. "But I don't have proof."

She wiped her face then, finally brushing away a tear that slipped free. “You won’t find any. Because I didn’t do it.”

I rose slowly, never taking my eyes off her. “Then someone else did,” I said. “But I’ll get to the bottom of it, one way or another.”

She looked away, but not before I saw the deep and buried fear behind the calm she was trying to wear like armor.

I walked to the door, paused with my hand on the knob. “You’re not out of this yet, Eleanor. Secrets don’t stay buried forever. Trust me. I make a living unearthing them.”

And with that, I left her alone in the silence, her past crashing down around her like a storm breaking against the shore.

~~~

The ceiling fans at the Palm Beach Police Station spun lazily overhead, stirring air thick with heat and stale cigarette smoke. I found Holcomb behind his desk, sleeves rolled up, tie loosened, and a scowl etched into his face like someone had carved it there. He looked like he hadn’t slept in a day and didn’t plan to.

“Well,” he grunted as I walked in. “You look like you’ve been to a funeral.”

“Close enough,” I said, dropping into the wooden chair across from him. “Just came from seeing Eleanor Cummings.”

His eyes sharpened. “She talk?”

“She listened,” I said. “Didn’t confess to anything outright, but I laid it all out: her mother, George, Mallory’s assault, the doubloon, the baby she gave up.”

He let out a low whistle, leaned back, and rubbed a hand over his chin. “She deny any involvement in George’s death?”
~~~

"Of course," I said. "But she cracked a little when I mentioned the daughter. She admitted the baby existed and that she and Alan covered it up. Said they paid people off to keep quiet."

"That's motive if it ever leaks," Holcomb muttered. "But it isn't murder." He tapped his fingers against his coffee mug, thinking. "So, what's our next move?"

"Alan's out of town until tomorrow. I say we visit them together when he's back. Ask them both to come in, no formal charges. Just a little chat."

He raised an eyebrow. "You think they'll come willingly?"

"They'll want to control the story," I said. "The best way to do that is to keep it friendly. For now."

"And if one of them starts talking?"

I gave a half-smile. "Then we lean on the other. They're both carrying secrets. If we put them in separate rooms and turn up the heat, one of 'em might spill to protect their own skin."

Holcomb gave a slow nod. "Classic squeeze play."

"It's all we've got. No proof where the poison came from, no prints, no eyewitness."

"But sometimes," he said, rising to his feet and stretching his back with a grunt, "that's enough. You start poking around in the dark long enough, something ugly always crawls out. Of course, once we start down this road, we might not be able to walk it back."

"I'm already halfway down it," I said. "Might as well see where it leads."

Holcomb nodded again, slower this time, like he was taking stock of what was coming. "All right. Tomorrow, then. We do it together."

I stood and took my hat from the chair arm. "I'll be here first thing."

Walking out of the station, I hoped tomorrow might tear the last veil off a secret that had stayed buried for over thirty years and expose the truth about who killed George and why. While that's the hope for any investigator, I wasn't sure either of the Cummins was ready for the truth to see the light of day.

~~~

The sun was starting to dip by the time I made it back to the office. The sky had turned a dusky gold, casting long shadows across the buildings.

Betty Lou was still at her desk, typing something with that same efficient rhythm I'd come to depend on more than I cared to admit. She looked up as I came in and arched an eyebrow. "Well?" she asked, already halfway into the question.

I dropped my hat on the rack and loosened my tie. "Eleanor cracked. Not wide open, but enough to show what's underneath. The baby story is true. She and Alan had a child, passed it off as dead, and paid to keep it quiet."

"Good grief." She blinked. "So Eleanor is Lisa's mother."

"Yes."

"Patrick Mallory's assault on Sharon changed everything for three generations," said Betty Lou, clucking her tongue.

I gave a tired nod. "We're seeing both Alan and Eleanor tomorrow. Holcomb and I are going to play them off each other, see who breaks first."

Betty Lou didn't say anything at first, just nodded and looked thoughtful. Then she said, "Be careful, Drake. People like that don't like being exposed. They'll do desperate things to stay in the dark."

"I know," I said quietly.
~~~

I stepped into my office and closed the door behind me. The quiet settled in like an old, familiar coat. I picked up the phone and dialed Mrs. Anderson's.

The maid put Constance on the phone, her voice warm and just the right amount of surprise. "Drake?"

"Hope I'm not calling too late."

"Not at all. I was just finishing up here."

I smiled a little. "I wanted to see if you're free tomorrow night. Thought we might take a walk, get some air, and spend time together. It seems like ages since we've spent time together alone."

"That sounds lovely," she said. "And how are things coming?"

"Hard to say just yet, but I'm close. Real close. Tomorrow should bring answers."

There was a brief pause on the line, like she was measuring something in her mind. "Well, in two days, my job is over here, at least for this season. After that…" Her voice softened. "Maybe we'll have more time together."

"I'm looking forward to that," I said.

We said good night, and I hung up. Then I locked up and headed home, the streets damp with evening air and the promise of rain. Tomorrow would bring something—confession, confrontation, maybe even closure. The Cummings story was about to end, but I didn't yet know whether it would end in peace or ruin.

Either way, it was time the truth prevailed.

Chapter 20

The overnight rain brought a low-hanging haze to the streets the next morning, clinging to them like the mist didn't want to let go. I met Holcomb out front of the station just after eight. He stood with his hands in his coat pockets, jaw set, eyes harder than usual.

"Ready?" I asked.

He gave a curt nod. "Let's hope they are."

The ride to the Cummings's house was quiet except for the occasional rumble of tires on the pavement. Palm trees lined the road like sentries, unmoved by what we were about to do. Holcomb drove, eyes on the road, as my mind turned over questions I kept asking myself. Would they lie again? Would one turn on the other? Would they slip up just enough to give us what we needed?

When we reached the house around ten, the maid, not Eleanor or Alan, answered the door. She looked flustered, nearly tripping over her words. "Oh, Mr. Marlow, I… I just arrived. Mrs. Cummings wanted me to stop by the market on my way in. I found the door unlocked and called out, but no one answered."

Holcomb narrowed his eyes. "Do you mean no one's here?"

She looked between us, confused and clearly upset. "I thought maybe something happened. Their car is gone. I… I haven't seen them since I left yesterday."

"You said, 'them.' Does that mean Mr. Commings was here before you left?" I asked.

She nodded. "Came home just before I left."

Holcomb and I exchanged a look, then stepped inside.

Downstairs was quiet. Everything looked undisturbed—silver polished, cushions fluffed, teacups washed and neatly shelved. If someone had walked in cold, they might think the owners had simply stepped out.

But upstairs told a different story.

The bedroom looked like a hurricane had blown through. Drawers hung open, half-full, some yanked entirely from their tracks. Strewn clothes blanketed the bed, and the closet doors gaped like open mouths.

"Someone packed in a hurry," Holcomb muttered.

"And didn't care who knew it," I added, stepping around a discarded shoe and a silk scarf caught in the edge of the dresser drawer.

The maid stood in the doorway, hands clasped tightly. "The family photo from the dresser is gone, too," she said softly. "One of Mr. Alan and Mrs. Eleanor at the yacht club. And the silver-framed one from their wedding. That's not like her. She always kept them right there."

Holcomb moved to the window and looked out across the drive. "Car's gone, alright. No note. No call. No sign of when they left."

I turned to the maid. "When did you leave last night?"

"The Mrs. requested I stay a little late, so I didn't leave until seven," she said.

I rubbed the back of my neck, the sting of disappointment setting in. "They ran."

Holcomb turned, frowning. "You think they knew we were coming?"

"I think Eleanor figured I'd tell you. And if Alan came home last night instead of today, as she told me, she might've spilled everything to him. Either way, it looks like they decided skipping town beat answering our questions and revealing Eleanor's past."

He exhaled hard, pacing a slow circle. "We've got no warrant. No formal charges. Just a lot of suspicion and a trail that's already cold."

"No proof," I said, more to myself than him. "Only a story and a hunch."

Holcomb nodded grimly. "Then they're gone for good, and no government position for Alan."

We stood in the disheveled bedroom, the silence stretching between us.

The maid lingered just inside the doorway, wringing her hands. "Are they in trouble? Should I… should I file a report or something?" she asked, her voice shaky. "They didn't say anything to me. I just showed up like always, and the place was open."

Holcomb gave her a reassuring nod. "We can take your statement if you'd like. Technically, adults can go missing if they choose, but we'll document everything. If foul play turns up later, it helps to have a paper trail."

"I'm just worried something happened," she said. "Mrs. Eleanor was on edge all week."

"She had her reasons," I muttered.

Holcomb took out a small notepad and jotted down a few notes. “Did they ever mention traveling? Any relatives they might go to?”

She shook her head. “No, sir. Not a word. They were supposed to attend the garden fundraiser this weekend. Mrs. Eleanor had already picked out her dress.”

We exchanged a look.

“I’ll need your contact information in case we have questions,” Holcomb said. “And if you remember anything unusual, let us know.”

She nodded, still looking dazed.

Back downstairs, we rechecked the study and kitchen, hoping to find a note, an itinerary, or something that would make sense of their vanishing. Nothing. Just the ticking of a grandfather clock and the faint scent of fading roses.

I found a small wooden box with spare house keys in the side drawer by the back door. I held one up. “Let’s not leave the place wide open.”

Holcomb took it and locked the front door behind us. “We’ll keep an eye on the property. If they come back, we’ll know.”

The maid looked at the house as if the dwelling she knew so well had become a stranger. “Should I still come by tomorrow?”

Holcomb hesitated, then nodded. “No need. For now, let’s get you to the station so we can take your statement. Then we’ll drive you home.”

~~~

I left the police station with no desire to head to the office. Instead, I turned and headed to Mama Dawson’s house, where it seemed only right for us to talk about what I’d learned. A car was parked down the street as I pulled up in front and saw her in her usual spot—the rocking chair on
~~~

the front porch, a crocheted blanket draped over her lap. Her head tilted slightly to one side, chin tucked to chest like she'd dozed off mid-thought.

"Mama Dawson?" I said gently as I climbed the steps.

No answer. The breeze stirred her skirt and nudged the rocker. I stepped closer. That's when I saw the voodoo doll cradled in her lap, the same one she'd shown me weeks ago. Only now, its threadbare face stared up at the ceiling with hollow button eyes, and her hand was no longer resting gently on the doll. Instead, her hand was limp and cold when I touched it.

She was gone.

I knelt beside her and checked for a pulse to be sure, even though I already knew. There was no tension in her skin, no resistance in her fingers. Just stillness. Whatever strength had kept her clinging to this world had finally slipped away.

I stood slowly, eyes sweeping over the porch and the house behind her. Something about how she sat was so peaceful, like she'd finished something. That alone kept me from calling it suspicious. Still, I had to be thorough.

I pushed open the screen door and stepped inside. The air smelled of its familiar mix of dried herbs, lemon polish, and something else. Calm and quiet. The kind that wraps itself around a room after the last heartbeat leaves.

Her teacup still sat on the kitchen counter. Everything else was perfectly in place—chairs tucked in, curtains drawn against the afternoon sun, not a speck of dust out of order. No signs of a struggle. No broken glass or overturned furniture. Just stillness. Tidy and final.

Then I saw her.

Max.

She stood in the far corner of the sitting room like a child caught sneaking sweets, eyes wide and red-rimmed, a bundle of letters clutched in her hand. A frayed string of twine in the other.

"What are you doing here?" I asked, sharper than I intended. The sight of her in Mama Dawson's home set off something hot in my chest.

Max winced. "I came to follow up after you mentioned her name at the paper," she said, her voice soft and brittle. "Thought she might shed some light on the story." She looked down at the letters. "I didn't think anyone would come by."

"Did you call the police?"

She shook her head slowly. "Not yet. I was with her when it happened. We were talking… and then she just…" Her breath hitched. "She just slipped away."

Tears welled in her eyes and broke free, trailing down her cheeks. Her voice shook, but not with performance. This was real. Raw.

"Did you get what you came for?" I asked, colder than I felt.

"Some of it," she said. "She passed before she could tell me the rest." She swiped at her tears with the sleeve of her blouse. "I came in to see if there'd been foul play, anything that might explain how she died."

"And?"

She looked around the room. "Nothing I could find. No marks, no sign of pain. She just… stopped..."

My gaze dropped to the letters in her hand. "And those?"

She hesitated, then stepped forward and offered them. "They're for you."

I took them, weighing them in my hand. Some envelopes had been opened, others remained sealed. My jaw clenched. “You read letters meant for me?”

Her eyes flickered with guilt. “I wanted the story. I’m sorry.”

“Sorry you pried into someone’s private correspondence, or sorry you got caught?”

She didn’t answer right away. “Both, I guess,” she said finally, voice small.

I turned over the top envelope. Bold, looping script noted the recipient: *For Mr. Marlow.*

There were others, too, letters postmarked from Marsh Harbour. Sharon. These were handwritten, intimate thoughts of the young girl’s life in the Bahamas, sent to Mama Dawson. A diary written in fragments, stitched together by hope and distance.

I crossed the room and picked up the rotary phone on the kitchen wall.

“I’m calling the police,” I said without looking at Max. “And you need to go. If they find you here, they’ll slap you with trespassing, interfering with a death investigation, and anything else they can get to stick. You’ll lose your job, your byline, and your reputation.”

Max’s mouth trembled. She stepped toward the door, pausing with one hand on the screen door knob. “I’m really sorry, Marlow. Please… call me later? Let’s work this out.”

“When I’m ready,” I said, keeping my voice even.

She walked out, giving one last glance toward the still form of Mama Dawson, blanketed now beneath a quilt on her rocking chair. Then Max disappeared down the sidewalk.

I turned back to the phone and dialed the station.

“Holcomb,” came the voice on the other end.

"It's Marlow. I'm at Mama Dawson's. She's passed."

A pause. "Natural?"

"Looks like it. Peaceful. But you'll want someone to check it out to be sure."

"I'll send a car. You staying put?"

"Until they arrive."

I hung up and returned to the porch, sitting on the rocker beside her. The voodoo doll still rested in her lap, like a sentinel keeping watch over her final breath. I didn't touch it.

When the patrol car pulled up twenty minutes later, I handed off the details, gave them a quiet nod, and left them to it.

The letters stayed with me.

~~~

Back at the office, Betty Lou was flipping through the society column with a distracted look when I came in. She sat up straighter when she saw the bundle in my hands. "Something happened?"

"Mama Dawson passed," I said, setting the letters gently on her desk.

"Oh," she breathed, one hand rising to her chest. "Drake, I'm sorry."

"She left these for me. Letters from Sharon. From when she was in the Bahamas, waiting to give birth."

Betty Lou's brows rose, then drew together in a worried frown. She reached for the twine and began to untie the bundle.

I poured us two cups of stale coffee and sat across from her. "Let's see what Mama thought I needed to know."

The office was quiet except for the creak of Betty Lou's chair and the faint ticking of the clock on the wall. The letters were aged and worn, the corners softened from
~~~

years of handling. I took the first one and began to read aloud while Betty Lou listened, her eyes trained on my face as if bracing for something she couldn't yet name.

"Dear Mama Dawson, I'm in Marsh Harbour now. The ocean reminds me of the one George and I used to sit beside in the evenings before everything changed. I'm expecting. I haven't told anyone but you. I don't know what comes next, but I know I still love him. I keep the doubloon with me. It's the only thing that makes me feel like he's near."

I paused, clearing my throat.

"She did love him," Betty Lou said softly. "It wasn't some youthful fling."

I nodded and moved to another letter, skipping several in between.

"The baby was born last night. A girl. Beautiful, with a tuft of dark hair and a reddish birthmark near her collarbone. I want to keep her. I held her against me and thought, maybe we could disappear. But Mama won't hear of it. She says no child of mixed blood ever made it, not in this world.' She's already made arrangements, but I'm begging you. Please help me find a white family to love her. Someone to raise her safe."

The words were soft, full of sorrow and resignation. I read the final envelope in the stack—Mama Dawson's note.

Mr. Marlow, if you readin' dis, it mean I done gone from this world. I ain't never mean to keep no secrets, but sometimes we carry burden for other people 'cause they can't carry it themself. Sharon trust me to find a home for her baby, and I do just that. I find a good family—one dat could give the child a life her mama couldn't.

I promise I wouldn't tell no one the truth—not Sharon, not George. I was tryin' to protect 'em best way I know how. George never know he had a daughter. That was me who keep it from him. That was my choice. And that story 'bout Patrick Mallory hurtin' Sharon? That one was Slater's. But that story in Sea Grape Cottage 'bout Bella and Kevin? That ain't no fiction, Mr. Marlow. That was Sharon and George. His memory, straight from heart.

The room fell silent.

Betty Lou looked up slowly, her voice hesitant. "Drake… if George never knew… and Sharon never told anyone who Eleanor's father was…"

It hit us both like a slow-motion train wreck. The letters dropped from my hand and fanned across the desk like falling leaves. "Alan and Eleanor…" I said, the words sticking in my throat.

"They're brother and sister," Betty Lou whispered. "And they don't even know it."

I stood, pacing to the window and back, hands on my hips, my mind unraveling all the assumptions I'd been stacking like dominoes. "George didn't know. Mama Dawson made sure of that. He never saw Sharon again, plain and simple. He carried her memory with him all those years, symbolized by the doubloon. Meanwhile, Eleanor was adopted, raised, and married Alan Cummings, unaware of any of it."

Betty Lou studied the letters, her brow furrowed. "Mama Dawson was trying to protect them… in her own way."

"Yeah," I muttered. "But secrets like that never stay buried. Not forever."

She was quiet for a while, then said softly, "Drake… if George didn't kill Patrick Mallory… then who did?"

I turned to her, surprised by the question, but not because I hadn't thought of it. I had. A thousand times. "No one ever figured that out," I said. "His body was found in the shack. Rumors swirled, but nothing stuck. No arrests. No leads."

"But George's notebook," she said, "those pages where he wrote that Mallory abducted Sharon and that George killed him—"

"They were fake notes," I said, cutting in. "Ones Slater showed Mallory to convince him that Cummings had murdered his father."

She stared at me. "So Mallory killed George because of those notes. He believed they were real."

I nodded slowly. "That's what it looks like. Slater believed George was going to tell the audience the story in Sea Grape Cottage was real, that he'd had a relationship with Hattie, who was really Sharon. That would have ruined George's career and Slater's livelihood. Silencing George was the only way to keep the secret at Sea Grape Cottage a secret."

"And now?" she asked, her voice small. "Do you know what the truth is?"

I looked out the window, the sky turning the color of bruised peaches as the sun began to slip toward the western horizon. A breeze rattled the palm fronds outside.

"I know pieces," I said. "I know Sharon and George loved each other. I know they had a daughter, Eleanor. I know Mama Dawson lied to protect them. I know Eleanor and Alan grew up strangers to their blood. But the rest…" I shook my head. "The rest is a mystery. I don't know who killed Patrick Mallory. I don't know how Slater and Mama Dawson wound up telling the same story of how Cummings killed him. Mama Dawson is dead, and I doubt Slater will ever talk."

Betty Lou rose and gently gathered the letters. "We know enough to end the story. Maybe not the way we wanted, but enough."

I watched her stack the letters and tie them with the twine, grateful for her steady hands and her steady heart.

"I'm not sure the story's over," I said. "With Alan and Eleanor on the run, there are still missing pieces. Yet, I have faith that the curse of this story turns into a blessing. I just don't know when."

Chapter 21

A week had passed since Mama Dawson's letters tore the lid off everything I thought I knew. The days dragged, gray and slow, with too much time to think and not enough to do. The truth had a way of settling in like dust after a storm—quiet, heavy, and hard to breathe.

That morning, like I did every morning, I stopped by Willie's newsstand. He handed me the paper with a nod. "You'll want to look at page four," he said, his voice low, eyes shifting to the street.

I gave him a subtle nod of thanks and tucked the paper under my arm. Back at the office, I slid into my chair and flipped the daily open. The article on page four caught me mid-sip of coffee.

"Cummings Estate Transferred to Missing Son"

George Cummings's will left everything to his son, Alan. The problem was that no one knew where Alan was. No forwarding address. No sightings. The lawyer couldn't find him, and neither could the bank. It was as if he and Eleanor had vanished into thin air.

I sat back in my chair, rubbing a hand over my face. They'd run. I should've expected it. But I didn't think it would end there.

The following week, another headline met me at the stand. Willie didn't say a word. He just tapped the front page before sliding it across the counter. I took the paper in silence and walked away, my heart already heavy.

"Explosion Aboard Passenger Vessel *Santa Estrella* Claims Dozens." The article went on to explain what happened. The *Santa Estrella,* a popular ship for those seeking new beginnings or lost fortunes, had been heading to Havana. Just after dusk, survivors said, an explosion rocked the vessel. Some thought it was the boiler. Others claimed it came from the kitchen. Whatever the cause, it tore through the decks like lightning through dry pine.

Flames chased passengers down corridors. Smoke turned the air into soot and screams. In the scramble, the crew lowered the lifeboats haphazardly. Some tipped. Others never made it into the water. The freighter *Gran Fortuna* spotted the fire on the horizon and pulled fifty people from the sea. The rest, the paper said, were presumed lost.

Among the confirmed dead: Alan and Eleanor Cummings.

I let the paper fall across my desk, the words still ringing in my ears like the crack of gunfire. They'd run from questions, from truths they didn't know. And now they were gone.

Betty Lou stepped in with a fresh cup of coffee and saw my face before I spoke. "What happened?" she asked.

I slid the paper toward her. "They didn't get far," I said.

She read the headline, and her hand flew to her mouth. Her eyes met mine, searching for sense, closure, and maybe even justice. "Guess that's the end of it," she said softly.

I shook my head.

"End of a chapter," I murmured. "Not the story."

~~~

A few days later, as I leaned back in my chair, the morning paper folded on my lap. Betty Lou tapped before cracking the door open.

"You've got a visitor," she said. "Max Shelton."

Max brushed past her, camera bag slung over one shoulder, eyes sharp as ever. She wasn't wearing her usual slacks and jacket. Today she wore a soft linen skirt and a blouse with just enough structure to look serious. Her expression said this wasn't a social call.

"I was going through my shots from the night of Cummings's talk," she said, dropping her bag on the chair beside my desk. "From the reception. I ducked into the hall early to test the light, figuring I'd get a few wide shots of the setup before the crowd poured in."

I raised a brow. "I thought the police had your film."

"Guess I forgot this one." She unzipped her satchel without another explanation and pulled out an envelope. Inside were a half-dozen glossy prints, still faintly smelling of chemicals. She slid one across the desk. "Take a look."

The photo showed the stage from a distance, just before the event—nothing unusual. But heading toward the podium, captured in mid-motion, was Mallory, one hand carrying a small serving tray. On the tray was the glass of water. The next photo showed him leaving without the glass.

Max leaned in. "I almost didn't notice. It's not crystal clear, but that's the person. And that's the glass."
~~~

I studied it a moment longer, my stomach tightening. The stage was empty except for him. No guests yet. Just Mallory and the glass of water.

"You're sure you took this before the crowd came in?"

She nodded. "About fifteen minutes before seven. The ushers weren't even calling people in yet. I was only in there a minute or two. But this… well, I thought you ought to see it."

I looked up. "Thanks, Max. This photo might change everything."

She gave a small shrug, but her eyes lingered on the photo like it held more questions than answers. "Friends, again?"

"That squares it," I said, grabbing the photos and leaving for the police station to show Borman and Holcomb.

The ceiling fans in Chief Borman's office turned slowly as I handed the black-and-white photos across the desk. Holcomb leaned in first, eyebrows raised as he thumbed through them.

"That's Mallory," I said, tapping one of the prints. "Not long before the talk started. And that's a tray in his hand with a glass of water."

Borman sat forward. "He wasn't supposed to be on stage."

Holcomb nodded once, grabbed his coat, and we were out the door five minutes later.

The Breakers kitchen was alive with the clang of pans and the thrum of lunchtime prep. Chef Tuttle met us at a narrow staff hallway off the main galley, his white coat slightly stained, his expression less than thrilled.

"Mallory's a dishwasher," he said after seeing the photo. "Not a waiter. He's not trained for service, wouldn't have had any reason to be near the podium. I don't know why he was carrying a tray."

Holcomb crossed his arms. "You mentioned earlier where you keep the strychnine."

Tuttle wiped his hands on a towel, clearly agitated. "Yes, yes—I told the officers already. It's in the dry supply room. Locked."

"Show us again," I said.

He nodded, turned, and led us down a side corridor. At the end, a narrow door sat recessed in the nondescript wall. The chef stepped up and reached above a spice rack to a small, painted-over hook. From it, he plucked a tarnished brass key.

"That's the key?" Holcomb asked sharply.

The chef paused. "Well… yes. It's where I keep it."

"Anyone else know it's up there?"

Tuttle hesitated a moment. "It's possible. Staff see everything, you know. But no one's supposed to touch it."

He unlocked the door. Inside, stacked shelves held bulk ingredients like sugar and flour. On the highest shelf was a small amber bottle with a yellowing label.

"Strychnine," Holcomb muttered. "Still there."

The chef nodded. "We hardly ever use it. Just for bait. And only when we see droppings. Rodents are most likely to come here for our dry ingredients."

We left the kitchen with more questions than answers, but one thing was clear—the locked room wasn't as secure as it should've been. And someone with just enough knowledge of where the key hung could've helped themselves without anyone being the wiser.

Back at the station, Mallory sat hunched at the end of a narrow table in the interview room, where even the walls felt accusatory. His eyes flicked between Holcomb and me as we stepped inside. Borman stayed in the hall, arms folded, watching through the glass.

Holcomb dropped the stack of photographs on the table. “Recognize this?”

Mallory’s face stiffened. He didn’t answer.

I leaned in, tapping the photo of him onstage. “You’re not a waiter, Mallory. So why were you carrying a tray? Why was there a glass of water headed for the podium?”

Mallory’s mouth opened, then closed again. He gave a feeble shrug. “I was just trying to help.”

“Funny,” Holcomb said, “we talked to the chef. He says you had no business being near that stage. And he showed us the closet where the strychnine’s kept.”

Mallory’s eyes widened just a hair.

“We saw where the key was hidden,” I added. “Not exactly Fort Knox. Anyone in the kitchen who paid attention could’ve found it. You had a motive. You had access. You had an opportunity.”

Holcomb crossed his arms. “We’re not fools, Mallory. The question is, who put you up to it?”

Mallory looked down, rubbing his hands together like he could scrub the guilt off. For a moment, it was quiet except for the ticking of the wall clock.

Then he broke.

“I’m not taking the blame alone,” he muttered. “Slater…. With Mr. Cummings speaking at the hotel, maybe it was time somebody evened the score for what happened to my father.”

“And you believed him?” I asked.

Mallory looked up. “He showed me the notebook. Said it was proof. That Cummings had written down how he did it. The notes were never meant for the public.”

I reached into my coat pocket and pulled out a folded page, one of the marked drafts from Cummings's writing desk. I placed it in front of him.

"Cummings didn't kill your father, Mallory. The pages Slater showed you? They weren't even in Cummings's handwriting. Slater wrote them to get you riled up enough to kill the man you thought did it. Your father's murder remains unsolved."

Mallory stared at the paper. His mouth hung slightly open. He leaned back, silent for a long moment, then buried his face in his hands.

We left him bent over the table, the weight of a story he'd believed pressing down at last.

Mallory's confession was enough to move things quickly.

By the time afternoon shadows crept long across the tiled floor of the Palm Beach police station, Borman had a warrant drawn up. Slater didn't put up a fight when Borman and Holcomb picked him up at The Breakers and brought him in quietly, cuffed and stone-faced.

Slater tried to play it cool in the interrogation room. "You can't pin this on me," he said. "I didn't touch the poison. Didn't put the glass on the podium. You got nothing."

Holcomb didn't blink. "You're being charged with criminal solicitation to commit murder and conspiracy. You gave Mallory the motive and the push. You set the fire. You just didn't light the match."

Slater scoffed. "That's not gonna stick. I was simply talking. You can't prove intent."

Holcomb slid the folder across the table, thick with statements and photographs. "I think the jury will see through you," he said calmly. "Especially once they hear what you told him. A son looking for someone to blame. You handed him a target and a reason."

"Did you think you were being clever?" I asked, watching him from across the table. "Using an old grudge like kindling and letting someone else do the burning?"

He didn't answer. Just gave me a sour little grin that faltered.

"Mallory has already signed his statement," I said. "He told us how you egged him on, showed him the notes you wrote about how Cummings killed your father, and played up the story of your father's murder until it was no longer a possibility but a certainty in his mind. Something that ate at him until..."

Borman stood beside me as Holcomb led Slater away. "You were right to keep digging," he said quietly.

I nodded, watching the hallway empty out.

Outside, the sea breeze stirred the palms and ruffled the edge of the morning edition abandoned under a bench. With George Cummings's name splashed across the front page, people would remember the man, the book, and the shock of his death.

But now they'd also know the truth.

Justice, slow-footed and tangled, maybe, but justice all the same. Thanks to Max.

~~~

A few days after the arrests, the air in the office felt heavier. Maybe it was the silence that followed a long, winding storm. Or maybe it was just unfinished business pressing on my chest.

I sat behind my desk, turning George Cummings's doubloon over in my hand, the images a symbol of love and promises made in secret. I looked up at Betty Lou. "Can you find the attorney from the article about George's will?"
~~~

She didn't ask why. She never had to. "Already did," she said, scribbling a name and number on my notepad. "Name's Winthrop Blakenship, in Philadelphia."

I leaned back in my chair, sunlight slanting through the blinds in golden bars across my desk. The doubloon sat heavy in my palm, warm from my touch, like it remembered everything I didn't. I turned it once more, then picked up the phone and dialed the number Betty Lou had scribbled on a slip of stationery.

Having asked for Mr. Blakenship, a voice answered—polished, deliberate, with clipped diction from years of prep schools and mahogany. "Winthrop Blakenship speaking."

"Mr. Blakenship," I said, sitting forward, "this is Drake Marlow. I'm a private investigator out of Palm Beach, Florida. I assisted the Palm Beach Police during their investigation into George Cummings's murder. I believe you're handling the Cummings estate?"

"I am," he replied, guarded but not impolite. "May I ask what this is regarding?"

"It's about a girl named Lisa. She's George Cummings's granddaughter," I said, watching the dust swirl in the sunlight and waiting for his reaction.

There was a pause—quiet, brief, but long enough to suggest his mind had started doing the math.

"George never mentioned a granddaughter. I'm going to need proof," he said at last, wariness in his tone but with a trace of curiosity as well.

"I'm sure you're familiar with George's novel, *Sea Grape Cottage*," I said.

"I've not only heard of it, Mr. Marlow, but I've read it. Quite the unconventional story for this era," Blakenship said, his voice more engaged now.

"Well," I said, "unconventional is a word one can use, but here's another: true. The story wasn't fiction. George had a romantic affair with a Negro girl named Sharon while visiting the Sea Grape Cottage one summer. Of course, he changed the names in the book, but Sharon was real, and so was the child they had together."

Silence on the other end. Not the awkward kind. The heavy kind.

"I've got letters," I said, pressing forward. "From Sharon to a woman named Mama Dawson, a trusted confidante. The letters detail everything: Sharon's love for George, their romantic liaison, their love, her pregnancy, the birth of her daughter Eleanor, and the arrangement to have her adopted by a white family."

"And you believe Eleanor was George's child?" he asked, his tone cooling into legal scrutiny.

"I don't believe it," I said. "I know it. The letters are clear. Sharon even refers to the gold Spanish doubloon. One of several she dug up on the sand and gave to George. A token of their love and a commitment to never speak of their encounter again. She gave the coin to Eleanor, who kept it her whole life. She wore the doubloon around her neck, knowing only that the coin came from her mother, not who she was."

"And Lisa?" he asked.

"She's Eleanor's daughter. Which makes her George's only living descendant."

Blakenship went quiet again, tapping something on his end. I could hear him flipping through mental ledgers, weighing obligations against reputations. "Letters help," he said finally. "But I'll need something more concrete. Anything else?"

"I've got the other doubloon," I said. "George kept his. I still have it. Won't be a coincidence if Lisa has a matching one, since Eleanor passed another to her daughter. It will be proof. Give me a couple of days. I'll track it down."

Blakenship hesitated. Then he sighed and relented. "Very well, Mr. Marlow. There is… one more thing that may or may not connect to George's death. Before he left for Florida, he instructed me to draft a letter, more of a termination-of-contract letter, for his literary agent, Mr. Slater. It was brief, but firm. George didn't explain, only that he'd deliver it in person. Do you happen to know if he followed through? Or if anyone recovered the letter among his belongings?"

"Not that I've heard. The police cataloged everything they found, but they didn't mention the letter. I'll follow up with them and call you back if it turns up."

"I'll await your call," said Blankenship.

The line went dead, but the weight of the conversation lingered. I picked up the phone again and dialed Holcomb.

"Holcomb," I said. "Meet me at the Cummings's house. Bring the key."

He didn't ask why. He just said, "On my way."

I left the office with the sun already pressing down like a judgment. Celia II coughed to life, and I pointed her north toward the Cummings estate. By the time I pulled into the drive, Holcomb was already there, leaning against his vehicle, sleeves rolled, cigarette burning.

He didn't speak immediately, just gave me a long look, then flicked the stub away.

"Well?" he asked as I approached. "What are we digging for now?" He held up the ring of brass keys, their dull gleam catching the afternoon sun, keys that could unlock more than just doors if we were lucky.

"Several things, it turns out. I spoke with George's attorney this morning. He said George had their office prepare a letter of dismissal for Slater. He wanted to cut ties. Seemed firm about that. The lawyer asked if Slater ever received the letter or if the police found the document among George's things."

Holcomb's brows lifted. "I don't recall a dismissal letter, so he must have given it to Slater, giving him a whopping motive for murder. Only he let Mallory do the dirty deed so he could keep his hands clean. Those charges will stick, and he won't be doing any public speaking for George."

"Good," I said. "I also told George's attorney about Lisa."

Holcomb's brow lifted. "The granddaughter."

"Right. He said the letters help, but they're not enough. He needs something more solid. Something that can hold up in court. I told him about the doubloons. But I want something that ties Sharon to the necklace and to Eleanor. Something irrefutable, since I'm sure the necklace went down with Eleanor when the ship sank."

Holcomb crossed his arms. "Like what?"

"A photograph. Preferably, one of Eleanor wearing the doubloon. And if we're lucky, one that shows the birthmark."

He arched an eyebrow. "Birthmark?"

"Left clavicle. Deep wine-red, shaped like a teardrop. Lisa's got the same one."

He gave a low whistle and turned toward the porch. He unlocked the door, and we stepped inside, the air stale and unmoved since the last time we'd been there.

We started in the study. Alan's writing desk was still cluttered with the detritus of a busy man—fountain pens, empty inkwells, and a leather-bound notebook that contained notes about his upcoming position. I thumbed through drawers while Holcomb scanned the bookshelves and file cabinets.

It wasn't until we reached the upstairs bedroom that we found what we were looking for. Tucked in the bottom drawer of a cedar-lined chest was a small, worn photo album. Holcomb handed it to me, and I flipped it open, scanning the pages.

Then I saw her.

Eleanor.

She was young, maybe seventeen, wearing a cotton sundress and a smile meant for someone just off-camera. Around her neck hung a gold chain, and from it dangled the unmistakable glint of the doubloon. My heart beat once, hard. There was no mistaking it. The curve of the coin, the way it rested on her chest like a promise.

A few pages later, there was another photo. A candid shot, less posed. Eleanor stood with her hair pinned up, the neckline of her dress dipped just enough to reveal the barest glimpse of skin near her collarbone.

There it was.

The birthmark.

A bloom just below her left clavicle, shaped like a teardrop or maybe a heart.

I looked at Holcomb. He saw it, too. Neither of us said anything for a long minute.

"This enough?" he asked, low.

"More than enough," I said, closing the album carefully. "We just found bloodline and legacy, both captured in silver nitrate."

"You gonna tell her?" Holcomb asked.

"Lisa?" I said. "Yeah. She deserves to know her grandfather didn't forget her. Even if he never knew she existed. But not until the court rules in her favor."

As we walked out, the sun slipped behind the palms, and I realized we hadn't just found photographs. We'd found proof that love leaves traces even when those involved try their best to bury them.

Chapter 22

I let myself into the office as the light outside started its slow fade to amber. The air inside was warm and still. I loosened my tie, tossed my hat on the desk, and reached for the phone.

The rotary dial clicked out a slow rhythm as I spun it—number by number—until the line rang through and Constance came on. "Mrs. Anderson's residence."

Her voice always had a touch of velvet to it, even when it carried an edge.

"It's Drake," I said. "I need a favor."

"Do I want to ask what kind?"

"It's not dangerous," I said, though the truth sat heavier than I liked. "I need to see Lisa. Tonight, if possible."

A pause.

"Why?" she asked, guarded now.

"I'm not trying to frighten her or stir things up. I need to talk to her. It's important. Has to do with the Cummings estate. With her family."

Constance exhaled softly. "And you think she'll listen if I'm there."

"I think she'll open the door."

Another pause, then, "All right. But you'd better start talking once I'm in the car."

"I will," I said. "I'll tell you everything on the way. I'll pick you up in twenty," I said.

She didn't say goodbye, just hung up.

I stared at the receiver for a moment longer, then reached for my coat.

We were about to rewrite a legacy, and it all depended on a girl who never knew the man who would soon shape her world.

~~~

I told Constance everything in the car. There was something in her silence. Something that told me she knew this wasn't just another twist in the case. It was the end of the maze. The place where all the threads came together—love, legacy, loss, and gain—wrapped up in one final truth.

And the last person in the legacy was about to learn it. Tonight.

I parked along the curb in front of the modest home tucked behind a hedgerow of bougainvillea and a rusting iron gate. The porch light was on. Good sign. We climbed the steps, and Constance knocked.

Footsteps padded across the floor, then the door cracked open a sliver. One eye peered through the gap. "Miss Constance?"

"It's me, Miss Lisa," she said gently. "I know it's late, but we need to speak with you. This is Mr. Marlow, my fiancé. He's a private detective. We need to speak with you. It's very important."

Lisa hesitated. Her gaze shifted to me, wary and unsure. I didn't blame her. A man showing up after hours in
~~~

this town didn't always mean good news. "I ain't dressed for company," she said, chin tilting ever so slightly.

"Just give us a few minutes," Constance replied. "Our visit could change your life."

The door opened wider. Lisa stepped back and motioned for us to come in. She sat on the edge of a worn sofa, arms folded. "So what's this about?" she asked.

Constance and I eased into nearby chairs. "Constance told me about the wedding dress. We'd be honored to have you make it.

That caught her off guard. Her eyes flickered with something between surprise and humility. "Well… thank you," she said softly. "Didn't expect that."

I nodded. "You've got a gift, and it deserves recognition. But that's not the only reason we're here."

Her gaze tightened. "Go on."

Constance took her hands. "Mr. Marlow has been working on a case and believes he knows who your parents were," she said, keeping her voice warm and even. "And that information may entitle you to a significant inheritance. But he has to prove the woman he thinks was your birth mother actually was."

Lisa's arms loosened, falling into her lap. She turned to me. "You… know who she was?"

"I believe so," I said. "But we need something more—something only you can help us with." I reached into my coat pocket and drew out the doubloon, glinting gold even in the dim light. "Have you ever seen something like this before?"

Lisa drew in a sharp breath. Her hand came up slowly, fingertips grazing her lips. Then, without a word, she rose and left the room. I heard a drawer open. Then soft footsteps returned. She sat down and opened her palm. A gold coin rested there.

"My adopted mother gave it to me when I was seventeen. She said it was given to her at the adoption by that attorney, Mr. Marlow." Suddenly, she put my name and that of the attorney together. "He your father?"

"Yes," I said. I leaned forward, gently placing George's doubloon beside hers. The two coins mirrored each other like twins separated at birth. "Would you mind if I took a photo of you holding this to show they match?" I asked.

Lisa hesitated, then nodded once.

I pulled out the camera and snapped a shot of her holding the coin, then passed the camera to Constance. "Would you take one of us? Like this?"

Lisa and I extended our palms side by side, the matching coins gleaming in the frame. The shutter clicked once, a wind of the film, another click. Then I knew I had to ask the harder question.

"There's one more thing," I said, sitting. "It's a bit delicate."

Lisa's eyes narrowed slightly.

"The woman we believe was your mother had a unique birthmark. Wine-colored. Left clavicle."

Lisa's hand instinctively went to her collarbone.

"I need a photo of it," I said, careful not to lean forward, not to rush her. "To confirm the match."

Her fingers clutched at the neckline of her blouse, eyes wide. "You want a picture of that?"

Before I could speak, Constance stepped in. "I'll take it, Miss Lisa," she said gently. "We can step into the back room. Just one quick photograph, that's all."

Lisa looked from her to me and back again. Then she stood. "All right."

She and Constance disappeared into the back, the hush of the house growing thicker with each passing second. I heard the faint click of the shutter. Then silence.

A minute later, they returned. Lisa looked as though she'd just stepped through a windswept storm.

I rose and gently took her hand. "Thank you, Miss Lisa. That photo may change everything."

"For who?" she asked quietly.

"For you," I said. "A granddaughter worth every ounce of the legacy your grandfather left behind."

We returned to the car, leaving her standing in the soft glow of the living room, a thousand questions written in her eyes.

But for once, I had more answers than doubts.

Chapter 23

It had been almost four weeks of waiting—long, drawn-out hours filled with busy work and paper shuffling, all to keep my mind from pacing a trench into the floorboards. The film had gone out the day after we visited Lisa. Betty Lou hand-delivered it to Stills's photography studio with a note scrawled in my chicken-scratch: *Rush. Top priority. Confidential.*

Stills took a week. Then we mailed off the photographs, the letters, and a personal note to Winthrop Blakenship, the kind written with care and enough gravity to let him know this wasn't some fishing expedition. My return address sat on the envelope in bold black ink, no mistake about where to find me.

After that, silence.

Long days. Longer nights. The kind where every ticking second echoed like a drumbeat down a hallway you couldn't see the end of.

Until this morning.

I was at my desk, pretending to read a newspaper I hadn't turned the page on in twenty minutes, the steady whir of the ceiling fan overhead like a metronome for my nerves. Then the office phone rang.

Betty Lou answered in the front room, her voice all business at first, smooth and bright, then, suddenly, she stopped talking.

A moment later, the intercom buzzed.

"Drake?" she called, and her voice had a tension in it I hadn't heard since the day Lillian Roth's body turned up behind a paneled wall in the secret passageway at The Breaker's.

I sat up straighter. "Yes?"

"It's Mr. Blakenship. For you."

My pulse kicked into gear like someone cranked the starter on an old Packard.

I picked up the phone, and Betty Lou burst through the doorway as if her feet couldn't wait outside. She stood there, arms folded across her chest, mouth drawn in a tight line, eyes wide with questions she didn't want to ask out loud.

"This is Marlow," I said into the receiver.

"Mr. Marlow," came the crisp, composed voice of Winthrop Blakenship. "I have news."

I braced myself.

"After a thorough review of the letters, the photographs—particularly the image of Miss Lisa with the matching coin—and the identifying birthmark, I'm satisfied. The evidence is compelling and conclusive."

I didn't move. Neither did Betty Lou.

"There is no doubt in my mind," Blakenship continued, "that Lisa is the biological granddaughter of George Cummings and the daughter of Eleanor Cummings.

And as such, she is also the sole heir to his and his late son's estate. We will begin the legal transfer immediately."

I let out a long breath, slow and steady. It felt like letting go of something I hadn't realized I'd been gripping so tightly for four long weeks. "That's mighty fine news, Mr. Blakenship," I said. "I appreciate your diligence."

"I should be thanking you," he replied. "You've helped correct a great wrong. Miss Lisa will be contacted officially within the next few days through your office. However, we'll need an attorney to finalize the transfer in court."

I didn't hesitate. "How about a retired attorney? My father, Frank Marlow."

There was a brief pause. "The attorney on the original adoption papers?"

"Yes, sir," I said with a quiet nod. "Same man."

"Well," he said, voice warming just a bit, "that would be quite fitting, wouldn't it?" He paused again. "There's one more thing," he added. "This is a considerable amount of property and money. Lisa will need someone she can trust to help manage the investments. Someone who can guide her and understands the complexity of her situation."

"I have the perfect person," I said without missing a beat. "He's the sharpest investor I know. And he's made quiet fortunes for others in the Negro community. He'll treat her like family."

"Then we're all set," Blakenship said, sounding pleased for the first time. "The papers will come to your office. Once you file them with the court, she'll receive the legal documents and gain full access to the estate's holdings and accounts. And, there'll be a check included for you, for handling the transactions and her case."

"We're much obliged, Mr. Blakenship," I said, my voice low with meaning. "This was a wrong that took far too long to set right, but I'm grateful it finally has been."

I knew Blakenship was too polished, too steeped in discretion, to speak aloud the deeper truth behind the documents. Yes, George Cummings was Lisa's grandfather—but more than that, her parents had been George's own son and his daughter-in-law, Eleanor, was his daughter, neither one ever knowing the blood they shared. A secret buried so deep, even the Cummings family had lived their lives blind to it.

When I hung up, I didn't say anything right away, just turned to Betty Lou, who hadn't moved an inch. I didn't need to say a word. The answer was all over my face.

Betty Lou let out a half-laugh, half-sob and flung her arms around me in a quick hug. Then she brushed her cheek with the back of her hand like she'd caught a speck of dust. "Well," she said, voice cracking, "I hope that girl's sittin' down when she comes into the office and we tell her the good news."

"She won't believe it," I said, easing back behind my desk. "But it's real."

For a long second, we sat in that quiet—no case to solve, no puzzle left on the board. Just the knowledge that somewhere out there, a girl who had once been invisible to the world was about to step into her name.

Lisa was about to get her life handed back to her.

~~~

We gathered in the office two weeks later, like the closing of a long, unfinished chapter. Detective Holcomb stood near the window, arms crossed, but a flicker of contentment in his eyes. His job was complete, and for once, justice hadn't arrived in handcuffs.
~~~

Cookie stood nearby, having brought refreshments. Betty Lou arranged the coffee and the assortment of pastries, as if we were about to discuss a garden party rather than rewrite a life.

Constance lingered by the door, her smile quiet but steady, while Willie adjusted his tie for the third time in ten minutes. My mother and father sat together, hands folded, a picture of calm authority, two bookends to the story now reaching its final page.

Then Lisa arrived, still dressed in her seamstress blouse and skirt, unaware of what was about to unfold. She stepped in hesitantly, never having set foot on Worth Avenue or in one of the couture dress shops, though her dresses had been worn by some of the most influential socialites in Palm Beach.

Her hair was pulled back, her eyes sharp, but wary. I stood and offered her the seat at the center of the room. Everyone followed suit, as if this were court or church, only quieter.

"I want to thank you for coming, Lisa," I said, motioning for her to sit. "What we're about to share with you might be a little overwhelming, but I promise, it's good."

She nodded once, eyes sweeping the room like she was still trying to piece together why all these people were here, and why a woman was taking photos.

I introduced each person and explained why they were here. Then, I reached into my jacket and pulled out a sealed envelope—thick, weighty, stamped with a notary seal and Winthrop Blakenship's signature in fine, slanted ink.

"But before I say anything else," I said, turning, "this honor belongs in the hands of someone I trust more than anyone." I passed the envelope to my father.

Frank Marlow stood slowly, cleared his throat, and looked Lisa directly in the eyes. “Miss Lisa,” he said, his voice firm but kind, “I was the attorney who filed the adoption paperwork for your birth mother and the Dandys, and I’ve been asked to oversee the legal restoration of what should have been your birthright.”

She stood, and Dad handed her the envelope. She took it with trembling hands and slid her thumb under the seal. As she pulled out the documents and unfolded the summary page, her eyes scanned the numbers, and her lips parted.

And then she wobbled.

“Whoa—whoa, there,” Willie said, catching her before she tipped. He guided her gently into the chair, steadying her with one hand on her shoulder.

“I… I don’t understand,” Lisa whispered. “This… this can’t be real.”

“It is,” I said softly. “That inheritance belongs to you. Every cent. Every acre. Every brick. Your grandfather left it to his son, your father, and now it passes to you.”

My father stepped in again. “We’ll be filing the legal paperwork with the court. Once complete, you’ll have full access to the estate. I’ll be helping you through every step. No need to worry about any of the complicated parts.”

Lisa stared at the papers in stunned silence, as if written in another language.

I reached into my pocket and pulled out one final thing. The doubloon. George’s. I stepped forward and held it out to her. “This was your grandfather’s. I believe it belongs next to yours now.”

She took it slowly, reverently, like it might vanish if she blinked too hard. Then she looked up, tears shimmering down her cheeks.

I turned to Willie. "And when it comes to managing the inheritance investments and decisions, you've got someone right here. Willie's the best man for the job. He's helped dozens of families, including Cracker Johnson, invest wisely and grow their wealth. You'll be in good hands."

Willie nodded once, touched his chest, and smiled. "I'm honored, Miss Lisa."

The room let out a collective breath as the weight of the moment settled. My mother dabbed her eyes with a handkerchief. Betty Lou sniffed but didn't say a word. Constance reached out and squeezed Lisa's hand.

There were no loud cheers, no champagne corks. Just a quiet joy, full and round, like the kind that filled a home during the first rain after a long drought.

After a few minutes of congratulations and soft laughter, Lisa leaned over to Constance and whispered something in her ear. Then she tugged her gently by the hand. "Come with me," she said. "Just a minute."

They slipped into the front room, leaving the rest of us to sip coffee and let the miracle settle. I moved to the door so I could hear.

Lisa's voice was soft but sure. "I'm going to make you the most beautiful wedding dress Palm Beach has ever seen," she said. "Fancier than anything the Worth Avenue ladies could dream up. Silk, lace, the works."

Constance chuckled. "That's not necessary."

"Oh yes, it is," Lisa said. "Without you, none of this would've happened. You walked me straight into my future, and I'm going to make sure you walk into yours like a queen."

They returned a moment later, Lisa glowing, Constance a little misty-eyed, and the office, for the first time in months, felt light again. We didn't need a toast to know something worth celebrating had happened.

The past had finally let go of the future.

And Lisa, for the first time in her life, could finally start living it.

I wasn't about to untangle the web of bloodlines that had brought her to this moment, or explain the twisted path that led to her inheritance. If she pieced it together in her own time, so be it.

Some truths are better discovered than delivered.

~~~

Max leaned forward across my desk the next day, eyes alive with the kind of fire that could set ink to page. "Drake, this story needs to be told. The whole sordid business—George, Sharon, the cover-ups. People need to know, and I'm ready to tell."

I rested my elbows on the blotter, meeting her gaze. "People might want to know, Max, but that doesn't mean they should. Sensationalism sells papers, sure—but in this case, it'll do more harm than good. Some stories are better left unsaid."

She arched a brow. "You're protecting their reputations?"

"No," I said, shaking my head. "I'm protecting those left behind. Dragging their names through the headlines won't fix anything. It'll just salt wounds that have started healing."

She leaned back in her chair, arms crossed. "So you're asking me to sit on it."

"I'm not asking," I said, soft but steady. "Remember Mama Dawson's? I let you off the hook there. We'll call your debt paid if you leave the story alone."
~~~

For several moments, her pencil tapped against her notebook. Then she pushed back her chair, rose, and extended her hand across the desk. “Deal.”

I watched Max step out of my office and eased back in my chair, the weight of the case settling like dust after a storm.

Truth has its place, but so does mercy. In this line of work, knowing the difference is half the battle.

NOTE TO THE READER

Thank you for reading *The Secret at Sea Grape Cottage*. I hope you enjoyed the mystery. As reviews are important to every author, please leave one on Amazon.

To become a ***Preferred Reader*** and receive updates and information on new releases, sign up at sallyjling.com.

COMING SOON!

TWICE GONE

A Drake Marlow Mystery

When a body turns up dead—twice—Drake Marlow is hired to untangle a web of secrets that refuses to stay buried. Each lead draws him deeper into a maze of dark riddles, whispered rendezvous, and carefully buried political cover-ups. The trail snakes from the sun-bleached wealth of Palm Beach to the hard edges of Chicago, and from the shadows of Cuba straight into the underbelly of American power.

As answers claw their way to the surface, Drake is forced to confront an unsettling reality: some ghosts don't stay dead, and some truths demand a brutal price. With a missing man's specter haunting every step and a widow's life balanced on a knife's edge, Drake must decide just how far he's willing to go, and what he's willing to sacrifice.

ABOUT THE AUTHOR

Sally J. Ling is an author, speaker, and historian who lives in South Florida. She writes mysteries with a Florida connection and historical nonfiction, specializing in obscure, unusual, or little-known stories of Florida history.

As a special correspondent, she wrote for the *Sun-Sentinel* newspaper for four years and was a contributing journalist for several South Florida magazines.

Based upon her knowledge as well as excerpts from her books, she has appeared in three feature-length TV documentaries—"Gangsters," the National Geographic Channel; "The Secret Weapon that Won World War II," and "Prohibition and the South Florida Connection," WLRN, Miami. She served as associate producer on the latter production. She has also appeared in and served as a production consultant for several short documentaries on South Florida history produced by WLRN, Miami.

She has been a repeat guest on South Florida PBS TV and radio stations, a guest presenter at Florida Atlantic University, and a guest speaker at numerous historical societies, libraries, organizations, and schools.

For information on current projects, or to become a "Preferred Reader" and receive notices on upcoming books. please visit Sally's website at:
sallyjling.com

To contact Sally, please do so at:
info@sallyjling.com

Sally's books include:

Fiction

- The Secret at Sea Grape Cottage: A Drake Marlow Mystery (Book7)
- Clandestine Encounters: A Drake Marlow Mystery (Book 6)
- Cyptic Marks: A Drake Marlow Mystery (Book 5)
- Deceptive Collision: A Drake Marlow Mystery (Book 4)
- Isabella: A Drake Marlow Mystery (Book 3)
- In the Gator's Grip: A Drake Marlow Mystery (Book 2)
- Della: A Drake MarlowMystery (Book 1)
- HalfGone: A Brooks and Romero Mystery (Book 1)
- Frayed Ends: A Randi Brooks Mystery (Book 1)
- Uncovered: A Randi Brooks Mystery (Book 2)
- Orchid Fever: A Randi Brooks Mystery (Book 3)
- Capone's Keys: A Randi Brooks Mystery (Book 4)
- Women of the Ring
- The Cloak: A Shea Baker Mystery (Book 1)
- The Spear of Destiny: A Shea Baker Mystery (Book 2)
- The Twelfth Stone: A Shea Baker Mystery (Book 3)
- The Tree and the Carpenter
- Spies, Root Beer and Alligators: Phillip's Great Adventures (Children's Novel)

Nonfiction

- Deerfield Beach: The Land and Its People
- Al Capone's Miami: Paradise or Purgatory?
- Out of Mind, Out of Sight: A Revealing History of the Florida State Hospital at Chattahoochee and Mental Health Care in Florida
- Sailin' on the Stranahan (commissioned coffee table book)
- Run the Rum In: South Florida during Prohibition
- Small Town, Big Secrets: Inside the Boca Raton Army Airfield during World War II (First and Second editions)
- A History of Boca Raton
- Fund Raising With Golf (out of print)

www.ingramcontent.com/pod-product-compliance
Lightning Source LLC
LaVergne TN
LVHW020708110826
845149LV00012B/2160

* 9 7 9 8 9 9 1 6 8 2 2 5 1 *